HIS OTHER WIFE

BOOKS BY NICOLE TROPE

My Daughter's Secret

The Boy in the Photo

The Nowhere Girl

The Life She Left Behind

The Girl Who Never Came Home

Bring Him Home

The Family Across the Street

The Mother's Fault

The Stepchild

HIS OTHER WIFE

NICOLE TROPE

bookouture

Published by Bookouture in 2022

An imprint of Storyfire Ltd.
Carmelite House
50 Victoria Embankment
London EC4Y 0DZ

www.bookouture.com

ISBN: 978-1-80314-345-3
eBook ISBN: 978-1-80314-344-6

For D, M, I, and J

PROLOGUE

NOW

'Daddy,' says a small, strained voice. 'Daddy, please wake up... please.'

He is surrounded by darkness – no, not darkness; there is light on his eyelids. His eyes are closed. Is he dreaming? This must be a dream.

'Daddy, please wake up, please wake up. I don't know what to do...' The voice again, still small, tears... She's crying.

His eyelids feel so... Is something holding them down? And his chest – there is something sitting on his chest, something heavy, pushing down, and pain... there is so much pain. Pain everywhere. He can't...

'Daddy... Daddy, don't leave me, please.' A touch on his cheek, a small hand, soft.

Emily.

He needs to...

'Daddy... Daddy.'

But he is gone; the darkness claims him and he cannot answer.

ONE
GIDEON
FOUR MONTHS AGO

The persistent ringing of his mobile phone drags Gideon from a deep champagne-induced slumber. He fumbles in the dark, knocking his watch off the bedside table before he grabs the phone. 'Yeah,' he answers, without even looking at who the caller is. He knows who it will be.

'Daddy?'

He sits up in bed, instantly alert. 'Em, Ladybug, what's wrong? Why are you calling me?'

'Can you come and help us please, Daddy? Mummy says the whispering man is back and she's scared.'

He pushes back the covers and stands up, moving towards the bathroom, the cold air from the softly humming air conditioner hitting his skin. 'Where is Mummy now, Ladybug?' He tries to keep his voice even, calm. If he panics, she will become hysterical.

'She's um... she's in the cupboard with me but she can't talk. She says the whispering man will hear her. Can you come, Daddy? We're very scared.'

He can see her there, hunched, holding the phone tightly,

dressed in her sunshine-yellow pyjamas, green eyes wide with fear and confusion.

'I'm coming, baby, I'm coming,' he says, even as he is pulling on tracksuit pants and a T-shirt, knowing that the February heat is still hanging heavy in the air. 'You just sit tight. I'll be there soon, okay, baby?'

'Okay, Daddy,' she sniffs, obviously crying. 'Okay. I have to go now in case he hears me.'

'Don't hang up, Em, don't... Stay...' But the call has ended.

'What's happening?' he hears, and a bedside lamp lights up the room, making him squint.

'I need to go over there. I think—'

'This can't go on, Gideon; you know that, don't you? She needs proper help.'

Gideon finds his shoes and slips them on, glancing quickly at Charlotte sitting up in bed, her blonde hair messy from sleep, concern in her blue eyes.

'I know, sweetheart, I know. I thought the therapy was helping, but you're right. It can't.' He is wide awake now, adrenaline coursing through him.

'So what are you going to do?' she asks, picking up her own phone to peer at the time. It's 2 a.m. He can only imagine Emily's terrified exhaustion as she hides in the cupboard with her mother.

'I'm going to get her admitted tonight and then we'll go from there. I thought she was doing so much better, but she's obviously not sleeping again. I'll bring Emily back here.' As he says the words, he realises he has made a decision right this minute. He hasn't wanted to, has kept hoping that things are actually okay, that they're getting better – but they're not and he can't hide from it any more.

'Do you want me to come with you?' Charlotte starts to climb out of bed, her slim body clad in deep blue silk, so different from Sarah, who never wore anything but his old T-shirts in bed.

'No, it's fine. I can sort it out.'

'Okay, but call me if you need me,' she says.

In his car, he races through silent streets to his ex-wife's apartment, hoping that the champagne and wine he consumed with dinner have not put him over the limit. Tonight was supposed to be all about celebrating his and Charlotte's engagement. She was completely surprised by his proposal, because they've only been dating for a few months.

'Oh my,' she said on seeing the ring on her dessert plate surrounded by delicate hand-made chocolate hearts, her eyes tearing up, a delighted smile on her face. 'Yes, yes, Gideon,' she laughed.

Their relationship has moved quickly, but Charlotte brings order and stability to his life and that's what he craves. It's what Emily needs as well. Five-year-old children should not be calling for help in the middle of the night. He slaps his steering wheel as he waits for a light to change in the empty street. He should have kept his daughter with him, but Sarah seemed so much better. She was cheerful on the phone when they talked, happy almost. There was no mention of all the things he knew she blamed herself for, the long list she carried around in her head that no one could make her forget. Emily was getting to school on time, enjoying her first weeks of the kindergarten year, and things were working well.

Even as he thinks this, he realises that he's noticed Sarah slipping in the last couple of weeks, noticed but not really taken proper notice. He has so much work on at the moment. The few months after Christmas and the summer holidays always bring a plethora of divorce cases into his firm; couples having spent too much time together realising that they no longer want to spend any time together at all. His days start at 7 a.m. and end at 7 p.m.

He accelerates away from the traffic light and shakes his head a little. 'You didn't want to know,' he says aloud, because he didn't. At the next light, he drums on the steering wheel as a sports car pulls up beside him, the top down, thumping music reverberating through his car too, with two young women giggling and dancing in their seats. He cannot remember being that young. He's only thirty-eight – hardly old. Hardly as old as he feels.

He and Sarah have been divorced for two years and he has spent a lot of that time worrying about her, wondering if he should file for full custody of Emily, hoping that Sarah would find a therapist who could help, because no one she went to lasted very long. She would see someone for a few sessions and then move on, saying, 'We didn't click' or 'She can't help me.' But two months ago, she finally found someone she really liked. Melanie is an older woman who used cognitive behavioural therapy to help Sarah manage her damaging thoughts, to guide her to the realisation that all the things she blamed herself for were not her fault, and to finally allow her to give herself permission to sleep. To Sarah, sleep was letting go, losing control, giving in. She confessed to Gideon tearfully on one occasion that she believed it led to the death of her loved ones – an idea that clung and damaged and she seemed unable to truly shake. Night after night she tortured herself, forcing her body to stay awake until it could no longer function. But he thought she was dealing with that now, was finally, finally dealing with it.

It was such a relief, but it hasn't lasted. He can't believe the whispering man is back, Sarah's terrifying, nightmarish, insomnia-induced hallucination, who it seemed appeared a few weeks after she moved into her new building – the lovely apartment she had finally bought with her part of the divorce settlement. The large building sprawls across many blocks and is secure and well populated enough for Sarah to be anonymous. He would have preferred something smaller for the two of them, a place where she knew her neighbours and maybe could call on them for help if she couldn't get hold of him. But it wasn't his choice to make.

And now... If the whispering man is back, then things have slipped further than he realised. He should have known.

When he gets to the apartment block, he uses the code to enter the building. At Sarah's door, he rings the bell and knocks loudly, calling, 'Em... Ladybug, it's Daddy, open up.' It is hot in the hallway, dense with humidity, and sweat prickles at the back of his neck.

He hears his daughter struggling to work the locks for a moment, small fingers working hard until, finally, she pulls the door open.

'Oh Ladybug,' he says when he sees her. Her brown hair is tangled and her green eyes red-rimmed. She is a miniature version of her beautiful mother and he should never have left her here. She reaches her arms towards him and he picks her up, smoothing her hair as she lays her head on his shoulder, her legs wrapping around his waist, her sweaty skin sticking to his. 'It's okay, it's going to be okay. I'm here now,' he says.

The apartment is baking, the air conditioner silent. Maybe it's broken, but he remembers Sarah complaining about how loud it is. Tonight she was listening for something. Tonight she heard it. Tonight the whispering man returned.

He knows that it's more likely the apparition has been back for some time. The signs he didn't want to recognise have been there for a few weeks at least. When he has picked Emily up, Sarah's movements have been quick, jerky with adrenaline, and her voice high-pitched, the words sounding like they're being forced out. There have been conversations on the phone where he's had to clarify arrangements with her more than once. Her eyes are dull and she has been making less and less effort to get dressed and do her hair. Some days ago, when he dropped Emily home on a Sunday night, he was sure he noticed a sour, unwashed smell coming off her and yet he left it. He didn't realise that things were this bad – or more truthfully, he hoped they would just get better without him having to do anything about it. Guilt settles on his shoulders. He has left his daughter in a potentially dangerous situation.

Holding her tightly, he takes her to her bedroom and turns on the air conditioner to cool the stifling room. He settles her in bed and tucks her in.

She looks up at him, her eyes wide. 'But the whispering man, Daddy. Mummy says he's outside.' Fear makes her clutch at his top.

'The whispering man is scared of me, so he's gone away now,' Gideon replies. 'I'm going to help Mummy and I want you to stay here in your bed, okay? Some people are coming over so she can get some sleep, and you mustn't come out of your room. Do you understand?' He doesn't want her to see her mother taken away on a stretcher. He has never wanted to do this, but he has no choice any more. Encouraging Sarah to check herself in to a clinic for intensive therapy has not worked. Outpatient therapy while living independently has not worked. Melanie is her fifth therapist in the last eighteen months, and each time Sarah has moved onto someone else, Gideon always hoped that he or she would be the person to finally help her get control of her life. He really believed that Melanie was finally the one. But she wasn't, and he needs to take control now.

Emily nods her head, clutching her stuffed pink rabbit with its one remaining eye. He wishes he could call his mother to take her while he does this, but his parents are in China on a long-planned-for holiday around Asia, and Sarah's parents are... He rubs his head. He should have brought Charlotte with him, but he didn't want her to see Sarah in such a vulnerable state, didn't want Sarah's pain to be visible. It felt wrong somehow. Sarah's pain is private, deep and dark, and he cannot expose it to anyone who doesn't love her as he and Emily love her.

'Try to sleep. I'll come back in a few minutes,' he says to Emily, as he feels the room cool. He can see that she is already drifting off, exhausted and knowing that she is safe because he's here now.

He goes into Sarah's bedroom and stands next to the large wardrobe. 'Sarah, sweetheart, it's me, can I open the door?' he says. The heat in the room is terrible and there is a thick, sweaty smell in the air. He used to associate the smell of peaches with Sarah, the smell of summer.

'Gideon...' Her voice is unsure, tremulous.

'Yeah, I'm going to open the door.' He slides the white melamine aside to find her sitting on the floor of the cupboard, surrounded by pairs of shoes and bags. Her brown hair is lank against her head, her green eyes dull. Violet shadows under her eyes tell the story of many, many sleepless nights. He knows that she's been tormenting herself, forcing herself to stay awake night after night, punishing herself for her crimes. His heart breaks for her and he has a vision of the girl he met at university, with her quick smile and abundance of energy.

He will never forget a lunch date at least fifteen years ago, when they went into the city for ramen and, walking to the train station, passed a sports car dealership. 'Let's go in,' she said.

'Why?'

'Just let's go,' she replied, laughing.

Inside she found a salesman in an expensive suit who glanced at them in their jeans and T-shirts and quickly got ready to dismiss them. 'My husband just inherited a huge amount of money from his grandfather,' she said to the man, whose eyes lit up. 'Old money, you know. I said he should spend some on a car, and we want to test-drive...' she looked around the showroom and pointed, 'that green Porsche. Green is his favourite colour.'

She giggled in the back of the car as they took the beautiful machine up and down the congested Sydney streets, loving the feel of it.

'We'll think about it,' she said imperiously to the salesman when the test drive was over, tossing her brown curls and offering him a smile he couldn't help but return.

She is so far removed from that girl now, so separated from her true self, and Gideon knows he has to help her. He crouches down next to her and strokes her cheek.

'He's back, Gideon. He was talking to me through the window, whispering things. I heard him.'

His heart breaks at how desperately sad she looks, at how thin she is. 'It's fine, he's gone now,' he replies. 'I'm here, and I'm going to find you somewhere to rest. I have to call someone, and you need to go with them.'

'I can't rest,' she says, reaching out to grab his shirt the way Emily did, imploring him to understand.

'I know, sweetheart, but you need to. I'll take care of everything else. I won't let him talk to you. He can't get you when I'm here, and I'm going to send you somewhere he's not allowed to go. You need to trust me.' He knows there's no point in telling her the whispering man doesn't exist. She can't think clearly now. There is also no point in trying to make her get into bed. Even if he stays here, she won't sleep. She needs strong drugs and more help than she has been given. He begins to stand up, but she grips his hand. 'Don't leave me,' she cries, and he sits down again, sighing. As he calls the emergency services, she watches him, but he has no idea if she understands what he's doing.

'I have to go open the door, but I'll be right back,' he tells her, gently loosening her grip so that she lets go of his hand. She nods her head and then she clutches her own hands together, comforting herself.

The paramedics arrive only minutes later. Both women

speak in soft, low voices. He explains quickly and he can feel their kindness in the way one of them crouches down next to Sarah and strokes her arm, encouraging her to come out of the cupboard. Sarah uncurls herself slowly, her focus on the window, where the whispering man stands. Gideon positions himself in front of it, protecting her from her terror. The paramedics keep talking, keep guiding her until she is lying on the stretcher.

He holds her hand while they give her the shot that will make it all go away. She stares into his eyes as the needle goes in, submitting because she trusts him. She has always trusted him on everything – except his opinion that nothing that happened is her fault. That she has never trusted him on.

'We will admit her for thirty-six hours and then they'll let you know the options,' says one of the paramedics as they place a blanket over Sarah, her head lolling against the stretched white sheet. Her hands are curled into fists, but even as he watches, her fingers uncurl and her body relaxes, the drug taking almost immediate effect. Yet she still fights sleep.

'Okay, I know. I thought this might be a possibility. I'll get her admitted somewhere. She needs specialist help.' He already knows which clinic he's going to call. It's close by, expensive and one of the best in Sydney.

The woman nods and she and her partner move the stretcher into the hallway and out the door of the apartment. Gideon has made sure that Emily's door is closed. His daughter does not need to see this.

Only when the paramedics have left does he go into her room, where she is fast asleep, curled up under her ballerina duvet, the room blissfully cool now. He lies down next to her, knowing that she is a deep sleeper, and calls Charlotte.

'I've had her admitted,' he says in a low voice. 'I'm going to stay here and get some sleep. We'll be home tomorrow.'

'Good,' says Charlotte. 'I'll have everything ready. You don't need to worry about a thing, just get some rest.'

His eyes close as he ends the call. Charlotte will take care of everything. And someone else will take care of Sarah. It's not what he wants, but it's the best he can do.

TWO
SARAH

She is fighting the drug, resisting it but at the same time letting go. She can't be awake any more. How many hours has it been? Not hours, days and days. She's not allowed to sleep or he will come for her child.

'Your fault,' he whispers outside her window at night. 'Your fault and you don't deserve her. Your fault and I will take everything.'

All night long he does it, the sibilant hiss of his words penetrating the glass, coming through the curtains, seeping through the air. She has to listen for him. She cannot turn on the air conditioner or put in ear plugs or hold a pillow over her head. She must listen to his words, must hear what he has to say, let him hurt her with his threats. All night he talks and she cannot sleep or he will take Emily as well. Her daughter is all she has left. She has lost everything else and she cannot lose Emily too, so she stays awake to guard her, to watch over her, to care for her as she never cared for those she lost. Even when Emily is with Gideon for the night, she has to stay awake, has to show him that she's sorry, so he doesn't take her child.

'All your fault,' he whispers all night long, so she refuses to close her eyes. And with each passing day her body gets heavier, harder to move, impossible to handle. Her arms jerk and twist and thoughts fly out of her head. Everything is funny and nothing is funny at all. She has stopped eating, hoping that it will make her feel lighter and help her stay awake, but nothing helps. She is tired inside her bones; the exhaustion has become her marrow.

The stretcher jolts and rumbles and then they are outside as she tries with all her might to stay awake. Where is Emily? Where is Gideon?

It is dark but so warm, the air holding the kiss of the day's heat, and there are flashing lights and people in their pyjamas, confused and worried at the noise, the lights, the drama.

Even as the drug begins to slow her thoughts, Sarah feels a deep well of humiliation open up inside her. They are looking at her, talking about her, judging her.

'It's this building,' says an older woman in a pink dressing gown, her hair in curlers, loud enough for Sarah to hear. 'They let anyone move in. I'm sure that one bloke is stealing underwear from the washing line. He's always looking at me, at all the women. This whole place is full of weirdos.'

Another woman standing next to her, her grey hair hanging down her back, says, 'Lead in the pipes,' and then Sarah watches as their faces warp and twist, their eyes growing larger, their teeth longer. Terror grips her. There are monsters everywhere.

Cool hands on her forehead. 'Try to rest now, love.' A kind, deep voice. She wants to explain about the whispering man, about the faces, about the monsters, but the hands are so gentle and they brush just above her eyes, which grow heavier and heavier.

Nothing she can do now. She can't fight this. Emily is safe

with Gideon and the whispering man is afraid of Gideon. Is he afraid of Gideon? Gideon forces him away. Does he? Her eyes blink, blink, blink. Gideon watches over Emily so she can rest. Emily is safe. Please, please, let Emily be safe. Then the world goes dark.

THREE
CHARLOTTE

In the kitchen, she is methodically chopping up watermelon into cubes, making sure that each cube is completely seed-free so that Emily will accept it. Her phone is clamped between her shoulder and her ear as she talks to her mother, Carol. Despite the heat, she has all the windows open, letting the outside shimmer in. She will close them soon, but the strong smell of the February honeysuckle is something she enjoys in the morning.

'Oops, another seed,' she says, more to herself than her mother.

Carol laughs. 'You were the same at that age, so fussy with your food. I remember you went through a stage of only wanting twenty peas on your plate. I used to stand and count them out. Your father thought I was crazy.'

Charlotte smiles. 'It's what mothers do, isn't it?' Even as she says the word – as she calls herself a mother – warmth spreads through her body. She is a stepmother, but she is a mother all the same and this little girl needs her now.

'It is. Are you ready to have her full-time, darling? You've only just moved in with Gideon and now there's a wedding to plan and a child in the mix. You're going to have a lot on your plate with work as well.' Her mother was overjoyed at the news of her engagement last night. She assumed Charlotte was calling her early this morning to begin wedding planning, but today the wedding is far from Charlotte's mind.

Charlotte covers the plate of watermelon with cling film and pops it into the fridge. She picks up a rag and wipes down the counter, admiring the shine on the pure white stone. 'I'm ready,' she sighs. 'I adore her. I can't quite believe I'm getting everything I wanted. It's terribly sad that Sarah can't take care of her, but I'm ready to step into the role. I can't wait to spend more time with her. And you're going to love her as well. She is the most delightful little girl. She reminds me so much of myself when I was her age that if she didn't look so much like Sarah, I would swear she was mine.'

Her mother is quiet for a moment. 'You're forty, darling. I know women have babies later and later these days, but you don't want to miss your chance. You should think about having one of your own soon. I would love a grandchild. You may need to go the IVF route, but so many women do. It's all very different these days. I struggled for years to have you and your brother, but we didn't have all this medical help then.'

'I know, Mum,' Charlotte says, 'but I don't want to do that. Firstly, I don't need to be reminded at every doctor's appointment that I'm two years older than Gideon, and also, I just... I've seen the heartbreak it's caused with my friends. There is a child right here who really needs a mother. I want her to feel like she is the centre of our universe. She's had such a hard time with Sarah. She needs stability and routine now.'

As she utters the words, she knows they are true, because she has made sure they are true, reinforcing them in her own mind, convincing herself over and again. Growing up, she always saw marriage and children in her future, never considered that finding a man to create a life with would be so difficult. The idea of having a child on her own never appealed to her, and as the years passed, she found herself trying to accept that she would never have that one dream. Before meeting Gideon, she was weary of dating, of swiping right again and again, only to be disappointed. She had high standards, but she knew she was right to have those standards when she met him. Once she knew that he was the man for her, she imagined that she would have her chance to have a child, but it has never been on the cards. She cannot share this with her mother, knowing that she would be devastated for her. 'I can't imagine going back to nappies and sleepless nights,' Gideon told her on their third date as they discussed Emily. 'I'm happy with one child.' Charlotte understood that she was being informed of where he stood. Gideon didn't want another child and she didn't want to lose Gideon. Now all she has to do is embrace the child already in her life, and she is delighted to do that. She is excited about the prospect of motherhood, in whatever way it comes.

Her mother says, 'Stability and routine. Just the way I raised you. Children like boundaries. And I respect your decision. All I want is for you to be happy. I know how difficult it has been dealing with Sarah and all her... issues, especially since Gideon seems determined to be supportive. It's very good of him, but there is a limit. Things should be easier now that she's getting professional help, away from outside distractions.'

'Yes, it is difficult... but you know that all of that is just between you and me. I probably shouldn't be sharing it with you. I knew she was struggling, but I never thought she would make up some ghoul who whispers to her. It's too much,' says Charlotte, popping a spare piece of watermelon into her mouth and savouring the burst of fresh sweetness.

'Yes, the whispering man, that is really odd,' agrees Carol. 'But I'm your mother; Gideon can't expect you to keep things from me.' Charlotte has always told her everything, appreciating her pragmatic point of view.

Charlotte fills a pot with some milk so she can make Emily a hot chocolate. Gideon has said they will be here soon and she wants to have everything ready.

'I'm sure he doesn't want me to keep secrets, but as you were saying, people need boundaries,' she says lightly, knowing that she doesn't have time for a discussion about her resentment of some of the boundaries she grew up with. Her mother controlled every aspect of her life, from what she ate to how she looked to what she did with her time. Now that she's older, she can see that her mother simply wanted the very best for her only daughter. And it worked, because Charlotte has a thriving career in the design world, a handsome successful lawyer for her soon-to-be husband and a beautiful little girl to take care of. She couldn't ask for more. Carol's occasional crossing of boundaries now that she's older is something she can deal with. Her younger brother, Edward, didn't fare as well with their mother's discipline, throwing himself against the wall of her control from the moment he could. And now he is living in an apartment paid for by Carol and gets by doing odd jobs for Charlotte. It is better to bend than to break, in Charlotte's opinion.

'Do you know what's going to happen to her – to Sarah? I mean, where is she going?' Carol asks. Charlotte pictures her mother seated at the small table and chair she uses to conduct telephone conversations. Even though the landline has long been cordless and she mostly uses her mobile phone, Carol Owens still insists on sitting down at the small carved timber table and matching chair with its red velvet upholstered seat. She would never think of whirling around a kitchen accomplishing tasks while she spoke to anyone. There is a set time and place for everything in her life. Charlotte would say it's her way of controlling her loneliness since her husband's death, but he died many years ago, and as far as she can remember her mother has always had an old-world elegance about her, a belief that nothing needs to be rushed. She will be dressed as though she is ready to go out, in a smart two-piece suit, even though today is her 'pottering about the house' day.

'Gideon has found her a space at the clinic you mentioned,' Charlotte replies. 'He says thank you for the suggestion, by the way. They are going to transfer her in the next couple of days and she'll get the help she needs.' The clinic is expensive, but Charlotte is more than happy for the money to be spent. Making sure that Sarah is safely tucked away and not damaging little Emily with her wild ramblings is the goal as far as she is concerned. As she and Gideon aren't yet married, the money is his to spend as he sees fit, but he still asked her for her opinion, which she appreciates. His consideration for her feelings has always been one of his best traits.

'Well, that is very fortunate,' says her mother. 'It's expensive but worth it, I believe. Pamela sent her son there to finally kick his little habit, and it worked. He's doing very well now.'

Charlotte stifles a laugh at her mother's choice of words. Pamela Turner's son is a drug addict. Her mother's generation prefer sweeping their problems under the carpet, minimising them into nothing and hoping they will disappear. Her mother and Pamela have been friends for years, so Charlotte has listened to many tales of her son's behaviour, a boy she disliked and a man she hoped never to see again. James was childhood friends with Charlotte's brother Edward, but that friendship has, thankfully, faded.

'Hopefully she'll get the help she needs, and by the time she is well, she may be happy to leave Emily with her father. I mean, she may never really recover enough to be a good mother again,' muses Charlotte. She cannot imagine being unable to care for your own child. Sarah must be devastated.

'It does sound like Emily will be better off with you anyway.'

Charlotte frowns at the words. Her mother is right, but only for now. Sarah will recover.

Her mother has never met Sarah and neither has Charlotte. Gideon wanted to introduce them as soon as the two of them became serious, but Charlotte didn't feel secure enough then to meet his first wife, his first love. She is embarrassed to admit that she has always been a little bothered by the amount of affection Gideon still has for Sarah. She would never have wanted to be with a man who said awful things about his ex-wife, knowing that was a large flapping red flag, but there are moments when Gideon still seems slightly in love with her.

'But he has chosen you, and from what you tell me, you and she are very different. He probably wants different,' her mother has counselled her whenever she complains that Gideon is too invested in his ex-wife's happiness, that he answers the phone whenever she calls, that his concern for her is over the top. Her mother has had to support her through some tearful phone calls when it's all become too much. It would be much easier if Gideon wasn't so involved in Sarah's life, but Gideon is the quintessential nice guy and only speaks about his ex-wife kindly. 'I've seen what happens to the kids of divorced parents who can't get along. It's not good,' is his reasoning.

'I won't argue if she does decide that Emily is better off with us, but time will tell,' says Charlotte. She hears the garage door opening. 'They're here,' she says, unable to hide a small buzz of excitement. Last night, after Gideon left, she couldn't help planning how her life would look with Emily in it full-time. She's already seen the gorgeous bridesmaid's dress she wants the little girl to wear when she and Gideon get married – a pale blue raw silk dress with a neckline of tiny embroidered pink roses. She and Gideon both want a small wedding, elegant and simple, and she's sure her mother will delight in being given the reins for that. A reception at their favourite Italian restaurant should be perfect, and she knows Carol will agree. The sooner they are married, the better it will be for Emily, and it will be a nice distraction for the child as well.

'Good luck,' says her mother. 'Say hello from me, and let's do lunch tomorrow, shall we? Much to be discussed in terms of the wedding, I think.'

'Absolutely. Love you, Mum, bye,' says Charlotte, and then she turns to greet Gideon and Emily as they come in. Both of them look exhausted. 'You poor darlings,' she says. 'I've got it from here, Gideon, you go and lie down. Emily and I are going to have a lovely breakfast of watermelon and hot chocolate and pancakes.'

'No seeds in my watermelon,' says Emily, her pale face lighting up a little. Charlotte crouches down next to her and takes her in her arms. 'I know you, Ladybug, no seeds at all.'

She watches Gideon's shoulders drop, relief on his face.

'Thanks, love,' he says. 'Will you be okay, Ladybug?'

'Mm hmm,' says Emily. 'Charlotte's here. Can I stir the hot chocolate?'

A flush of warmth rushes through Charlotte at Emily's trust in her, but she also feels a touch of despair for the child and what she's gone through with her mother. Although Gideon has told her some of what Sarah suffers from, until last night they had no idea just how bad things had become. There have been some very odd late-night phone calls, but Charlotte has assumed, perhaps wrongly, that Sarah calls Gideon late at night as a way to pull him away from his new life. She is glad she has never expressed this resentful thought to Gideon now that she knows what has actually been going on. Now she feels some guilt at not pushing him to find out what was happening sooner. But she is still treading the delicate line between girlfriend and wife, so pushing might have been a bad idea. Things will be different now that she's going to be his wife.

Emily grabs a wooden spoon from a kitchen drawer and stands expectantly in front of Charlotte. 'Can I stir?' she asks again.

'Yes, you can. I'll get a chair and an apron so you don't mess up your pretty dress,' says Charlotte, thinking that the dress will be one of the first things she gets rid of. It's plain denim, functional and simple. Emily is such a beautiful little girl. She deserves beautiful things.

'Love you both,' says Gideon, and he turns to go.

'We love you too, Daddy,' sings Charlotte as she lifts Emily onto a chair and ties the child-sized apron, bought specially for her, around her waist.

'Slowly now,' she says to Emily as the little girl dips her spoon into the pot. 'Slowly.'

FOUR
GIDEON
ONE MONTH AGO

Are you sure I can't pick you up?

No, I told you it's absolutely fine. I've booked a cab. I can't tell you how thankful I am to you and Charlotte for setting this up for me. I'll contact you in a few days to organise the first visit with Emily. I'm so excited but I want to make sure I have everything ready.

Okay, no problem. Enjoy! Gideon replies, and starts to type *I love you*, but then realises his mistake and adds a smile emoji instead. It's strange to think that they have been divorced for over two years and yet he still wants to add those words at the end of a text to her.

It was not his choice to end their marriage. It would never have been his choice, but a switch flipped in Sarah after she lost the baby – after she blamed herself for losing the baby, despite what every single doctor told her. She could not be reasoned with, and every time he tried, she grew angry at him, pushed him away, hated him.

'I think we should have some time apart,' she told him, four months after she had miscarried, her arms crossed and her face pale. She had lost weight and she hadn't been for a haircut for months. She didn't seem to be able to manage the house, spending all her time taking care of Emily. Most nights he came home to silence, an empty fridge, washing piled everywhere. She wouldn't let him get her domestic help, wouldn't discuss getting psychological help, wouldn't talk to him about anything. Their dream home, with its wide timber floorboards and stone fireplace, was a constant mess, the chaos of Sarah's grief covering every surface.

'I think you should get counselling and try to find a way to move forward,' Gideon replied. 'I love you and you love me, Sarah. This is your grief affecting things – it's not really how you feel. You've lost a baby and your parents in the last few months and you need... help.' They were in the living room, toys scattered everywhere, something sticky on the cream rug. He poured himself a drink, double what he usually would, and sat on the sofa, pushing aside an open Tupperware box filled with half-eaten crackers.

'You know what I would love?' she said, pulling her hair back irritably.

'What? Tell me... anything,' he replied, not realising that the flat tone of her voice was not a prelude to something he could do to help change the way she was feeling.

'I would love it if people would stop telling me that this is grief. I know the difference between grief and what I'm feeling. The grief lives inside me, deep inside me, colouring every day, but losing Adam has made me question things. And then Mum and Dad... Life is short, Gideon. I don't want to be married any more. I want you to leave. I don't know how much clearer I can make that.' She had become immovable, impossible to speak to.

'I'm not leaving,' he said. 'You don't really want this.' He took a large sip of his drink, letting the burn of the whisky focus his thoughts.

'I can call the police,' she said simply, raising an eyebrow, a spot of red appearing on each cheek. 'I just want you to go.' She began pacing, and Gideon felt a tide of alarm rise in his chest. He couldn't believe she could possibly be serious, but she was.

He downed his drink. 'Listen, Sarah...' he began, but she stopped pacing and looked at him, her hands grabbing her hair and pulling.

'Please go... just get out, get out, get out,' she yelled, her voice rising.

It was frightening to watch her baring her teeth and to see the hate for him in her eyes. For months he had been calm and patient and had tried every way he could think to get his wife help. Now his own anger rose inside him.

'Fine, but I'm taking Emily with me,' he replied, standing up and slamming his glass onto a side table, its surface covered in the sticky rings of previous drinks.

'You would say that, wouldn't you?' she spat. 'I've lost everything, so take the one thing I still love.'

'You still love *me*, Sarah,' he protested, his anger fading and concern growing about how confused she seemed, how mixed up.

She stepped right up to him, placed her hands on his shoulders and looked at him with something like sympathy. 'No, I don't. I haven't done for some time. I'm sorry, Gideon. Even before I lost Adam I wanted out, and I need you to know that and respect my choice.'

His hand went to his chest, pushing down on the pain that had appeared. Until that moment he had thought physical heartache wasn't possible. There was no way to change her mind.

He had no choice. He left that night.

The next day, still battered and bruised, he called her. 'How are you?' he asked tentatively.

'I'm okay,' she replied. 'I'm sorry about last night. I just couldn't… You weren't listening and I need you to listen. This is what I want, Gideon, it really is. Could you give me some space? You can see Emily whenever you want, just send me a text.'

Her voice was calmer on the phone and she did seem to be okay, so he agreed.

He called again the next day, hoping she would be ready for a real conversation, but she would only discuss Emily. He began turning up at the house on the pretext of visiting his daughter, needing to talk to his wife. 'Oh great, you're here,' she would say. 'I needed to get some food. You can have some time with Ladybug.' And she was out the door and gone before he could say anything. She did it every time he came over. There were moments when he hoped she would fail at being a single parent, and he fantasised about her calling him in the middle of the night for help, but it never happened. Eventually, and as much as it broke his heart, he accepted that she was happier without him.

'I'm getting the house ready to sell – my lawyer suggested it,' she told him one night.

'I'm going for a job interview tomorrow, at the high school across the road from where Emily will start school when she's five – isn't that perfect?' she said only a week later.

She was happy without him and it hurt, but he couldn't help being pleased for her as well. He was glad that she was managing to pull herself out of the hole of grief she had fallen into after losing Adam, losing her mother and father.

And then the papers were signed and everything was in place and she laughed about how well they were doing as a divorced couple. 'Conscious uncoupling,' she said with a giggle. 'No longer married but still friends.'

But as more time passed, she seemed to falter. When he went to pick his daughter up one day, he could see that Sarah had lost weight and that she looked tired. 'Is everything okay?' he asked.

'Fine,' she snapped, 'I'm just exhausted.'

The next time he saw her, she was even thinner, and he noticed, as she handed him Emily's backpack, that her nails were torn and ragged. Every time he called, Emily would answer the phone and say, 'Mummy's having a rest.'

One night Sarah phoned him in tears. 'I dreamed about him, Gideon, about our baby. He told me... he told me that I was the one who lost him, that it was my fault.'

'Sarah, it was a dream,' he comforted her, 'just a dream. It was never your fault. It couldn't have been. Every doctor told you that. Sometimes these things happen.'

'No, no... you don't understand,' she wailed.

'I'm coming over,' he said. 'I'll come and stay. I can help you with Emily so you can rest.'

'No,' she snapped, suddenly angry. 'I'm fine without you.'

'You're not fine,' he shouted, emotion getting the better of him.

'Leave me alone,' she responded, and slammed down the phone. The next day she sent him a text. *Sorry about last night. I'm going to see a therapist to get a handle on things. I have an appointment tomorrow.*

Gideon didn't know what to do, so he took himself off to his own therapist. 'How do I help her?' he asked. 'I want to be married again. I don't want this.'

'You can't force someone to love you back,' said Peter, a psychologist he had chosen at random from the internet, just needing someone to talk to. 'You have to let her be and move on with your life. Your only duty is to your child, and from what you say, Emily is doing fine.'

'Something is wrong with Sarah. I think she's depressed,' he said.

Peter shrugged his shoulders. 'I can't comment on that. But

if she's getting help, that's the best thing. Perhaps we can discuss you. I imagine that losing the baby was hard on you too, that you also experienced a lot of grief.'

Gideon felt tears prick at his eyes as the night they lost Adam returned to him. 'I didn't get a chance to grieve. All I've done is help and support Sarah.'

'Perhaps you have some anger about that?' the therapist asked. 'Perhaps we should work on that.'

Gideon finally allowed himself to feel everything he had been pushing away so he could help Sarah. He was devastated at the loss of the baby, angry with Sarah for not talking to him, furious that his whole life had disintegrated even though he had tried so hard to keep everything together. He and Peter worked through it all and Gideon accepted that he and Sarah would never be a couple again.

Even as Sarah continued to struggle, he developed the ability to sympathise with her but not allow it to break his heart that he couldn't be with her and hold her and somehow try to make it better.

But he failed her and he knows that. He should not have moved on with his life while she was still struggling. Maybe then the whispering man would never have appeared.

He sighs. She has endured so much, and now she's coming home and he's happy for her and excited for Emily, who will get to spend time with her mother. But he's also terrified, because what if it happens again? She seems completely changed, but what if she is still hiding the truth?

He shakes his head. He doesn't want to let his mind wander down that particular path now. He just wants to help Sarah get back on her feet so his daughter can have a fully present mother in her life.

He puts his phone down and looks over the paperwork he is supposed to be checking for a client, but he can't seem to concentrate on someone else's divorce. In truth, he had his doubts three months ago that Sarah would get to this point, that she would recover and be able to rejoin the world.

He stands up from his chair, bending his body backwards a little to stretch out his back, and then turns and looks out of his office window and down on the city of Sydney, beautiful in the autumn sunshine. In the harbour, sunlight dances off the water and the white sails of the yachts look bright and fresh.

If he had forced Sarah to get help when he first realised she was not herself, would they still be together? It's not something he lets himself think about too much. He's with Charlotte now and his life is... serene, calm, ordered. That's the best thing for him – and the best thing for their daughter.

A couple of weeks ago, when he told Charlotte that Sarah was coming home, he got the sense that she was unhappy about it.

'So soon?' she asked. She handed him a drink and poured one for herself. He liked that Charlotte was a whisky drinker as well, enjoying the discussions about smoky and deep flavours with her.

'I know it's only been a couple of months, but I can tell that everything has changed. She's so much better, like the old Sarah again,' he explained.

Charlotte frowned. 'Are you sure about that? I mean, it's not like you've had that much contact with her.'

Gideon felt a jolt of alarm at her question. He hadn't thought to mention that he and Sarah talked regularly. He was the only person she could call, really. She had friends but no one she felt ready to completely open up to, and so she used her one weekly call to speak to him.

'Yeah, but...' he began.

'How often are you talking to her?' Charlotte asked, her brow furrowed, able to read his hesitation.

Instead of telling her the truth, he fibbed – just a little.

'Only every now and again, but I can tell that everything is different.'

Without fail, the first thing they talked about when Sarah called was Emily. She sent daily emails to her daughter filled with jokes and pictures and questions. Emily answered each email right before she went to bed, taking pleasure in sitting in her dad's office, a pillow on the chair as she used his computer to talk to Mummy with his help. He had explained to her that her mother was getting help so she could be happy instead of sad. Emily missed Sarah but accepted this explanation. 'I want Mum to be happy,' she said.

But Emily was not the only thing they talked about. After they had caught up on their daughter's life, they found themselves discussing other things, like their time at university, where he had studied law and she had studied history and education. Sarah talked about how much she missed her mother and father, and asked about Gideon's parents, who were still on their trip of a lifetime.

'We can cut it short,' his mother had said anxiously on the phone when he had called to tell her what had happened with Sarah. 'We can come home and help with Emily. She can be with us during the week.'

'It's fine, Mum. Charlotte is doing brilliantly.'

'Of course she is,' his mother said, her tone betraying her feelings. Both his parents had been unhappy that he had got into a relationship again so quickly, believing that at some point he and Sarah would work it out. They had always loved Sarah – her warmth and humour made her a favourite everywhere she went – but they had never seen the dark side of her depression, the person she became.

Now she is back to being more like the Sarah he knew from that first moment in the university coffee shop, when they both reached for the last giant chocolate chip cookie and she laughed and offered to split it with him.

Small twitches of regret at rushing into another relationship are there, but he won't allow himself to think about that too much. In the weeks he and Sarah have been talking, he has admitted to himself that marriage to Charlotte was more her idea than his. They started dating and suddenly she was basically living with him. Proposing just felt like the next step as she pointed out rings she liked and discussed their future and developed such a good relationship with Emily. But it's been a blessing in disguise, and so he doesn't like to think about him and Sarah too deeply.

'What if she does it again?' Charlotte asked. 'What if she puts Emily in harm's way? How do you know you can trust her? It's hard not to worry. Perhaps if she had some outside supervision, we could be sure that Emily is safe.'

'I'm not going to do that,' he said. 'She's got the help she needed and moved forward. Emily will stay with us primarily until Sarah says she's ready to share custody. Sarah is her mother and she would never hurt her.' He felt anger rising inside him. Charlotte was wonderful with Emily, but Sarah was her mother and Emily needed her in her life.

'And what if the whispering man comes back?' Charlotte snapped, and then covered her mouth with her hand. 'I'm sorry,' she said quickly. 'That was uncalled for.'

'It was,' he said quietly. He let it go and sipped his whisky, and Charlotte did the same.

'I've made pasta puttanesca for dinner,' she said.

'Perfect,' he smiled, finishing his drink. 'I'll choose the wine.' The uncomfortable conversation was over. One thing about Charlotte is that she never pushes. If he doesn't want to talk, she leaves him to it. He would never say this to anyone, but he enjoys the fact that she is so aware of his moods, is always watching him and making sure he's happy. It's a nice change.

Now, as he watches a cruise liner moving slowly through

the harbour, he wonders if it's possible that Sarah will remain happy and healthy.

He will make sure that she is rested and well, and he won't take no for an answer if she needs help. Satisfied with this decision, he sits down at his desk again and tries to focus on the divorce papers, concentrating on someone else's life for a moment.

FIVE
SARAH

'Are you ready? Do you feel ready?' Dr Augustine asks.

Sarah's first instinct is to say yes, to move her lips against her teeth so that a smile appears, to lie. But she knows Dr Augustine won't accept that.

Three months ago, in her first session with him, she told him, 'I'm fine. I don't need to be here,' even as she scratched at the skin on the back of her hand and jiggled her foot. That was a lie and he knew it. Three days of drug-induced sleep in a hospital had not solved her problem. The doctor removed his round glasses and peered at them, searching for specks on the lenses, then replaced them in silence. He allowed the silence to go on for at least a minute as Sarah looked around his office at the walls lined with dark wood bookshelves. When she returned her gaze to him, he was waiting for her, his bushy grey eyebrows slightly raised.

'Now, that was a lie, wasn't it?' he said gently, and Sarah burst into tears, relieved at being called out, at being forced to confront what she was dealing with. Of course it was a lie. She had been sectioned for three days and Gideon had arranged for her to come here to Pacific Green, a small private hospital where everyone was fighting their own demons.

She has learned over the past few months that it's fine to let go, to sleep, to forgive herself. There is so much she has done wrong, but blaming herself for all of it won't bring anyone back. It's not as simple as that, not even close, but she knows that when she wakes up in the morning now, she is not exhausted because she only let herself doze, fearful of deep sleep, terrified of dreams, scared of sinking into her subconscious and losing control. And she is not immediately overwhelmed with the hideousness of simply being alive. A few months ago, nothing mattered except Emily and Gideon, but the fact that Gideon mattered was a secret she kept from herself. And now Gideon is with Charlotte and he is happy – and he deserves to be happy. But she is happy too, in a small way; she is here and happy to be alive, happy that on the nights when there seemed to be only one way out of her situation, she didn't take it.

But is she ready? She has no idea, so she needs to be truthful about that because it all starts with her being truthful with herself.

'Not really,' she says to the doctor now. 'I'm not really ready.'

He nods. 'And that's okay, because you can't ever be totally ready for this. You've been in this safe space for many weeks, and the world outside can seem scary and uncontrollable. But you have the tools to manage now, don't you?'

'Yes,' breathes Sarah, relieved to be reminded of this by her doctor, even though she reminds herself of it every day.

'And when will you be seeing your daughter again?'

'I've told Gideon to give me a few days to settle into the apartment he's rented for me. I'm looking forward to being somewhere new. And then we can start visits. He'll come the first few times and... well, supervise, I guess, and then when

Emily is comfortable enough, I'll pick her up from his house or school or his new wife can drop her off.'

Sarah is nervous about finally meeting Charlotte, the woman who has so effortlessly stepped into her shoes as a mother to Emily and done it so well while still flourishing in her career. When Gideon talks about her, she can hear the admiration and respect he feels for her in his voice. He deems her to be capable of anything and everything – which is certainly not how he thinks of Sarah, not how he has thought of her in a long time, and with good reason. But she's working on getting back to her old self, becoming a better self really, every day a step forward.

'Good, good,' the doctor says. 'Take it slow, Sarah. Take it as slowly as you need to.'

'I've missed her so much,' she says. 'I can't wait to just... just hold her.' Her daughter's face comes to her, a memory of the two of them looking in a mirror together, Emily touching Sarah's chin, saying, 'Just like mine,' and stroking her mouth, 'Just like mine,' and brushing her finger near her eye, 'Just like mine. We're the same, Mummy, but you're bigger.'

'I'm bigger,' she agreed, and she knows that at the time she hoped that certain parts of Emily would not be just like her; that she would be stronger and more resilient than her mother.

'And you have your first therapy session booked with Amelia, so that's good,' says the doctor.

'Yes.' Sarah nods. Amelia comes highly recommended by Dr Augustine. The new psychologist is part of Sarah's recovery plan, just like the sleeping pills are, so that she never descends into the same space she was three months ago, but Sarah is not looking forward to meeting her. The idea of starting with a new therapist, of telling her story again from the beginning, feels overwhelming but she has the appointment in her phone and she will attend it because she has to so she can be with her daughter for every precious moment in Emily's life. That's all she wants and thinks about. It is her reason for getting up in the morning and working to be better each day.

'I think you're going to be fine,' says Dr Augustine, standing up from the leather tub chair he likes to sit in during sessions. He smiles. 'You've worked really hard to accept everything that happened over the past few years and you are prepared to move forward with your life. Good luck.' He extends a hand, but Sarah impulsively stands up and steps forward to hug him. She is grateful that he hugs her back.

'Thank you,' she says, 'for everything.'

'You did the work,' he replies.

Back in her room, she checks the bathroom and her cupboard one last time to make sure she hasn't left anything. All Emily's drawings, everything she has sent over the past few months, have been carefully packed into a box for her to take home. She will put them up in the room at the new apartment where Emily will one day hopefully sleep over.

The new apartment was Gideon's idea. It's on the second floor of a small block. 'It will feel safer,' he told her. She will rent there until she finds somewhere she would like to buy. Her old apartment has to sell first – something else Gideon has organised for her. She is relying on Gideon too much right now, but she hopes to change that soon.

'Why will it feel safer?' she asked. 'The last apartment was in a secure block.'

'Yes,' he agreed, 'but it was on the ground floor and... I mean...'

'You mean he can't get to me on the second floor,' she said, and then she laughed, actually laughed. At this point, the whispering man seems like something from a movie, a child's nightmare come to life. At her worst, he was so clearly there. She never saw him, only heard his sibilant threats, but his image is burned into her brain. His drawn face, scraggly grey hair and skeletal fingers ending in curled nails will never leave her.

Even now, she remembers the throat-closing fear she would feel when he visited her. She would be in bed, her eyes darting from side to side, having checked on Emily for the tenth time in an hour, and as time passed and the night grew deeper and darker, her body would struggle to remain awake. She would fall, tumbling into sleep, and then jerk awake again, jumping up to check on Emily. Back in bed, she would hear his nails on the window, hear him whispering, 'It's your fault, Sarah, all your fault. They are all gone because of you. It's your fault.' She understood what he was saying, what he was threatening, even without him actually speaking the words. She knew Emily would be taken from her next. She would leap out of bed and run to her daughter's room, spend the night curled up next to her on her small bed, her arm draped protectively over her. On very bad nights, it wasn't enough to simply be next to Emily. Instead, she had to hide them both.

She feels something like shame rise inside her now when she remembers how some mornings Emily would wake up on the floor of the walk-in wardrobe with her. She is grateful, deeply grateful now, for the night her daughter demanded to go back to bed or she was calling her daddy. 'I'm not scared of him,' the little girl said, pretending to be brave and strong but obviously terrified.

'He'll get us, Em. Please, baby, don't go out.' Sarah was totally convinced he was there. Her exhausted brain could not separate fact from fiction.

'Then let me call Daddy, let me call him. The whispering man is scared of him.'

Once or twice Sarah herself called Gideon late at night, made an excuse about hearing a noise, about fearing that someone was trying to break in. To his credit, he understood the ruse and came over instead of instructing her to call the police. He would walk around the apartment checking the windows and go out into the small garden to look around. He would encourage her to make herself a hot drink and then sit with her until she could calm her nerves.

But that night, the night she was taken away on a stretcher, Emily told Gideon the truth, begged him to save them both from the whispering man. He came when she needed him the most. She pushed him away, but he has never let her down.

Just before she leaves, she sits down on the single bed she has slept in for the last few months and takes a deep breath. A certain giddy joy fills her. She's finally here, finally leaving. Finally ready to rejoin the world, to really embrace it, not to simply exist in order to take care of her daughter.

Standing up, she glances in the mirror on the wall opposite her bed. Her chestnut hair sits just below her shoulders and her green eyes are bright and clear. There is a long road ahead of her as she rebuilds her relationship with her little girl, but she's determined to get there. Taking one last look in the mirror, she smiles, a smile she can feel, and then she leaves the room, closing the door behind her, vacating the space for the next person who needs the help of the Pacific Green Clinic.

As she wheels her suitcase down the hushed, carpeted hallway, she remembers to feel grateful that she got to recover in a place like this, where there are nice rooms with large windows and soft beds, where the food is good and the gardens beautifully tended, with bright green grass and towering trees.

She stops outside a room close to the end of the hallway and knocks softly.

'Come in,' the person inside calls, and she opens the door.

'I wanted to say goodbye,' she says to the man lying on the bed, a book in his hands.

Damien gets up and comes to stand close to her. 'I've been dreading that, to be honest,' he replies.

'You'll be fine,' says Sarah, and then she puts her arms

around him, pulling him into a hug that he returns, holding on tightly. He has been here for her on her worst days and her best days, cheering her on just as she has done for him.

When she first arrived at the clinic, she was bewildered and sad as she tried to adjust to where she was and cope with not seeing Emily. A few days later, a man sat down next to her at dinner. 'You look like I feel,' he said simply.

Sarah had been staring down at her tray of food, concentrating on the orangeness of the orange she had taken to eat for dessert and wondering if she would have the energy to peel it. But when he spoke, she turned to look at him, noting how thin he was, his cool blue eyes the most arresting thing about him, his mouth slightly hidden by a neat beard.

'I feel...' she began, finding her voice scratchy. She had barely spoken to anyone yet. She sat up a little, cleared her throat and dredged up the energy for social niceties from somewhere deep inside herself. 'How long have you been here?' she asked him.

'Long enough to want to leave, not long enough to be able to leave,' he said. 'Only since yesterday.'

Sarah nodded, understanding the out-of-body feeling of finding yourself at a mental health facility.

'I'm Sarah,' she said, and held out her hand, formal despite the situation.

He took it gently and met her gaze. 'I'm... Damien,' he said. 'I just thought I would say hello. You look so sad.'

Sarah nodded again, confirming her sadness, the deep well of it inside her. Picking up the orange, she rolled it around in her hands, then she said, 'I miss my daughter,' and burst into tears.

She expected that Damien would walk away from the awkward situation. But he didn't. Instead, he put his arms around her and held her while she cried, murmuring, 'Of course you do, of course you do.'

They quickly became good friends and shared their stories. Damien struggles with the outside world and getting through every day, believing he is always being judged, stared at, mocked. 'I feel like everyone, just everyone, is laughing at me, and even though I know that's not logical, the anxiety makes it impossible to get out of bed on too many days. I feel like I'm completely controlled by my anxiety and I have turned to things that are not good for me to help that. I want to be better,' he told her, sharing this in halting sentences, watching her face to see if she too would laugh at him.

'I understand,' she told him the first time and has told him every time they talk. 'I understand.'

Now she lets go of the hug before he does. 'You'll email me, won't you?' she asks.

'I will, but you won't want to speak to me; you'll be too busy getting your life back together,' he says morosely.

'I'll never be too busy for a friend, especially one I've confided so much in,' replies Sarah, making sure that Damien meets her gaze so he understands she means it. 'And when you feel ready to leave here, we'll catch up and have coffee or get a drink or something.'

'Like good friends do,' he says, his tone sullen and slightly resentful.

In the weeks they have known each other, she has been careful to make sure he understands that she is not looking for anything more than friendship, even as she has sometimes thought how easy it would be to be with him. He understands her completely and she never feels the need to explain her anguish. He suffers as she does on the bad days. He also struggles with depression and chronic shyness, making it difficult for him to speak to people and to be out in the world. He has not bonded with any of the other patients, hurrying away if someone came up to talk to her and sitting alone rather than joining her if she was with a group of people. She has been his only friend at the clinic and she is concerned about how he will be now that she is leaving.

'It took me a whole day of watching you before I found the courage to speak to you,' he confided in her, 'but I reasoned that you were struggling too, so maybe you wouldn't just reject me.' Their friendship has helped Sarah as she worked her way towards recovery, but she has always been aware that there were days when she needed to distance herself from Damien and his need for her approval and attention. Most importantly, she has her child to think of before she can think about anyone else.

She has not discussed their friendship with Dr Augustine, knowing that he might caution her against it, but he has seen them sitting together at dinner, waved at them as they played a board game in the recreation room, so she has assumed that if there was a real problem with her getting to know Damien, the doctor would have said something.

'I have to go now,' she says, 'but I'll be waiting for your first email.' Sometimes it's easier to let Damien work through things himself without trying to constantly reassure him.

'I'll miss you,' he says, and she smiles in reply, stepping out of his room and continuing her journey out of the clinic and into the autumn sunshine, bright and glaring in a perfect blue sky.

A cab is waiting for her, the driver quiet and respectful of where he has picked up his fare from.

'It's a beautiful day,' Sarah finally says as they drive past a beach, where waves lap at the shore and those not at work are soaking up the slight warmth in the air.

'Yes,' he agrees. 'It surely is. Warmer than usual, but that will change. We're expecting a huge drop in temperature in the next couple of days. Winter will be here soon.'

'It will be fine,' Sarah murmurs, more to herself than the

driver, and then she closes her eyes and takes a deep breath. *Are you listening, Mum? Dad? My baby Adam? Are you listening? Please help me. It needs to be fine. It has to be.*

SIX
CHARLOTTE

Charlotte takes one last look around the apartment and breathes a sigh of satisfaction. It looks perfect, because she has done a perfect job. It's light and serene but cosy at the same time. It was a good choice to paint the walls in white with blue undertones, to bring out the blue in the sofa and armchairs. She has left the bedroom plain because Gideon said Sarah wanted to decorate that herself, but she has created a pretty bedroom for Emily with one yellow wall and matching bed linen. At home, Emily has a room decorated in pale blue with stars painted on the ceiling, the kind of bedroom Charlotte longed for as a child, unimpressed with the dark pieces of antique furniture handed down from her grandmother that she had instead. Emily's favourite colours are blue and yellow. She is remarkably clever and even at five knows that one day she wants to be a scientist and study the stars. Every night Gideon turns off her light and together they identify the constellations on her ceiling. It's adorable to see, and listening to Gideon talk to his daughter makes Charlotte love him just a little more.

She tweaks a curtain in dusty blue so that it hangs correctly and then plumps a cushion on the sofa before snapping a few quick pictures for her portfolio. There is a limited amount you can do with a rental apartment, but she is good at making such places feel like home, although the clients she usually works with are high-end bankers and lawyers and doctors from overseas who are only in Australia for a few months.

'You don't have to be involved at all,' Gideon told her when he explained that he was going to rent a new apartment for Sarah to come home to. 'She has some stuff she wants to keep, but I thought I would get a new sofa and some chairs, something to make it feel like a different place. I want her to feel like it's a new start.'

'I'd like to,' Charlotte said. 'She's part of your life and we all need to be friends. I want everything to be easy. The last thing you need to worry about is your ex-wife and your new wife not getting along.' The words sounded sincere because she wanted them to. She has worked very hard on squashing her resentment towards Sarah, trying to see her as a person who needs compassion instead of someone who takes up more of Gideon's time than she should. She is still working on it. It helps to be able to tell the truth to her mother, to listen to her mum's perspective while still feeling supported.

'Of course you'll get along,' Gideon said. 'Sarah is incredibly grateful to you for stepping up, and she wants Emily to be happy, as we all do. It's going to be fine.' Gideon is an optimist, a glass-half-full kind of man.

'Absolutely fine,' agreed Charlotte, with a brisk smile. Even as she said the words, she hoped Gideon couldn't hear that she was concerned. It will be an adjustment for all of them, especially Emily, who is happily in a routine now. Charlotte has expressed some of her worries to her mother, who has cautioned her against saying anything. 'You don't want to make things difficult,' she said. 'Let everyone find their place and give it some time. You never know how things are going to play out. Perhaps now would be a good time to think about having a baby – Sarah is back and you can concentrate on your own family.'

'Emily is my family,' Charlotte replied, not willing to confess that Gideon was against a return to the baby years.

'Of course, and the best thing you can do is make sure Gideon sees you as a partner and an ally now that Sarah is home.'

Her mother has a pragmatic way of looking at things and Charlotte trusts her judgement. So she actively helped Gideon find this apartment and then she decorated it with a practised eye. Emily will be staying here eventually and Charlotte wants her stepdaughter to be happy.

Taking one last look around, she smiles and then checks her outfit in the mirror she has hung by the front door. 'We may not be the most beautiful women in the world, but we have the dollars and sense to make the most of ourselves'; that was her mother's mantra and now it's hers. She and Sarah are very different-looking. Gideon's first wife is pretty, almost beautiful, but she wears her beauty as though it doesn't have anything to do with her. So far Charlotte has only seen pictures of her, but she can tell that there is nothing posed or studied about the way she looks. Beauty has come easily for Sarah, and like most beautiful women, she probably doesn't think about it too much.

Charlotte, on the other hand, has dieted, exercised, buffed and polished her way to beauty. Her blonde hair is cut by the best hairdresser in Sydney, her body is shaped by daily workouts and her skin treated with the best creams and lotions she can afford. It's hard work, but any time she has complained about this, her mother's reply is always the same. 'If it matters enough to you, you'll work for it.' Another one of her mantras, and true of everything in life.

It does matter to Charlotte. It matters when Gideon tells her she looks good, or when she walks into a meeting with new clients and they are instantly at ease with her decisions for their home – because of her past work, but also because of the way she looks. Her job is all about image, and she is very good at that. She has worked hard to become one of the most sought-after designers in the city because she wanted it. And when she first saw Gideon, she wanted him as well, knowing almost immediately that he was the perfect man for her.

Her mother was married to her father for fifteen years before he died, and in that time, Carol did everything she could to be the perfect wife. Whatever her husband was interested in, she was interested in. He liked bushwalks, so she joined him, despite the fact that she preferred the indoors. He enjoyed watching cricket, so she became proficient at watching the game, able to comment on where each team was in the competition and have a conversation about the players' performances. He liked shooting, so she joined the gun club with him and together they spent hours on a Sunday there, despite Carol hating the feel of a weapon in her hands. Charlotte understands that her mother was trying to keep her marriage alive and interesting, though it didn't work. Her father died early, but the marriage was already faltering, nearly over.

Charlotte doesn't subscribe completely to her mother's theory of marriage, although she has acquired a taste for whisky because Gideon enjoys it so much. She also works hard on creating a calm environment at home, because she understands that's something Gideon values. 'It's so easy to relax here,' he has told her. He likes being at home with her and Emily, and that's important. Home is his safe space, a safe space for him and his daughter.

Getting along with Sarah is also important, because it will mean that Gideon doesn't feel he's in the middle of two women, and she means to work hard at it. It's good for Emily as well, an angel of a child who deserves the best possible life.

Things are going to be very different now that Sarah is coming home and returning to her role as another primary caregiver, and Charlotte is determined to make the situation work well for all of them. The end goal is shared custody, with Emily spending half the time with her mother and half with her and Gideon. It's important that the little girl knows they are all there for her. And taking care of a child is a lot of work, especially for someone who is fragile. Charlotte needs to be ready to step in full-time again if she needs to.

Her phone pings and she sees it's a message from Edward. *Now what?*

She grits her teeth, struggling with a flare of irritation towards her brother, who needs to be given instructions over and over again. *You know what to do – I sent a list!!!!*, she types quickly.

Her mother's soft spot when it comes to Edward borders on the ridiculous. He's only just returned from a holiday in Europe. Her mother paid, saying, 'He needs a little break, and who knows – he might meet a nice girl and finally get married.'

'Why would you spend so much money on him?' Charlotte replied. 'He doesn't deserve it, and what does he need a break from anyway?'

'Trust me, darling. In the end, your life will be improved by your brother having some time away.'

Now she feels like she has to train him all over again, explaining the simplest pick-ups of furniture and every other task in detail.

She switches off the light in the hallway, pleased that she thought to put a bunch of flowers on the round table in the centre of the room, because the blue hydrangeas smell sweet and bring everything together.

Sarah will be happy and she will tell Gideon, so he will be happy too, and Charlotte has made it her business to keep Gideon happy.

She is aware that Gideon would have waited a lot longer to propose to her if she hadn't pushed, just a little, hadn't moved in bit by bit before he realised what was happening, hadn't taken steps to make his life easier with her in it. When he proposed, she played the role of surprised girlfriend very well, acting as though she'd never expected it, as though she hadn't stopped to stare longingly in the windows of jewellery stores, remarking at how pretty some of the rings were. She knew what she was doing. He thinks proposing was his idea, but 'there's nothing wrong with giving a man a little shove as long as he doesn't feel your hands on his back', as her mother says.

The first time she saw him, she felt her breath catch, literally catch. She had been brought in to redecorate his firm's boardroom and some of the offices, to take the whole feeling from 'a bunch of stuffy old men work here' to 'this is a place that is young, dynamic, filled with different people and genders'. The firm now had four women partners and they needed the space to reflect that.

Charlotte brightened the walls in the boardroom by removing the panelling and adding a light-coloured parquetry table to go with the aged leather chairs. She improved the look of the reception area with slimline Scandinavian sofas and stunning prints filled with colour on the walls. When it was time to move on to the offices, one of the partners – a woman named Shana, who Charlotte got along with very well and shared some lunches and after-work drinks with – said, 'That's Gideon's office and he has no desire to change, mostly because he hates the idea of having to stop working for even a moment. He got divorced a year ago and the poor man is still not over it, which is strange for a divorce lawyer.' She laughed, a hollow, brittle laugh that told Charlotte that Shana wanted to help him get over his divorce.

And then the office door opened and she understood why. Gideon was tall and slim, with broad shoulders, a head full of grey-brown curls, and dark brown eyes, a light stubble on his square jaw.

'Oh Gideon, this is Charlotte, the designer. Sure you don't want your office done?'

Gideon looked at her and smiled. 'Well maybe,' he said, and Charlotte smiled back and right then made a decision. She was drawn to his smile, to the light in his eyes, to the way he held himself.

They went from one after-work drink to marriage in a matter of months.

'Well done, darling,' her mother whispered on the day of her small wedding, organised quickly while she tried to adjust to caring for Emily full-time. 'I had almost given up hope that you would find someone, but Gideon is just perfect.'

Charlotte smiled as she adjusted her cream silk gown. The material clung to her body just enough, falling beautifully to the floor.

It was a lovely wedding and Emily spent the whole evening right next to her, beaming at everyone, beautiful in her bridesmaid's dress. Charlotte felt complete in a way she had never imagined she would, her happiness only marred by her needing to accept that she would never have a baby of her own.

The only fly in the ointment – yet another of her mother's phrases – was Sarah, who was lovely and kind according to Gideon but fragile and damaged by so much loss. Charlotte understood, but she also understood that when Sarah called, Gideon went. It was something she was still striving to get used to.

Three months ago, Sarah went from fragile and holding on to completely delusional and in need of help. Now she is back, and Charlotte can hear from the way Gideon speaks that he will not hear a word against her. If she pushes too hard, if she criticises too much, he will turn on her, but she's not too worried about that. There's more than one way to skin a cat, as her mother would say.

SEVEN
GIDEON
THREE AND A HALF WEEKS AGO

'Stop jumping, Em, she's coming,' says Gideon as they stand at the door to Sarah's apartment.

The door opens and his heart lurches, because standing in front of him is the woman he fell in love with. She has gained some weight, so she no longer looks like a strong wind could blow her away, and there is colour in her cheeks, freckles across her nose and light in her green eyes. But the best part is her smile, wide and genuine and all the way to her eyes. He can literally feel her happiness radiating off her.

'Ladybug, Ladybug,' she says, and she crouches down and enfolds her daughter in a hug, lifting her up. 'You look so lovely and you smell so good and I have so many fun things planned for us today.' She whirls around with Emily in her arms and the little girl giggles.

'Granny Carol says pretty girls should always smell nice, so she gave me some of her perfume.'

Sarah looks at Gideon and he shrugs his shoulders. Carol is not his favourite person in the world, but she does love Emily. She likes to give her gifts, nearly empty bottles of expensive perfume and old designer bags for her to play with. She often asks to spend the afternoon with her, and she will take her to get her curls straightened and her nails done. Charlotte thinks it's good for Emily to have time with her, because Gideon's parents are away and Sarah's parents are both dead. He knows that Sarah would not like the emphasis Carol places on looking good and on how pretty Emily is, but he has also decided that she is not doing any real harm.

'Well, lucky you,' says Sarah, and Gideon is grateful that she has let it go. 'Now, the most important thing we need to do is bake cupcakes.'

'Yay,' shouts Emily as her mother puts her down. 'But first I have to see my room.'

'Absolutely,' agrees Sarah.

Emily looks round the room with wide eyes. 'It's the best,' she says. 'Charlotte told me she made it pretty just for me, and it is – I love it. When can I sleep here?'

'Not tonight, but soon, Ladybug,' says Sarah, and Gideon can see it pains her to say that, but they need to take things slowly. The woman she was three months ago is completely gone. She is so different that the transformation feels miraculous, and he experiences a fleeting wish that he had forced her to get help sooner, but as Charlotte says, there's no guarantee it would have worked before now. 'She was ready to get help, Gideon, there's nothing to blame yourself for.'

He looks around the apartment, admiring what Charlotte has done with the place. 'I'll take care of everything,' she told him, and so he left her to it. It amazes him that his wife can take any space and turn it into a home, and he feels a glow of pride.

'Charlotte did a beautiful job,' says Sarah. 'I've texted her to thank her, but do you think I should call?'

'A text is fine,' he says, knowing that even though Charlotte has been really good about Sarah coming home, she is feeling a little pushed to the side. 'Wouldn't it be nice if Sarah could finally meet someone new to be with?' she said last night as they discussed what was happening today. They were in bed, doing last-minute checks on emails on their phones and coordinating their schedules.

'It would be,' he agreed, closing his calendar, 'but I don't think she's ready for that.' He hated the idea of Sarah with another man, though he knew it shouldn't bother him.

'Maybe we could introduce her to Edward, he's single,' Charlotte laughed, and he laughed along with her, knowing she couldn't possibly mean that. He has only met Edward a couple of times, but he's heard all about how he frustrates his mother and sister with his inability to get his life together.

'I think Sarah can find her own dates,' he said, making sure Charlotte understood not to get involved. She is forever trying to fix her brother up with single women. 'He needs someone to run his life for him, and when my mother is no longer here, I don't want to have to do it,' she often says. Edward would obviously not be a good match for Sarah. Gideon doesn't want to think about what man would be.

'Let's hope she finds someone soon. I'm sure you want her to be happy,' Charlotte murmured, and then she climbed out of bed and left the room. 'Just checking I switched the dishwasher on,' she said over her shoulder. But she didn't return for a long time and he eventually switched off his bedside light and closed his eyes. They had both felt the conversation moving in the wrong direction. Charlotte is good at avoiding an argument. He knew she was probably in the kitchen, cleaning out a drawer or wiping a shelf in a cupboard so that the things she wanted to say were wiped away with the dirt she thought was there. He would like to tell her that she shouldn't feel she needs to keep her opinions to herself, but when it comes to Sarah, he would prefer her to stay out of it. The whole thing is difficult enough already.

He wants to believe that Charlotte has no reason to be jealous of his feelings for his first wife, but looking at Sarah now, he can't help questioning that. She is the mother of his child, and there is still something there, something he needs to keep under control.

'Cupcake time,' he says, and Emily claps her hands.

While Emily and Sarah mix and talk, he sits in the living room of the small apartment, listening while he pretends to be on his phone. He explicitly told Sarah during their last conversation before she was released from the clinic that he would need to be here when she and Emily first reconnected, so that Emily felt safe and so that—

'So that you can supervise me,' Sarah said.

'No, it's not that,' he replied.

'Yes, it is, and that's fine, Gideon. I understand, and if things were different, if you were the one who'd had a breakdown, I would do the same thing, so you don't need to feel guilty about it.'

He breathed a sigh of relief at her words. He couldn't simply drop Emily off and leave. Charlotte thought they should get social services involved to make sure that Sarah was fine to be with her daughter, but there is no way Gideon would have allowed that. Sarah is better – he can see that now.

'I may just go and get some petrol,' he says, standing up. 'Will you be okay for a bit?'

'Sure,' smiles Sarah. 'Ladybug, you watch those cupcakes – not too close, but watch carefully and you'll see them rise like magic as they cook. But don't touch, because it's—'

'Hot, I know, Mum. I bake all the time with Charlotte and I never touch the oven.'

'Good, I'm just going to open the door for Daddy.'

He starts to protest, but then realises that she wants to speak to him. They stand outside the apartment with the door slightly open.

'Are you sure you're happy to leave her with me for a bit?' Sarah asks, uncertainty on her face.

He squeezes her shoulder. 'I'm sure, but what matters is

that you're sure. I can stay, but if I go, it will only be for a short time. It's up to you.'

She leans forward and hugs him, tight and hard. 'Thank you,' she whispers, and then she goes back inside.

Gideon realises he's smiling when he reaches his car. A rumble of thunder warns him of an impending storm, and he gets in quickly, Sarah's face on his mind. As he pulls away from the kerb, he shakes his head. He's in trouble here. He knows he is.

He cannot allow his feelings for Sarah to resurface. He needs to distance himself from her, make sure that their relationship remains strictly as co-parents.

Charlotte is worried and he can feel that. When they started dating, she insisted on seeing a picture of Sarah and he noticed her slight frown as she looked at one he had on his phone. 'She's very pretty. Why did you get divorced?'

'Not my choice,' he answered. 'But that's the past and I'm looking forward to the future.'

In the last few days, he has felt her get a little jittery, has seen some cracks appear in her perfect self-control. She essentially stepped into the role of mother for Emily and he knows she doesn't want to give it up. He can't blame her. But they will all find a way to get along and everything will be okay.

As he pulls into the petrol station, he whispers it aloud: 'Everything will be okay.' And prays that the words remain true.

EIGHT
SARAH

Alone in her apartment with her daughter for the first time, Sarah practises breathing slowly. She can do this, she knows she can; the anxiety tapping at her heart is just unfamiliarity, that's all.

The timer on the oven pings and Emily leaps up from her cross-legged position on the floor of the tiny kitchen. 'They're done, they're done!' she shouts.

'Yes, they are,' agrees Sarah. 'Now stand back. See, we'll put them up here,' she takes the tray from the oven, 'and they can cool while we make icing. What colour would you like?'

'Pink and blue and green,' says Emily, clapping her hands. The caramel-sweet smell of cooling cupcakes fills the air.

'Right, lots of colours,' says Sarah, and she gets everything they need.

An hour later, they have iced all the cupcakes and eaten one each. They have had a meandering conversation about school and friends and Charlotte and Granny Carol and the reasons why Emily still has to go to bed at 7.30.

To Sarah it feels like they have simply picked up where they left off. Her anxiety has diminished with each passing minute and she even found herself giggling over a dab of icing on her nose. She has missed this feeling, this living right in the moment feeling of being with her little girl. It has been such a long time since they have been able to be together like this, since way before she went to the clinic. She can see that Emily is slightly wary of her, of how she will react, watching to see if she is okay in a way that a five-year-old child should never have to, but Emily, too, has relaxed as Sarah has shown her that she is back to being the mother she remembers.

After they have cleaned up the kitchen, Sarah gets a text from Gideon. He's been gone longer than she thought he would be but she has loved every minute alone with Emily.

Are you doing okay? I went to grab some coffee as well. Should I come back?

A touch of irritation at being checked up on flares, but she grits her teeth against the feeling. He's only doing what needs to be done.

We're having a great time. All good 😊

'Now what are we going to do?' asks Emily, her energy unwavering.

'Now we are going to colour in this book of magical pictures,' Sarah says, taking out the colouring book and crayons that Charlotte so kindly left in the kitchen.

'I love colouring!' squeals Emily.

Together they page through the book, looking at the black and white pictures of fairies and elves and dragons. On one page is a picture of a witch with long grey hair and curled fingernails, and Sarah feels her heart jump as she quickly turns the page.

Finally they settle on two unicorns by a river, a rainbow

arching above them. They each pick up a crayon and start on a separate piece of the picture.

'Are we going to go back to our old house?' Emily asks after a minute of silence, her yellow crayon moving over the unicorn's body.

Sarah keeps colouring, her fingers tightening around the blue crayon she is holding for the sky, and takes a deep breath. 'You mean the house where we lived with Daddy? We sold that one, baby, you remember.'

'No, um... I'm going to make his horn pink... the house where it was just you and me and the whispering man came.'

Sarah puts down the blue crayon and flexes her fingers, which have cramped around it. She picks up a purple crayon and starts on the rainbow at the top of the page. 'No... that's going to be sold. We'll stay here for a bit and then find somewhere new.'

'And will he come there?' Emily asks softly, her tongue jutting out of her mouth a little as she concentrates. Sarah understands that her daughter can only ask her this because they aren't looking at each other, and her heart breaks for her little girl who is trying to figure out who her mother is now.

'Em, Ladybug,' she says, 'the whispering man isn't real. Something was wrong in my brain, but it's all fixed now. He was my imagination and he won't come back.'

Emily puts down the pink crayon and picks up her cup of water. 'Was he part of my 'magination too, Mum?' she asks, staring down into the drink.

Sarah's breath catches, her heart thumping inside her chest. 'Did you... did you hear him too?' she asks.

'Sometimes,' says Emily, lifting her head to meet her gaze.

'Well, he's gone for ever now,' Sarah says firmly, reaching out to touch her daughter's chin, knowing that this was her fault. She told Emily that the whispering man was outside, told her child that he was going to get them. She was not in her right mind. She feels guilt seeping through her body at what she has done. Other parents make Santa Claus and the Tooth Fairy real, but she has given her child a hideous apparition to worry about. Emily probably hears the spectre in her dreams. She will need to watch her carefully and perhaps suggest a child psychologist if things seem off.

'Gone for ever,' says Emily, and she smiles, her relief obvious.

They finish their colouring mostly in silence until Gideon returns, dragging the winter cold in with him, his shirt damp from the rain that has arrived. When Emily realises that he has come to fetch her, she bursts into tears. 'No, no,' she says, clinging to Sarah's leg. 'I want to stay here with you.'

Sarah feels her own tears on her cheeks and quickly wipes them away before crouching down to hug her. 'Very soon you will, Ladybug. So soon that you won't even remember a time when you didn't sleep over here. But today you don't have any of your stuff. You don't have Bunny or your toothbrush or your pyjamas. Next time you come, bring those with you and then we can have a proper sleepover.' As she says the words, she looks up at Gideon, hoping, praying that he will agree. If he doesn't, she won't fight him on his decision. She's rushing things, but everything just feels right. She wants to be back in her daughter's life right now. She wants to have never left, but there is no way to change that.

'Come on, Em,' he says. 'You heard what Mum said. Next time you can sleep over. Maybe we can stop for an ice cream on the way home.' Sarah's eyes well up as relief rushes through her. Next time her little girl won't have to leave after a few hours.

'But I already had a cupcake, and Charlotte says that too many sweets will make me roly-poly,' says Emily, her tears ceasing.

Sarah feels her shoulders tense. She and Gideon had very clear ideas on raising a daughter in the age of social media, and making food purely something to be enjoyed was high on the list of their priorities. She really hopes that Charlotte hasn't changed his mind about this.

'Well, I say that today is an ice cream and cupcake day. Come on, give Mum one last kiss and then you can call her when we get home,' he says jovially.

'Can I use your phone?' asks Emily, excited now as she waits by the door.

'You can,' says Gideon.

'And can I play a game on it?' she adds, sensing that this is the time to push for everything she wants.

'We'll see,' laughs Gideon, and he looks at Sarah, who laughs with him. The jolt in her stomach is just happiness, or that's what she tells herself. Gideon was her first real love, but he belongs to someone else now.

Even so, as she closes the door behind her ex-husband and her daughter, the whole- body ache that ripples through her takes her breath away. She stands still, her hands clenched into fists, stopping herself from wrenching open the door and screaming, 'Come back, come back to me.' She lets the hideous feeling wash over her until she can breathe normally. Then, shivering, she grabs a warm jumper from her room and boils the kettle for a cup of tea.

'Camomile for calm,' she hears Damien say as she puts a tea bag in her cup, and she smiles, remembering afternoons when they sat together watching the rain through the clinic windows, giant mugs of camomile tea in their hands.

Yesterday she had her first appointment with Amelia, her new psychologist, and the young woman suggested this technique of simply being in the moment and accepting her pain instead of trying to push it away. Sarah was taken aback when she first saw Amelia, who is obviously under thirty, with short blonde hair and big brown eyes. She wanted to turn and run but sat down on Amelia's cream-coloured sofa, knowing that Dr

Augustine trusted her. 'I hope I'm going to be able to be here for you, Sarah,' the young woman said, her voice deep and full of warmth. 'I know that this may feel like you're starting again, but you're a different person to the Sarah who went to the clinic three months ago and sometimes it helps to look back from this new perspective.'

Sarah felt immediately at ease, even managing a smile by the end of the session, which felt a little like speaking to a new girlfriend, someone she could trust to guide her through the next few months. She left confident that her days would soon be ordinary and average as she raised her little girl, routines repeating and small joys everywhere.

Yet seeing Gideon and Emily has washed away some of her confidence. She hates that her child isn't with her, but she has no choice. 'Next time,' she whispers as she feels her body relax, 'next time she'll stay with me.'

NINE
CHARLOTTE

'Looking at your phone won't make the time go any faster,' says her mother, and Charlotte puts the phone down on the table, deliberately turning it over so that she doesn't have to see that only one or two minutes have passed.

'I'm just worried,' she replies. 'It's the first visit and I can't help thinking of everything that could go wrong. What if she seems fine but isn't?' In front of her, her grilled fish and steamed vegetables remain untouched. The restaurant is Carol's favourite because of its simple food and elegant decor. To Charlotte it looks old and tired, with its oversized fabric dining chairs and white tablecloths, but the food is still fine and the waiters stand patiently while her mother reels off her list of requirements.

'Didn't you say that Gideon was going to stay there the whole time? What could go wrong?' Her mother picks up another piece of lemon, squeezing it over her fish and vegetables. It's the only flavouring she has, so the waiters know to bring her plenty of it.

'He said he would, but what if he leaves? I think he trusts Sarah too much. He seems to think she's completely cured and back to being exactly who she was before...' Charlotte flaps her hand, not wanting to go over Sarah's tragedies again, 'everything,' she finishes.

'I suppose he hopes she will be fine. Please eat, Charlotte, it's getting cold.'

Charlotte picks up her fork and spears a piece of zucchini. Her food too has been cooked with little flavouring, and the vegetable tastes bland in her mouth.

'I wish Sarah had a boyfriend,' she confesses. 'It would make everything so much easier. I even...' She stops and shakes her head; she's not sure she should say this out loud, but then she decides that it makes no difference. Her mother will understand. 'I even thought of setting up a dating profile for her and finding someone and then introducing them.'

Carol laughs. 'That's almost a good idea. A man who could distract her so that you can stop worrying about losing Gideon. I know you're fretting about that all the time, darling.'

Charlotte puts down her fork, giving up the pretence of eating, and instead finishes her glass of white wine, the crisp tartness pleasant on her tongue. 'It's hard not to worry,' she says softly. 'I've shown you pictures of her, and he gets this look on his face when he talks about her... I don't know. Maybe I'm imagining it.'

'I'm not saying you have no reason to be worried. But you need to think carefully before you turn this into an issue.' Her mother dabs the side of her mouth with a white cloth napkin and then takes a sip of her own glass of wine.

'I am,' says Charlotte as she turns her phone over and sees that Gideon has still not texted her. 'I'm thinking about it all the time. I think before I say anything or do anything. I spend a lot of time cleaning the kitchen so that I don't overstep, but I hate having to watch what I say. I wish he had some anger towards her; even a touch of hate would be good. I don't know any divorced couples who are like this. It's not normal and it's driving me mad. If Sarah had a man in her life, it would make things easier. I told Gideon I wanted to introduce her to Edward – he's not dating anyone, is he?'

'I don't think so. What did Gideon think of that suggestion? I've always seen Edward with a practical girl, someone who can push him in the right direction. I'm not sure Sarah would be the right kind of person for him.'

'Yes, well there's no need to worry about that. Gideon has no interest in his ex-wife dating anyone as far as I can tell.' Charlotte sighs, then lifts her hand to summon a waiter so she can order another glass of wine. She has work to do this afternoon, but she doesn't care. She needs to find a way to stop the endless loop of thoughts. 'What would be good,' she says ruefully, 'is if she just went back to the clinic for another stay.'

Her mother studies her for a moment. 'I suppose it could happen. Sometimes people need more than one visit to a place like that. Pamela's son has had to return because he's still struggling with his little problem.'

'I have a feeling he'll always be struggling,' says Charlotte. 'He was never a very strong person, always easily led. I'm sure he just did whatever Edward told him to do to upset me when we were kids. I've never liked him.'

'Yes, I do remember he and Edward took delight in tormenting you with insects and the like. But poor Pamela is absolutely devastated.' Carol takes a small sip of her own wine and Charlotte catches a tiny smile. Despite being friends for decades, there has always been an element of competition between her mother and Pamela. Pamela's husband was loyal for their entire marriage, something that grates on her mother, but James and his little problem more than make up for it.

'It's a shame he's had to go back,' says Charlotte, even though she doesn't care one way or the other about the man. 'I'm sure if Sarah were to return there, she'd have no chance of getting anything except supervised visits after that.'

'Well, yes, but is that what you really want?' her mother asks, laying her knife and fork together neatly on her half-full plate.

'Of course not,' Charlotte lies, copying her mother's gesture. 'Of course not.'

TEN
GIDEON

Emily cannot stop talking about her mum, about everything they did together and what Sarah said, even though he was there for most of it.

'It was just...' she sighs, 'the best, best, best.'

Gideon laughs, relief running through him at how well the first visit has gone. He should have texted Charlotte, but it slipped his mind – he was enjoying just being with Sarah and Emily, enjoying the relaxed atmosphere that he remembered from a long time ago. His ex-wife is so different to Charlotte. Sarah's whole approach to things is casual and spontaneous. Today she allowed Emily to choose what she wanted to do next and didn't police what their little girl was doing or how she was doing it. He knows it's early days, but it was wonderful to see her like that. He didn't believe it was truly possible until he had witnessed it for himself.

He smiles as Emily sings a song she and Sarah sang together. *Alice the camel has five humps, Alice the camel has five humps...*

Today could not have gone any better, although he needs to be careful when he tells Charlotte about it, not wanting to give her any more reasons to be concerned about his relationship with Sarah. He is lucky to have Charlotte, who came into his life at exactly the right time.

It's true that she likes things to be just so, but he enjoys coming home to her and Emily at the kitchen table, doing homework or just chatting. He feels a sense of peace when he walks through the door, as though it's okay to leave his work behind him.

He knew when he and Charlotte got serious that there was no guarantee that she would get on with his daughter, despite how lovely Emily is. But Charlotte adores her, something he thanks his lucky stars for every day. There are a few divorced partners in the firm who complain that children make for difficult dating lives, and even more difficult blended families. But Charlotte has stepped into the mother role with Emily as naturally and as well as she does everything else, and their marriage has only strengthened their family unit.

It was a perfect late-summer wedding – simple but filled with joy. Emily was fizzing with excitement all day about being the only bridesmaid, and she took her role very seriously, straightening the small train on Charlotte's elegant dress every time it moved and watching her stepmother all the time in case she needed anything. By the time they got to dinner, she was exhausted, but she didn't fuss or cry, just curled up on two restaurant chairs and drifted off to sleep, leaving Gideon and Charlotte to enjoy the delicious Italian food and the wonderful tiramisu wedding cake. There were moments of guilt when he remembered where Sarah was, working through her issues while he slow-danced with his new bride, but he knew she was getting the help she needed and there was nothing more he could do.

'We should go away for a few days. It will be the shortest honeymoon ever, but we should,' he told Charlotte the next day, happiness running through him as he looked at his beautiful wife.

'There'll be plenty of time for that later,' she smiled. 'We need to give Emily stability now. She's doing so well and is so happy and settled.'

'You're a wonder,' he told her, and he meant it. He was grateful that she had accepted he didn't want another child. He felt too old to return to nappies and he liked his life the way it was. For her to embrace his daughter so completely was more than he'd dreamed of asking for.

Now he tunes back in to what Emily is saying, realising that he should be listening. '... and Mum says,' she states, her little voice firm, 'that the whispering man is never ever coming back again, never, never, never.'

His heart lurches. Why would Sarah have been talking to Emily about that? 'What else did Mum say about the whispering man?' he asks slowly, the words making him feel sick.

'Nothing,' says Emily, and she returns to her song, but it feels as if the ghoul who tormented Sarah for months is back. Gideon knows that's not the case, but he can't help remembering a time when he felt his life was dominated by the phantom.

He's aware now that the whispering man plagued Sarah for weeks before she confided in anyone about him. He stood outside her window and told her everything was her fault. He scraped his fingers up and down the glass to let her know he was there. And he told her he would come for her child.

The first time Gideon heard any mention of the strange hallucination, he was picking Emily up for a sleepover. Sarah and Emily had only just moved, and he had been late because he'd got lost trying to find the apartment in the large sprawling building. When he finally arrived, Sarah opened the door with Emily standing behind her, her backpack already on her back. He had expected to be invited in to see the new place, offered a cup of tea even, but Sarah was in no mood for conversation.

'Give me a kiss goodbye,' she said to Emily, not even greeting him, and he tried not to notice that she was pale and thin and exhausted.

'Bye, Mum,' trilled Emily. 'Don't let the whispering man come tonight, okay?'

'Okay, baby,' said Sarah, her voice catching.

'Who's the whispering man?' Gideon asked, and Sarah looked at her feet.

'Nothing... nothing. Just... a game,' she said, almost shoving him out of the door.

'Who's the whispering man, Emily?' he asked his daughter in the car.

Emily was walking her pink bunny up and down the side of her car seat. 'He's... um... well, sometimes he comes in the night and he says stuff to Mum. He's always outside and he... um...' She looked out of the window. 'Look – a kitty, a kitty, Daddy.'

'I see, yes,' he said, not taking his eyes from the road. 'Em, Ladybug, tell me more about the whispering man.'

'I don't like him,' said Emily seriously. 'When he comes, Mum puts me into the cupboard to hide. Can we get an ice cream? What's for dinner? My friend at school eats bugs and that's yuck.'

'Does Mum put you in the cupboard alone, Emily?' he asked, a slow wave of horror moving through him. That sounded cruel and strange and not like Sarah at all.

'No,' she sighed, irritated at having to answer any more questions. 'She comes with me. She's scared of the whispering man.' Gideon glanced in his rear-view mirror, seeing Emily hugging her bunny to her. 'Scared, scared, scared,' she sang.

'Are you getting enough sleep?' he asked Sarah bluntly when he dropped Emily off the next day.

'I'm fine,' she answered lightly.

'Who is the whispering man and why does Emily say you have to hide in the cupboard?' His tone was more strident than he meant it to be, but he wanted an answer. Despite a night without Emily, Sarah looked even more exhausted than she had the day before. 'Just ask her about it,' Charlotte had advised him when he reluctantly told her the story as they shared some take-away Thai food after Emily had gone to sleep. He hadn't wanted to say anything to his girlfriend, but his concentration was off as he worried and fretted, and Charlotte noticed, saying, 'I feel like you're not really here tonight.'

'I'll ask her about it,' he'd said, and this morning he had arrived determined to figure out what was going on.

Sarah folded her arms, anger colouring her cheeks. 'She had a bad dream, Gideon, nothing more. She's just turned five and it happens. Stop worrying about me. Don't you have a girlfriend to think about now?' she spat, her shoulders back, defiance etched on her face.

Stung, he simply nodded and left. It was unlike Sarah to be nasty.

The next time he saw Emily he asked about the whispering man again, but she didn't want to discuss it, desperate to tell him about all the words she could spell and where tigers lived instead.

A week later, when he called Sarah, she seemed to be slurring her words. 'Are you drunk?' he yelled, not caring that Emily could hear him over the phone.

'No,' she protested. 'I'm just tired, so tired,' and she burst into tears, making his heart lurch.

'Something is wrong with her,' Charlotte said when he called to discuss what had happened, needing to speak to someone with an outsider's perspective even as he felt bad for doing it.

You need to get some help, he texted his ex-wife the next day. *I am concerned about you taking care of Emily.*

He expected an angry message in return but that wasn't what he got. *You don't need to be concerned. I have been struggling with insomnia, as you know. I did see someone after we got divorced but he isn't really helping any more. I'm seeing someone else now. I am getting help. Please don't worry. I do sometimes hear him at night, the thing I call the whispering man. I hear him.*

Bewildered, he called her immediately. 'What are you talking about? What do you mean, you hear him?' he asked so loudly that someone walking past his open office door stopped to peer at him.

'Calm down, Gideon,' Sarah said, her tone flat. 'I know it's not real. It's just a trick my brain plays and I'm getting help, so you don't need to worry, okay?'

'But I am worried,' he began, his stomach churning with anxiety.

'I wish I'd never said anything. I'm handling it – back off,' she yelled, and then she ended the call.

'Are things getting better?' he asked her a couple of weeks later when he went to pick Emily up.

She sighed and shook her head. 'I knew I should never have said anything. It was a momentary lapse, but I'm fine now. Just let it go, Gideon.'

But two nights later, she called him saying that the power was out in her apartment and she wasn't sure if it was the fuse box.

'If you come running every time she calls, she knows she can manipulate you,' Charlotte said, angry at having their night interrupted.

'I have to help her,' he replied. 'I'm not leaving my child in an apartment without power.'

It was after 11 p.m., and when he got there, he found every light in the apartment on and Emily tearful and sleepy. 'It just came back,' Sarah said. 'Do you want a cup of tea?'

He knew it was an excuse, knew she needed him there because something was scaring her. He put Emily back to bed and then sipped his tea slowly, letting the camomile soothe him. 'Perhaps you need a new therapist,' he said, watching Sarah as she lay on the sofa. She seemed to be struggling to stay awake.

'Yes, this one's not working,' she admitted, and he was so relieved at her honesty that he didn't push.

When Sarah finally started working with a new therapist, Melanie, Emily stopped talking about the whispering man and things seemed more settled again. It didn't last. The horrible spectre returned with a vengeance, and the middle-of-the-night phone calls began again, culminating in that night when he finally understood that Sarah needed more help than she was getting.

'It won't be like that now,' he says aloud now, reassuring himself.

'Won't be like what?' asks Emily.

'Oh, nothing, Ladybug,' he says.

The whispering man only appeared when Sarah was so sleep-deprived she began hallucinating. She wouldn't let that happen again.

He won't let that happen again.

ELEVEN
SARAH

When she finishes her tea, her mind and body calm, she tidies up, missing her child but not letting the emotion drown her, missing Gideon and the easy way they have been able to speak to each other in the last month, but not dwelling on the feeling. By the time she left for the clinic, there was so much between them they didn't discuss, didn't confront. They had never really discussed what losing Adam had done to their family, to her, to him. She knows she is guilty of not wanting to see anyone else's grief but her own. She would like to talk about this with Gideon one day – apologise and acknowledge that he lost a child as well – but now is not the time. Now she needs to get things back on track with her daughter, sell her old apartment and buy something new, even find a part-time teaching job.

It is quiet as she eats dinner, the television not enough of a distraction. She likes the apartment, loves what Charlotte has so kindly done for her, but she knows that this is not where she meant to end up. The truth is she would like to be home with her husband and child, getting Emily ready for bed, sharing a bottle of wine with Gideon, getting to the end of an average day in an average life.

She knows there is no point in wishing away the past, and she wouldn't want to. The most painful memories also hold moments of joy, the most awful nights have taught her she can break, and the hard days have taught her she can rebuild.

When she lost her baby boy at twenty-five weeks, she never imagined that her life would spiral so completely out of control. Even now, as she picks at a plate of pasta tossed with garlic and chilli, she remembers the night it happened, remembers the bone-chilling fear she felt as she lay in bed and began to understand that the baby wasn't just sleeping. It was midnight, and ever since she had climbed into bed at eleven, she had been waiting for some movement. Usually if she tapped the side of her belly, her son responded with a kick, with a fist, with a twirl, but he hadn't moved at all. She kept tapping her belly, even pushed at it in the hope that something would happen, and when she couldn't lie there any more, she woke Gideon. 'We need to go to the hospital,' she said.

A flurry of movement and organisation kept her going as they called her mother to come over and babysit Emily, packed a bag just in case she needed it, and drove to the hospital through silent, empty streets.

'My baby hasn't moved,' she told the nurse in the emergency room.

'How long?' the nurse asked, the question forcing Sarah to think, to really think, because time got away from her. During the day, while Emily was at pre-school, she was teaching history at a school ten minutes' drive away. And then there was the afternoon rush of Emily's gymnastics or swimming class, and homework and dinner and marking and prep for the next day.

'Hours, I think,' she said, and the nurse nodded.

'And how many weeks are you?'

'Twenty-five,' she said, the words catching in her throat along with the antiseptic smell. She was so close and yet so far from the wished-for end of her pregnancy.

They were shown into a cubicle, and as Sarah lay on the narrow bed covered in starched cold sheets, she kept tapping her stomach, kept poking and prodding, whispering, 'Wake up, wake up.'

The registrar on duty didn't even bother listening for a heartbeat. He came in with a portable sonogram machine, spoke kindly and softly, asked lots of questions as he spread gel across her stomach. Neither Sarah nor Gideon could see the screen, but the registrar could, and so could the young woman he'd brought in with him, saying, 'This is Penelope, she's a medical student. Do you mind if she observes?'

The girl had seemed impossibly young, but Sarah had nodded, 'That's fine,' not caring who was there.

It was the young woman's gasp that let Sarah know that her fear, her great and terrible fear, was realised. The registrar turned and gave the student a stern look, then resumed his kind, soft words. 'I'm afraid...' he began.

And Sarah sank like a stone into an ocean of grief.

In the days and weeks that followed, the only thing she did well was sleep, allowing the prescribed pills to wash everything else away. Even when she was awake, her brain was mostly dormant as she drifted through her days just waiting to return to bed. A few weeks turned into a month, then two months, and she still could not find her way back to normal. She quit her job without even asking about taking leave. She saw a psychologist, who counselled acceptance, but her mind wouldn't allow that. She had done too much, not rested enough, not eaten the right things, not paid enough attention. The accusations against herself whirled through her mind whenever she was awake, letting her know that she and she alone was to blame for her child's death. Only when she was asleep, the drugs washing away all thoughts, was she okay.

But because she was asleep, she missed her mother's rapid weight loss. Because she was asleep, she didn't notice her mother's eyes yellow slightly. Because she was asleep, she didn't listen when her mother told her she was absolutely exhausted. Her brain was not functioning, and so by the time her mother was diagnosed with pancreatic cancer, it had spread like wildfire through her body. 'Even if you had noticed and taken her to the doctor sooner, it wouldn't have helped. She could have gone to the doctor herself. It wasn't your job to notice,' Gideon said.

'But you notice when your mother changes her hairstyle, Gideon,' she protested as they sat in bed late one night and Sarah catalogued her failings as a daughter, which she had now added to her failings as a mother. 'Sometimes people need someone else to say something before they realise they need help.' She knew that her mother had been too busy helping taking care of Emily and encouraging Sarah to eat or rest. She'd been consumed with listening to Sarah talk about how awful she was for losing her baby. Sarah hadn't noticed something was wrong, and while her mother knew she was unwell, she had pretended she wasn't so she could help her daughter.

When Sarah thought about it, she saw herself as carrying the rock of guilt at losing her baby, and after her mother got sick, she added another rock to her already overburdened shoulders. Every step was impossible and staying awake was torture. Her mother's funeral nearly broke her, not just because of her own loss but because of the loss she read on her father's face, the tears he shed as he eulogised his wife. Her parents had been her strength throughout her life. As she clutched Gideon's hand by her mother's graveside, her tall, strong father, a retired builder who had still seemed capable of anything, looked small and thin and horribly sad.

She thought about ending her life, but she couldn't leave Emily, her one great joy. Gideon tried being positive, tried to suggest things that would help, mentioned the idea of another baby. But each time he walked out of their front door and went out into the world to function, she hated him for it, for not being as weighed down by grief as she was. She began to distance herself from him. Distance was easier because then she didn't care what he felt.

'She was my life,' her father told her after her mother's funeral. 'I'm not sure how I'm going to survive without her.'

'You have me and Gideon and Emily,' Sarah said, but then she returned to her bed, unable to take in two such great losses in the space of only a few months.

Officially, her father, who still sneaked the odd cigarette, had a heart attack four months after he lost his wife, but according to his doctor, broken heart syndrome was actually something that happened. 'It's the stress of grief,' he said.

In six months, Sarah had lost both her parents and her unborn child. When she did make it out of bed, out of the house, friends and acquaintances crossed the road to avoid her, and she knew they were terrified of going near all that grief, all that pain, all that bad luck. She took Emily to school and then came home to climb back into bed, only getting up again in time to fetch her. She couldn't bear the thought of looking for a new job, unable to deal with the classes filled with the fresh faces of teenagers. They were full of expectation for their lives ahead and all she could see for her own future was the unending darkness that had already engulfed her.

But then, three weeks after her father died, Sarah opened her eyes in the middle of the night and sat up in bed, realising that there was one thing left that she loved with all her heart, and that if she slept, if she drifted away into her dreams, she would lose her. She didn't understand how she knew this, only that it was the absolute truth. She didn't go back to sleep properly for ten days.

Her life spiralled out of control with each wakeful night. She couldn't seem to concentrate enough to even get a load of washing done. Every day her husband came home and she saw the way he looked around in despair, judging her and hating her for her weakness. She hated him right back, and at some point, deep in the dawn hours, she decided that everything would be okay if she wasn't married any more.

She told Gideon she wanted a divorce. He refused, but she was determined. She pulled away from him if he tried to hug her or touch her in any way. She started sleeping – or not sleeping – in the spare room and she stopped taking his calls during the day. When he asked her what was wrong, she refused to discuss it. He suggested marriage counselling and counselling just for her, but she wouldn't even consider it. One night he got down on his knees in front of her and said, 'Please, I'm asking you to tell me what I can do to help you.' She was sitting on the sofa at the time, chewing on a fingernail that was already bleeding, her eyes burning and her heart racing, the lack of sleep making her feel high. She stood up and walked away from him, sick of having to think about his needs, about anything except Emily.

She told him she wanted a divorce again, screamed and yelled, and finally he left. She watched him from the living room as he put his suitcase into his car, and some part of her understood that she had broken him. His shoulders were hunched, his head down and he kept swiping at the tears on his face. She wanted to feel something for him, but she had nothing left to give anyone except Emily. She didn't even have anything left for herself.

When she discussed her decision with Dr Augustine at the clinic nearly two years later, she realised that by asking Gideon for a divorce, she was trying desperately to start her life again and get it right. But nothing could make it right.

'And perhaps you were punishing yourself,' Dr Augustine suggested.

'How?' Sarah asked. 'I had been punished enough.'

'Yes, but perhaps you felt you didn't deserve a man who

loved you like Gideon loved you. You made him go so you could suffer alone, so that he couldn't help you in any way.'

'Yes,' she whispered, knowing that this was true.

Whatever her reasoning had been, when Gideon finally agreed to time apart, she was gratified to feel slightly better. Purpose filled her life now that she had to pack up and sell a house. She lived on coffee and energy drinks, only collapsing into the oblivion of sleep when her body could no longer function. She avoided her friends and extended family, hating the way people looked at her, hating the awful pity she saw in their eyes. She even shopped two suburbs away so she wouldn't bump into anyone from Emily's pre-school and have to suffer their kind questions about how she was.

Over the next year, she bounced between therapists, going for a few weeks or a month and then giving up when she felt it wasn't working. How could anyone counsel her out of her terrible grief if they had not lived it? What did they know? How could they possibly understand?

There would be some good weeks when she managed to close her eyes and rest, but inevitably her sleep issues would return and become chronic again. Nights were spent staying awake, being watchful, protecting her daughter. She kept repeating the pattern until the night she was woken by the whispering man.

He appeared just after Sarah bought a lovely open apartment on the ground level of a big building where people came and went all day long, where she knew she would be able to keep herself and her grief private. It was Charlotte who had told Gideon the apartment was for sale. Sarah didn't know what to think about Charlotte at that stage. Emily had begun mentioning her, as had Gideon, and to Sarah it seemed that Charlotte was everything she was not – a woman in complete control of her life.

Sarah was jealous, she wasn't jealous. She cared, she didn't care. She was trying to move on and let go of any regret over her divorce.

'How did she find out about the apartment?' she asked Gideon when he called to tell her it was going on the market.

'She knows real estate agents across the city because she is often called in to style a house before it sells. She says you'll love it.'

'What does she know about me?' Sarah asked. She hated that she sounded peevish, but she was exhausted and drained of any ability to pretend.

'Only what I've told her,' Gideon replied, and Sarah heard the truth behind those words: that Charlotte knew of her failings, her weaknesses.

'Do you and your girlfriend spend a lot of time discussing me?' she spat.

'If you don't want to see it, fine. I don't care.' Gideon's patience with her seemed shorter each time they spoke.

Yet she went to see the apartment. It was beautifully done in tasteful cream and gold and was in a very exclusive area, according to Charlotte. Sarah hadn't wanted to like the space, but the small garden was perfect and all she needed to do was move in and unpack. Maybe I will be able to sleep here, she thought hopefully as she walked through the rooms.

But she wasn't able to sleep.

Now she shivers as she remembers the first time the whispering man appeared, just as she had finally drifted off to sleep one night, exhausted from having finished the last of the unpacking. '*Saraaah,*' he whispered through her window. '*Sarah, wake up, wake up.*' She knew what he looked like even before he appeared, and then he scraped his long, yellowed nails against the glass and whispered her name again. She froze in bed, terrified. She heard the things he wasn't saying, knew that he had come for Emily, knew that he had come to take the last thing she still loved.

The next morning, after many cups of coffee, she convinced herself that he was a dream. But he returned again and again. Her hours of sleep whittled away to nothing.

Desperate for a solution, she returned to her search for the perfect therapist and that's when she found Melanie, who really helped her, pointing out the lack of logic behind some of her thoughts. Melanie herself had lost a child, so Sarah felt a real connection to her. But even Melanie could not keep the whispering man at bay, could not help Sarah sleep, and so she stopped seeing Melanie, determined to fight her demon alone.

In the six months she spent in the apartment, she never managed to say more than two words to any of the neighbours, and even today she can recall the deep feeling of humiliation that washed over her as she was taken from the building on a stretcher, gawked at by neighbours who were strangers.

Everything is different now. Her medication is right, her mind is clear and she sleeps well at night.

'I've got this,' she says aloud as she gets up to take her uneaten plate of pasta to the kitchen. She picks up an apple instead, biting into the slick red skin and enjoying the sweet crunch of the fruit.

She cleans and tidies, a tiny spark of alarm igniting in her at the thought of getting into bed. She has only been out of the clinic for three days and she has slept well each night, exhausted from unpacking. But tonight feels different and she can't figure out why. She is probably just on edge from seeing Emily and then having to say goodbye again. Or it could be seeing Gideon. She tries a meditation and then goes to her bookshelf. Charlotte has left a few of the latest novels for her, and Sarah looks at each one, thinking how nice it is of her to have done something like this.

Her breath catches as she picks up one with a dark cover, a figure in the shadows appearing to peer through a window. She hurriedly returns it to the shelf, wondering at Charlotte's choice of a horror novel, and switches on the television again, watching a comedy for twenty minutes until her heart slows and she can laugh at her reaction to the book. She gets up and grabs it from the shelf, tossing it in the bin without looking at it again. She doesn't know Charlotte very well and Charlotte doesn't know her, so perhaps it was just chosen randomly, one among many.

She hopes they can get along, but they've only spoken over text, and Sarah's tentative offer of meeting up for a coffee next week was met with silence. Charlotte is busy with work and Emily and obviously doesn't have time, but Sarah is sure they will eventually get to know each other so they can be the best parents to Emily. *Emily's happiness is more important than anything. Emily's happiness is more important than anything.* That's what she keeps telling herself, repeating it, making it a mantra whenever she feels overwhelmed and resentful of the woman's presence in her daughter's life.

The day of Gideon and Charlotte's wedding was a dark day for her. She was unable to leave her bed at the clinic, feeling exhausted and sad and devastated at how she had ruined her own life. No matter how she tried to frame it, she couldn't see it as anything other than another woman stepping in to take her place as though she had died. She tried not to imagine her little girl in the bridesmaid dress she had been sent a picture of, to see Gideon, handsome in a suit, waiting for a faceless woman who would take away Sarah's little family. She had pushed Gideon away so she knew she had no right to feel the jealousy that wound its way around her heart, but she felt it anyway.

She hopes that in time she will find a way to accept Charlotte's place in Emily's life, but right now she is still struggling. The woman is obviously kind, and Emily seems to love her, but the fact that Charlotte is the one sharing a bottle of wine with Gideon, that she is the one discussing things Emily said and did, forces acid into Sarah's throat. She gets up from the sofa and moves around the room, swinging her arms as she pushes thoughts of Gideon's wife away, not wanting her sleep to be affected by a churning mind.

It is after eleven when she finally gets into bed after a long, hot shower.

On her phone, an email pings, and she opens the app to find a message from Damien.

Hey Sarah,

I hope you've had a good few days. Things feel kind of grey without you here. Dr Augustine told me I need to work a little harder on moving on and moving forward. I am trying, I really am.

The thought of seeing you again, outside of all this, is helping.

In the world outside the clinic, I would never dream of approaching a woman I liked. Maybe it will be different now and I can just ask a nice woman, a woman like you, out instead of obsessing and then doing things I regret. Maybe.

I want to leave here but… I don't know. I think I have a long way to go.

Please write back

xx

She thinks for a moment before she replies, knowing that Damien is a lovely man whose depression and anxiety led him to do things he regrets. He has explained some of the things he struggled with, like being unable to hold down a job, and his terrible relationship with his father. He got into trouble all through school and was teased a lot by girls and called a weirdo.

'I may have taken revenge a bit too far sometimes,' he told

her. 'I just wanted them to understand how they'd hurt me. But I'm not like that anymore now that I'm getting the help I need.'

The tone of the email worries her. She has made her feelings clear, but perhaps he hasn't understood.

As she's thinking about what to say that will sound supportive, another email comes through – again from Damien.

Hey Sarah,

Did you get my email?

She experiences a moment of disquiet. He has barely given her time to compose a reply. She types quickly.

Hi Damien,

Yes, I got it – was just in the shower. I'm sorry you're feeling a bit low, but you and I both know that Dr Augustine is the best there is. All you need to do is work with him and he will really help you feel better.

I'm going to get some sleep now, but I wish you a restful night and a morning filled with colour. You can do this, Damien. I believe in you.

Sarah

She deliberately doesn't add any kisses at the bottom. She considers whether she should try and distance herself from him now that she's left the clinic, but that feels terribly cruel. He was a good friend to her when she needed someone, and he's trying to get better. She needs to be a good friend to him now that she's home.

She turns off her phone and then remembers that there is always a possibility that Gideon may need her for something to do with Emily. The memory of a midnight visit to the emergency room when Emily was two and her temperature spiked, sending both of them into a panic, returns to her. She turns the phone back on again, but puts a 'do not disturb' lock on everything except Gideon's number.

As she feels herself finally drifting off, she hears a scraping sound outside her bedroom window. She is instantly awake, sitting up straight, her heart thrumming in her ears. She clicks on her bedside lamp and listens carefully. The rain has stopped and there is only the slight whistle of the winter wind.

With jelly-like legs, she climbs out of bed and takes the torch from her bedside table, swallowing her fear as she pulls open the curtains to the small balcony that leads off her bedroom. She shines the beam of the torch through the window, watches the light bounce off the window of an apartment in the building next to hers. Taking a deep breath, she opens the sliding glass door, stepping into the dark and the cold, her feet recoiling at the touch of the cool concrete. Her eyes follow the torch beam as she moves it back and forth, but there is nothing to see except a ladder leaning up against the wall of the building next to hers. She remembers seeing painters there this morning. They are obviously coming back tomorrow.

She shuts the door and gets back into bed, closing her eyes determinedly, but she feels the minutes and hours pass and sleep refuses to come.

'Please,' she finds herself begging, 'please let me sleep.' But whoever she is talking to is not listening, and it is only when the first dawn calls from birds outside her window filter through that she feels herself finally succumbing and sinking into a dreamless slumber.

TWELVE
CHARLOTTE

'And then next week,' says Emily, as Charlotte wraps her in a towel and rubs her back, 'I'm going to have a sleepover at Mummy's house and she said we can watch two Disney movies, whichever ones I want, and she said that she's going to buy me some sparkly sneakers like my friend Tamira has and she said—'

'I bet you're going to have a wonderful time,' interrupts Charlotte, trying to ignore her irritation at Emily's endless babbling about her mother. Sarah has been home for a couple of weeks, and she calls Emily in the morning on Gideon's phone to wish her daughter a good day and at night to wish her lovely dreams. Every time Charlotte turns around, it seems as though either Gideon or Emily is on the phone to the woman.

'Mummy says she wants me to bring the picture I drew at school when I see her,' Emily said before bath time.

'Sarah said could you let her know what cereal Emily likes? I can see the box in my head but I forgot the name,' Gideon said on the phone as he was driving home from work yesterday.

Mummy says, Sarah says. Mummy says, Sarah says.

Sarah doesn't live in their house but after three silent months she is suddenly everywhere and the only topic of conversation between Gideon and Emily. They are excited to have her back, and Charlotte is sure that eventually things will settle down. But there is a look Gideon gets on his face, a certain softening that she has noticed when he mentions his ex-wife, and she doesn't like it. The green-eyed monster is sitting firmly on her shoulder, and she hates it.

Emily pulls one arm out of the towel wrap and pats Charlotte's cheek. 'Don't worry, Charlotte. I'll be home soon. If you miss me, you can call me,' she says, obviously parroting the things Gideon and Sarah have said to her.

'I know, sweetheart, and I am so happy that you're going to have such fun with your mum. But I want you to know that if you need me or Daddy, you can call us too. You remember my mobile number, don't you? We practised it this morning.'

Emily nods and rattles off Charlotte's number.

'Good girl, you're so clever,' says Charlotte.

'I know, you tell me all the time,' replies the little girl, and then she lifts both arms so Charlotte can slip her pyjama top on.

She smells like coconut from the organic body wash Charlotte's mother bought for her. Charlotte wants to grab her and hold her tight and never let go.

'Teeth time,' she says instead, and she tries not to laugh as Emily keeps talking even while she is brushing her teeth.

When she is in bed, the novel they are reading in her hand, Emily asks, 'Can I take *Charlotte's Web* with me when I sleep at Mummy's so she can read it to me?'

'But that's our book, because I'm Charlotte, remember. You can read a new book with Mummy,' Charlotte says before she can stop herself. *Stop being so petty*, she admonishes herself, but she can't seem to help it.

'But I want to read this one. I want to see if the spider can write some other things.'

Charlotte takes a deep breath, feeling herself on the edge of something, knowing that she wants to shout and stamp like a child. Instead, she sits down next to Emily on the bed and slips her arm around her shoulders. 'If you want to, that's fine. I'm glad you're so excited, but...' She pauses, unsure if she should say anything, but at the same time needing to say it.

Emily waits patiently, watching her.

'If the whispering man comes back to talk to Mummy, you will tell me, won't you?' Charlotte doesn't want her step-daughter to ever have to go through that again. Emily has never talked about that final night with her mother before Sarah went to the clinic, perhaps wiping it from her memory to protect herself.

'He won't come back,' says Emily confidently. 'Mummy told me that he was just her 'magination and he isn't real and he won't come back because she is all better now.'

'Oh, I'm sure she is, but if he does ever come back, you tell me and I'll sort it out. Also...'

'Also?' asks Emily as Charlotte opens the book to find the right chapter.

'Also don't tell Daddy if the whispering man comes back, because he would be sad. It can be a secret between you and me, okay? A Charlotte and Emily secret.'

'Okay,' says Emily agreeably, and then she snuggles down and grabs her bunny, holding it tightly around its shabby neck. 'Now read, Charlotte,' she commands, and Charlotte finds her place and begins, even though what she most wants to do is scream.

Sarah is capable and present, sleeping well and taking excellent care of Emily when they are together.

'Like the woman I fell in love with,' Gideon said last night, and then he blushed when he realised his slip. 'I mean, not like... It's the past, and I'm just happy that she's healthy again.'

'So am I,' said Charlotte drily, wishing she could inject some enthusiasm into her voice as she poured herself another glass of wine, one more than she should have. 'So am I.'

Tonight, it is just her and Emily at home because Gideon is working late. She wouldn't tell him, but she loves evenings like these. Emily is all hers and she doesn't have to share her with anyone. Once she is sure the little girl is asleep, she prepares herself a small salad, pours a glass of good Merlot and puts both on a tray to take into the living room, adding the bottle as an afterthought. Once she's settled on the sofa with the tray on the coffee table, she calls her mother.

'Darling, how are things going? Is Gideon not home tonight?' Her mother doesn't believe Charlotte should be on the phone to her if Gideon is home, because couples need time together.

'No, working late, which to be honest is a bit of a relief. If I hear him mention his ex-wife again...'

'Now, Charlotte,' says her mother, and Charlotte hears her uncork her ever-present sherry bottle, and then the swish of her filling a small glass to take back to her telephone table with her. 'You knew that this would be a little difficult after her being away for three months, but things can simply go back to the way they were before she went to the clinic.'

Charlotte holds her breath for a moment, reining in the anger that flares inside her. She doesn't want to yell at her mother over something that isn't her fault. She also doesn't want things to go back to the way they were before the clinic. She doesn't want Sarah here at all. She lets the breath out slowly and takes a sip of wine, and then she knows she can speak calmly. 'I understand, but it feels different now. Before, she was something that Gideon had to deal with and worry about, and I could see that he was genuinely happy to see me and be with me because she was so unstable. But now, she's... I mean, I have no idea what she was like before she got sick, but he keeps saying she's like she was when they first met. I feel like he's being pulled away, like there's something magnetic about her and she just draws him to her.' Her face flushes, humiliation at feeling this way making her take another long sip of wine.

'I'm sure that's not true. It just feels like that because she's back in your lives. Everything will settle down soon enough and the three of you will work it out. And if you can't... well, then you have to figure a different way forward.'

Charlotte pokes at her unappetising salad, wishing she had something different to eat. She finishes her glass of wine instead. 'What if he's falling back in love with her? Maybe he was never *out* of love with her. It's driving me mad. I can't lose them, I just can't.' She is surprised and embarrassed to find her cheeks wet. The wine on an empty stomach has allowed her to lose some of the control she prides herself on having at all times. Her mother doesn't believe in feeling sorry for yourself. She believes in finding a solution to your problem so you can feel better.

'Oh sweetheart,' says Carol. 'I hate to hear you so unhappy. I wish I could assure you that nothing will rock the boat, but that's not life. You know it's not. Your father... Well.'

She stops speaking, and Charlotte knows that this is because she hates discussing her late husband. Paul, Charlotte's father, died before he could leave his wife and children. It's not something she and her mother have ever discussed, but they both know it's the truth. Charlotte was thirteen, Edward eleven, and she remembers the whispered conversations her parents had late at night, remembers her father getting up from the dinner table and running for the phone, remembers the nights he came home with a bunch of flowers for her mother and some small trinket for her, a gift for her brother, a sheepish look on his face.

He was having an affair and was planning to leave, despite everything her mother had done to be the perfect wife. A heart attack took him one night and Carol found him slumped on a bench next to the lake at the back of their house. Charlotte loved her childhood home – her mother had spent a lot of money recreating the feeling of an English garden to go with the gabled house – but after her father died there, she was never able to appreciate the beautifully kept rural property again. She wishes Carol would sell it and move, unable to understand how she can stand being alone there, despite the visiting gardener and cleaner and home organiser. 'It's my safe space darling,' her mother always says. 'I have no need of anything else.'

'What if Gideon is exactly like Dad, Mum? What if he's hiding something?' she says now, broaching the taboo subject out of desperation, wishing she could ask her mother how long it took her to realise what was going on. Did she know all along, or did she only figure it out when it was too late?

'All that was a long time ago,' says her mother, and Charlotte hears her move, knows that she is returning to the glass and gold trolley in the living room where the alcohol is kept. She feels bad for pushing her, but she doesn't want to be dismissed.

'You know how you felt when Daddy told you he was leaving,' she says. 'It's not like you didn't try and convince him to stay.' She has no idea what was said in the discussions between her mother and father beyond overheard phrases like 'think of Charlotte and Edward' and 'I can't bear this any longer'. She was convinced that she herself might be the problem. It was a difficult time for her, because she knew she couldn't ask her mother about private, adult things.

'I did,' agrees Carol, 'but once his mind was made up, there was nothing I could do. If he'd been inside instead of out by the lake, I might have found him sooner, got him help. And then he would have been fine and living with that woman, and I would have had to accept it.' Her tone betrays her, and Charlotte knows that she would not have simply accepted it. Her mother has never accepted less than perfect from anyone or anything, except Edward, who she regards with pity.

'At least you had two children of your own,' says Charlotte, unable to hide her sullen tone. 'If Gideon leaves me, I'll be alone again.'

'You and Edward were and still are my world,' agrees her mother. 'Perhaps you need to discuss the idea of a baby? A child connects you and you would—'

'He doesn't want another baby,' snaps Charlotte. 'He said he's done with all that.'

'Oh.' Her mother is silent for a moment. 'I had hoped... Well, now is really not the right time anyway.'

'Obviously not,' spits Charlotte, cursing herself for having told her mother the truth. She pulls the soft cream-coloured blanket off the back of the sofa and wraps it around herself, taking comfort in the velvety material.

'I don't think you're at the point where you need to worry about this, darling,' Carol says firmly. 'You need to relax a bit. Don't go assuming Gideon is feeling one way when he may not be. And if he is, then we can think again. If you become shrill and demanding now, you may push him right into that woman's arms, and you don't want that.'

'No,' agrees Charlotte. 'I definitely don't want that.'

'I spoke to Edward today,' says her mother, changing the subject, irritating Charlotte further. 'He mentioned that you've been a little short with him. You know that he's doing his best.'

'That's ridiculous,' says Charlotte. 'Don't take him seriously. I'm only short with him because he keeps messing up the tasks I give him. My clients blame me when things go wrong, and then I have to explain that I have people working for me who make mistakes. You asked me to fill his empty hours and I'm doing that.'

She shifts around on the sofa, kicking off her shoes and pulling her legs up under her, aggravated that her mother has spoken to her on behalf of her brother. She has enough to worry about without including him in the mix.

'You're a good sister,' says her mother, 'but perhaps Edward needs a little more patience from you.'

'Hmm,' says Charlotte. 'I have to go now, Mum. I'll call you tomorrow.' She didn't call her mother to talk about Edward.

'All right, darling, and try to relax. You don't want to turn into a nag. Men hate that. Just be your usual wonderful self. Gideon must realise what he has with you. He would be a stupid man if he didn't.'

'I know, Mum, thanks,' says Charlotte, and she ends the call.

She lays her head back against the cream sofa, staring up at the stark white ceiling, where there is not a ripple or a crack to be seen. She finds peace in this room. Everything is in shades of cream and white, from the champagne-coloured carpet to the raw silk curtains. The marble side tables go with the sofa and everything is highlighted by the large picture on the wall, a riot of shapes and colours that make it a focal point. They call it the grown-up living room, so that Emily knows she must not come in here. She is such a good child that she has never questioned why. She is a lot like Charlotte was at that age: accepting and agreeable. There were a lot of grown-up rooms in Charlotte's childhood home, and she is pleased to have at least one adult space here, although everywhere else is for the whole family.

She drops the blanket from around her shoulders and leans forward to fill her glass again, then takes a long drink of wine, feeling herself getting sleepy. As she closes her eyes, a sudden stray thought appears.

She remembers her father's funeral, sees herself in the black dress with long sleeves that made her hot and itchy on the warm spring day. She was sitting next to her mother as the priest droned on and on about what a wonderful man her dad was. She listened to the words and couldn't imagine the man he was talking about. Her father went to work and came home to a perfect house and a lovely dinner and a daughter who sat silently at the table, a son who was usually in his room for some misdemeanour. He would ask her how school was, talk to his wife about the garden and maybe mention a client. Beyond that she had no idea who he was. Her relationship was with her mother. They were mother and daughter but best friends as well. Charlotte preferred spending time with Carol over everything else. There was nothing her mother didn't know about. She always looked beautiful and she was a brilliant cook. But mostly she was fascinated with her children, and Charlotte grew up knowing that however much she sometimes resented her mum's boundaries, they were only there because she was loved so much.

She thinks back to the day of the funeral; the heat, the slight smell of body odour that permeated the large, overfilled church, competing with the sickly scent of the gigantic floral arrangements in front of the coffin. Edward was hunched over next to her, bored and hot. Her mother was sitting ramrod straight, her make-up immaculate, her lips pressed together, a delicate lace handkerchief in her hand that she occasionally touched to one eye, despite there being no tears that Charlotte could see. Her mother's best friend, Pamela, also immaculate, also blonde with blue eyes, was sitting next to her. Pamela's son James was there as well, fidgety and desperate to leave. Charlotte hated James. He and Edward always found ways to irritate her, like moving the bookmark in her book, throwing live spiders at her, and once, putting a dead frog in her bed. Charlotte threw a scowl his way whenever their eyes met, hating him more than ever that day. His father was sitting in the row behind them, occasionally patting his son on the shoulder to make him sit still.

At some point Pamela turned a little in her seat and scanned the crowd.

'I can't believe she had the gall to turn up,' she whispered to Charlotte's mother. 'And what kind of a slut wears red to a funeral? Hideous.'

Her mother didn't say anything, just lifted her eyebrows slightly. Charlotte turned her head quickly, trying to spot the woman Pamela was talking about.

She had known that her father was cheating and that he planned to leave, but Carol would never speak about it. 'Please, tell me what's happening,' Charlotte had finally begged when she could no longer take the secrecy and tense silence between her parents.

'You do not need to worry about what goes on between a husband and wife. You and your brother are my priority and that will always be the case,' her mother told her, and that was the end of any discussion.

Charlotte looked around the church, her eyes moving as she tried to pretend she wasn't looking for the 'slut'. There was a young woman seated in a row near the back, dressed in vibrant red. Charlotte could see that she was very different to her mum, pretty, with dark hair, and tears running down her face. Her mother shifted in her seat, and Charlotte quickly looked away and returned her attention to the priest.

'Better to be a widow than to be betrayed,' Pamela whispered.

Her mother didn't reply, but Pamela's attempt to comfort her stayed with Charlotte, her words something she thought about for a long time after her father's death.

Is it? she wonders now. Is it better to be a widow than to be betrayed?

She shakes her head and pours more wine, gulping down most of the glass as she swallows her morbid thoughts. Gideon doesn't have a heart problem and nothing is going to happen to him. She doesn't want to lose him or Emily.

In an ideal world, the only person who would be lost is Sarah.

THIRTEEN
GIDEON
TWO WEEKS AGO

'Do you want to come in and have something to eat?' asks Sarah as she stands at the front door to her apartment. Tonight is Emily's first sleepover, and the little girl is beyond excited. Gideon can see in Sarah's shining eyes that she is thrilled too, so happy to have her child with her all night. Her hair is tied back, a stray wisp of hair curling over her ear. He restrains himself from reaching out and tucking it back into place as he used to do.

'I'm good, thanks,' he says. 'Charlotte is preparing dinner for us.'

'No problem,' says Sarah, her smile lighting up her face. She turns to Emily and says, 'Say goodbye to Daddy, Ladybug.'

'Bye bye, Daddy, I'll see you in the morning, okay? Don't be sad without me,' says Emily, but she is already running to her bedroom, her backpack filled with things for tonight and things she wants to leave here.

Gideon blows a kiss at her, then, without thinking, blows one at Sarah as well.

She laughs and says, 'Old habits.'

He colours, because it's true. It feels like every time he sees her, he slips further and further back into old routines, old conversations, old ways of connecting with each other.

He hesitates. 'Maybe I will stay for a snack,' he says, not wanting to leave just yet, not wanting to return to his quiet home where it will be just him and Charlotte and he will struggle to fill the silence as he watches everything he says.

Charlotte hates it when he talks about Sarah, and lately he finds it impossible not to mention her. He doesn't know why this is – or at least he does, but he doesn't want to think about it. It's not right. He and Sarah are divorced and their closeness right now is only because they are connected by their daughter and because they've been through such a tough time. Each time he sees her, each time she is like she was before, the old Sarah, he feels something he knows he shouldn't. The desire to grab her and hold tight is so strong sometimes he has to shove his hands in his pockets. He would never betray Charlotte; would never cheat on a woman he was married to – that's not who he is.

He remembers a conversation with his father when he was sixteen, when he was just beginning to date and found himself spoilt for choice. He was good-looking and clever, and being captain of the school soccer team helped. At one stage he was dating two girls at the same time, and finding himself struggling with the juggle, he went to his dad for help. He found him in his shed, contemplating a chest of drawers he was sanding. His father was a lawyer, but he was also a craftsman at heart, and he spent his free hours finding and rescuing old furniture, restoring it to perfection. He was drinking a beer and he absent-mindedly offered Gideon a sip, which he gratefully took.

'I don't know what to do,' he said. 'There are these two girls and I'm seeing them both but it's kind of exhausting. I like them both.'

'Actually, you don't really like either of them,' replied his father, moving sandpaper in slow, smooth strokes over the top of the chest of drawers, dust drifting into the air, which smelled pleasantly of old timber. He was a measured man who always thought before he spoke, knowing that his words had weight.

'What? Of course I do. They're both pretty and smart and–'

'Gideon, son, let me tell you something. When you really like a girl, when you really want to be with her – when you fall in love – there is no one else you want. One day you will meet a girl and she will be your whole world and you won't have to ask this question.' He changed the sandpaper for a finer piece, getting out the very last of the roughness on the top of the chest.

'You and Mum have been married for like twenty-five years. Are you telling me you've never looked at another woman in all that time?' asked Gideon brashly, grabbing the beer for another sneaky sip.

'Looked, yes – I'm only human – but wanted to be with, never. If you want to be with someone else, it's because you're not happy with the person you are with. Simple as that.'

Gideon knows it isn't really as simple as that, especially now, when the wife he wanted to be with forever is back and his new wife is waiting for him at home. He loves them both, and he's as confused as that sixteen-year-old boy, wondering what he should do. He could call his father and talk it over, but he fears that his dad will judge him and he doesn't want to interrupt his parents' trip with any more of his worries. He is already judging himself, already struggling with himself. But right now, he doesn't want to think about that. Right now, he wants to stay here in this cosy apartment, where there is a feeling of warmth in the air, where Sarah has draped soft blankets over the sofa and left a couple of Emily's teddy bears on an armchair, ostensibly watching television.

He sits on a stool next to the kitchen counter as Sarah cuts up apple and cucumber and carrot for Emily and plates up some carrot sticks with dip for him. Emily eats while she talks and watches television and goes in and out of her room.

'It's a small apartment, but it looks like she'll exhaust herself soon enough,' says Sarah.

'I'm sure she'll sleep well, and you'll call me if anything...'

'Gideon,' she says seriously, 'I'm fine. It's going to be fine. I promise you.' She takes out some fish fingers and lays them on a baking tray, then adds a few extra because she knows he loves them.

In the end, he stays longer than he should. As he drives home, he prepares his excuse of needing to help Sarah fix something. What could it be? Light bulbs – he needed to change some light bulbs. And then the electricity fused. The elaborate lie forms in his head even as he mentally chastises himself for being dishonest, but he tells himself it's only to protect his wife.

When he gets home, the house is dark, which is unusual since Charlotte always leaves the outside light on until he returns. He fumbles his way from the garage into the kitchen, using his phone as a torch, and then turns on the lights, calling, 'Char, I'm home... Sorry I'm late.' He is met with silence.

He takes a beer from the fridge and opens it, thinking that perhaps she had a headache and went to lie down, but then he sees a note propped next to the kettle.

Didn't know how long you would be so spending the night at Mum's.

He feels cold in the white kitchen. She could have texted him or called him. Before Emily was with them all the time, she would sometimes go and stay with her mother if he was going out of town for an interstate client or a conference, but she never did it when she knew he would be home. He opens the cupboard with the garbage bin inside it to throw away the bottle cap and sees a whole golden roast chicken dumped in there, along with grilled asparagus and what looks like some kind of fruit tart. He shakes his head at the wastefulness as he pulls the bag out to take it outside. She didn't text him or call him; she just sat here and fumed and then chucked out a whole dinner to make a point.

He can feel her anger in the curt note, see it in the garbage, and he knows it's going to be a rocky few days as he finds the right way to apologise. He tries her phone, but she doesn't answer, and he's just about to call Carol on her landline when he decides to leave it. If she is angry, she will feel better in the morning. Her mother has a way of making her feel better about everything. He will let Carol work her magic and take it from there.

He adds a reminder to his phone to buy flowers for her tomorrow. She is fetching Emily from Sarah in the morning, and now he wonders if that was the best idea, but it can't be helped; he has a 7.30 meeting with a client who wants to keep the beginnings of his divorce proceedings quiet. He drains his beer and then opens another one as he contemplates what to do.

He is suddenly completely exhausted, tired of being in his head. He orders a pizza, drinks another beer, and eventually feels himself falling asleep in front of the television.

His thoughts as he begins to drift off are of Sarah, of her face, her voice, her body.

Even though he's half asleep, he gives himself a mental shove for thinking about his ex-wife, for wishing she was still his wife, sitting next to him on the sofa chatting about what one of her students did to make her laugh. He reminds himself that she wasn't like that for a long time before her breakdown, and jerks himself awake.

He sets an alarm on his phone and covers himself with the blanket that is kept folded neatly on the sofa. Sleep does not come quickly as he stares into the dark, tormented by memories of a previous life with another woman, a life that will only ever exist in the past.

FOURTEEN
SARAH

The most amazing thing to Sarah is how different the apartment feels with Emily tucked up in bed only a few steps away from where she is cleaning the kitchen.

Tonight is a test, and she knows that, but so far she feels completely relaxed. She even navigated the usual bedtime argument the same way she used to.

'Just one more chapter,' Emily begged.

'No, Ladybug, it's time for sleep. Otherwise you'll be very grumpy in the morning when Charlotte picks you up for school.'

'I don't care, I want another chapter.' Emily pouted, her eyes shining with forced tears.

'Well, I do care. It's time for lights off, but I'll lie next to you until you fall asleep, how's that?' She thought it was possible Emily was worried about being in an unfamiliar space; perhaps she still held memories of the last night they spent together, and feared the return of the whispering man. Small children are suggestible and Sarah hates what she did to her daughter. She has caught her looking at her once or twice, studying her as if she's expecting her to start saying some of the things she used to say. She doesn't quite trust Sarah yet, and this weighs heavily on her, but as Dr Augustine told her, there is no way to rewrite the past. The best thing she can do is move forward, to create a future.

I am moving forward. I am safe and well and moving forward, she repeated to herself as she lay down next to her daughter and circled her arms around her, snuggling her until she could hear the deep, even breathing that signalled proper sleep.

Now she switches on the dishwasher and leaves the kitchen. She peeks in on Emily, pleased to see her fast asleep, Bunny clutched tightly in her arms.

It's early for her to go to bed, but she is really tired. The anticipation of this first night has worn her out, so she showers and gets into bed, reading a few pages of the romance novel she is enjoying. It's one of the books added to the bookshelf by Charlotte, but this one is light and easy to read. Charlotte has done more for her than she can thank her for, which is why Sarah feels so guilty about the way she is looking at Gideon. It's not fair to either of them.

The ping of an email coming in causes a jolt of apprehension in her body. She knows without looking that it's from Damien. He emails her every night at around this time. She needs him to take a step back. It's getting too much. Biting down on her lip, she opens it.

Hey Sarah,

I know I shouldn't be contacting you this much, but I'm kind of stuck here while you're getting on with your life. I think about you and what you're doing. I hope that you are reconnecting with Emily and that all is going well. You don't have to answer my emails, I just like knowing that you're reading them and thinking of me. Don't worry, I'm not getting weird. I know we probably won't see each other if I ever leave here, and that's not looking likely, to be honest. I am trying to be positive and grateful for all the progress I have made, but you know as well as I do that some days are worse than others. Hope you sleep well.

Damien xx

She sighs, hating that he sounds so down when he seemed to be making real progress before she left. But she also knows that she can't let him keep contacting her like this. If he does leave the clinic, the last thing she wants is to have to worry about him contacting her. Her priority is her little girl – that's what matters. She decides on a generic reply, hoping that he will get the message and start to back off, or she may have to put in a call to Dr Augustine.

Hey Damien,

I'm well and really busy. I hope there are more good days than bad.

Sarah

Putting the phone back on her bedside table, she picks up her novel again. Her eyes start to close even as she is holding the book, and she feels the delicious floating feeling that means sleep is on the way. Suddenly she hears, distinctly, a knock at the front door. Her eyes spring open and she sits up, certain that she must be mistaken, but the knock comes again.

She slides out of bed and goes to the front door of the apartment, peering through the peephole. No one is there. It's after ten and she would be surprised if anyone was dropping round at this hour. She has made a decision to get to know her neighbours in this new apartment. She wants to connect with people rather than withdraw. It's difficult to go up to strangers and introduce herself, but she is trying, taking longer at her letter box, which is mostly filled with junk mail, so she can greet anyone passing by, and dropping off a tin of biscuits at the apartments on either side of her with a note saying hello and introducing herself and Emily. She's met the neighbours now; they are both older couples with adult children. She has received a tray of muffins from the Larsons on one side, and a bottle of wine from the Gilberts on the other, but so far she hasn't had a full conversation with anyone.

She peers through the peephole for a moment more and then decides she must have imagined the knock. Turning to go back to bed, she shakes her head at herself. She needs to get to sleep so she can be fresh in the morning. She doesn't want Charlotte to turn up and find her looking frazzled, sure that the woman will be watching her as closely as Gideon does. She hates to think of Charlotte knowing everything that happened to her, but she's in Gideon and Emily's life, so Sarah has to accept that.

Back in her room, she picks up her phone and has a look at her messages to Charlotte over the last couple of weeks. The first one she sent as soon as she arrived home from the clinic.

Hi Charlotte, thank you so much for everything you did at the apartment. I would love to be able to take you to lunch to properly thank you. Let me know what day suits you. I won't be working for a couple of months so any time is good for me.

That message was met with silence. Sarah wanted to say something to Gideon but decided against it.

A week later she sent another.

Hi Charlotte, I would really love to get together to have a chat about Emily, just so we're all on the same page. I am so grateful to you for taking such good care of her and I wanted to know if there were any routines or things you do together so that we can keep things as similar as possible between the two homes. Kids like routine.

That message at least got a reply.

Emily understands that different homes have different routines.

Rude and abrupt, but again, Sarah has not mentioned this to Gideon. She gets it. She left Emily in Charlotte's care while she was in the clinic, and now she's back and trying to take over. Charlotte doesn't seem like the kind of woman who would appreciate that. Sarah has looked her up, finding the slick designer website where she recognises the names of several rich and famous clients. Her own career as a high school history teacher feels small and insignificant in comparison. It is harder than she thought it would be not to wish Charlotte gone in her darker moments. Her mantra about Emily's happiness is not working as well as she would like it to. She wants to be enlightened and inclusive and parent with her ex-husband and his new wife in a positive way, but Charlotte seems to have no desire for them to even get to know each other. Sarah is trying to find a way to think about things in a good light, but it's difficult.

Tomorrow she and Charlotte will finally meet face to face, and she hopes they can forge some sort of relationship for Emily's sake.

There is another knock at the door, and this time, because she is fully awake, Sarah knows she heard it. Irritation rises inside her, and she stomps to the front door, unlocking it and wrenching it open, ready to yell at whoever it is.

The hallway is empty, silent. No one is there.

A prickle of unease makes her shiver. She closes and locks the door, turning around just as Emily's scream pierces the air. She is in the room in seconds, reaching for her daughter, who is sitting up in bed, sobbing.

'What's wrong? What's wrong?' she says as she wraps her arms around the little girl and strokes her hair. Finally Emily's sobs subside and she is calm enough to speak.

'I got scared,' she says. 'You weren't here and I didn't know where you were and I didn't know where Daddy was.'

'I'm here, Ladybug, right here,' Sarah says, and she plumps up Emily's pillow, laying the child back down. 'I'm here,' she repeats, 'and I'm not going anywhere.' She dries Emily's face with her hand. 'If you wake up, you just have to call me and I'll come. My room is right next door.' She contemplates moving Emily into her bed with her, but she knows the little girl is a restless sleeper and she will fidget all night, keeping her awake. She and Gideon were always quite firm about Emily being in her own bed, knowing that she would be reluctant to ever sleep on her own given the chance to sleep with them. There is no them anymore, but Sarah still knows that it is best for Emily to get used to her own bedroom at the apartment.

'Don't go away again,' commands Emily, and Sarah has a feeling that her daughter is not just talking about right now but also the months she spent getting well.

'I won't,' she says. 'I promise.'

She continues to stroke Emily's hair until her daughter's eyes grow heavy and finally close. When she's sure she's asleep again, she slips out of the room on silent feet, holding her breath as she did when Emily was a fretful baby.

In the kitchen, she warms some milk and makes hot chocolate, hoping that it will relax her. This is not how she wanted her first night with her daughter to go. Who would have knocked on her front door? Why knock and leave? Maybe it was some sort of prank... but no one from outside could get in. There are a couple of teenagers in the building – she's seen them slouching out in the morning with school backpacks – but it feels like an odd thing to do on a week night, an odd thing to do altogether. She takes a deep breath and closes her eyes, hoping that she didn't imagine the knocks, that her anxiety wasn't making her hear things. That can't happen again.

She checks on Emily, then climbs into bed, picking up her book. She reads for longer than she thought she would as she decompresses from the night. The novel makes her laugh out loud once or twice, and she is soon able to dismiss the knocking as a mistake or a joke. It's all going to be fine, she knows it is.

By the time she turns out the light, her eyes are closing, and she sinks into a deep sleep.

The scraping of fingernails against the glass drags her abruptly from her rest. A high-pitched sound, like nails on a blackboard.

Saraaah, Saraaah. I'm here. Saarah.

She sits up in bed, her heart hammering, her skin prickling and her mouth dry. She turns on the bedside lamp, then gets out of bed and looks in on Emily, who is still fast asleep. Her bedside clock tells her it is just after midnight. She has been asleep for only forty minutes.

'A dream,' she whispers to herself, 'it was just a dream.' Feeling overwhelmed but needing to know, needing to dispel his presence and prove to herself that there is nothing there, she takes the torch from beside her bed and roughly flings open the curtain and the door to the balcony, cold air rushing in to chill her. She moves the torch all around, up and down, daring something to appear, but there is nothing except the painter's ladder, still leaning against the wall on the opposite building, creepy and shadowed in the torchlight.

When she gets back into bed, it is impossible to sleep, and

she finds herself reading until she finishes the novel. Only when the dawn light peeks through the curtains just before 7 a.m. is she able to doze, half listening for Emily, who she knows will be awake soon.

Half an hour later, Emily bounces into her room and jumps onto the bed. 'I'm awake, I'm awake,' she says, and Sarah drags herself from sleep, determined to greet her daughter with a smile. Her eyes are gritty and her head is pounding, a fierce headache on its way.

'Did you sleep well, Ladybug?' she asks, sitting up and opening her arms for a hug.

'I held Bunny tight and he kept me safe from the whispering man,' says Emily, and Sarah swallows quickly, her mouth horribly dry.

'I told you he won't come back, Em. He isn't real.'

'I know, but Bunny was worried,' says Emily. 'Can I watch television before breakfast?'

'Yes... yes,' says Sarah, touching her chest as if to still her racing heart. *Has he come back? Did I really hear him, or was it a dream?*

Emily is out of the room and in front of the television before Sarah even gets out of bed. A sing-song tune in a high-pitched voice fills the apartment, ramping up Sarah's headache. She climbs out of bed and has a quick shower, hoping to wake herself up. By the time Charlotte arrives, she has energised herself with two cups of coffee and applied some concealer under her eyes to cover the shadows.

She pastes a smile on her face after buzzing Charlotte up and opens the door, instantly feeling underdressed as she sees the cool blonde woman in front of her, immaculately made up and dressed in a beautifully tailored pants suit and high heels.

'Hello, Charlotte,' she says softly. 'It's nice to finally meet you.'

'How did it go?' asks Charlotte with a nod, her body stiff with tension, her face devoid of a smile. Sarah decides it is best to respond in kind, so she stands a little straighter. Charlotte has no desire for the two of them to be friends, that much is abundantly clear. Sarah can feel that everything is going to be more difficult because of this. 'Just go away,' she would like to say to the woman, but she doesn't have that luxury right now.

'Really well,' she answers firmly. 'Emily is just getting Bunny. Come on, Ladybug, Charlotte is here to take you to school.'

'You look tired,' says Charlotte, concern on her face. *Is* it concern, or is it judgement?

'Not at all,' lies Sarah, trying not to feel shabby in her tracksuit pants and light hoodie as she looks at the woman opposite her.

'Are you sure?' presses Charlotte, and Sarah allows the resentment she feels towards this woman to rise inside her. She has spent so much time trying to simply be grateful to her, but there is something there she cannot deny. In all honesty, she wishes Charlotte didn't exist.

'Mummy, I can't find Bunny,' calls Emily, and Sarah turns to go and help her daughter, leaving the door open but hoping Charlotte won't come in. The apartment is a mess because she knew she had the whole day to clean up. Her jacket is lying on a chair and the toys she has bought are scattered everywhere. The sink is still filled with breakfast dishes and the smell of cold coffee lingers.

In Emily's room it takes some hunting to find Bunny, who has become wedged between the wall and the bed. 'Finally,' sighs the little girl when her mother locates the toy, her world-weary tone making Sarah laugh.

'Hold him tightly now,' she says.

When she emerges from the room, she sees that Charlotte has come in and is standing near the kitchen, her lips pursed and her arms crossed as though reluctant to touch anything.

'Hello, Charlotte, did you miss me?' asks Emily. 'We watched Disney movies and Mummy made fish fingers for dinner and Daddy had some too, but he likes his with mayonnaise and I like tomato sauce, and Bunny likes it here and can I have fish fingers at home?'

'We like home-made food in our house,' says Charlotte, and she offers Sarah a small smug smile.

'But Emily loves fish fingers, so she can have them when she's here,' says Sarah, hating Charlotte even more.

Charlotte holds her gaze for a moment before she smiles, showing a row of perfect white teeth. 'Each to their own, as my mother would say,' she says. 'Kiss Mummy goodbye, Ladybug, and then have a quick visit to the bathroom.'

'I don't need to go,' says Emily.

'Always a good idea, quick sticks,' says Charlotte, and Sarah hates the way Emily simply obeys, despite the fact that she would have advised the same thing.

When she comes out, Sarah wraps her arms around her little girl. She knows now that she's determined to have her back in her life in a permanent shared custody arrangement. She had a dream last night, that's all. There is no way the whispering man has returned. She can't let him return. She simply can't.

Tears prick at her eyes and she blinks quickly, telling herself she is being ridiculous. Emily is coming again on Thursday night for another sleepover.

'I'll see you on Thursday afternoon,' she says, and the little girl nods and takes Charlotte's hand, already talking to her stepmother about what she did with Sarah and what she's going to do in school today. Sarah doesn't fully close the door until she can no longer hear her daughter's voice, and then she takes herself back to bed, her body and mind exhausted from pretending that everything is okay.

Her sleep is deep and thick, but she still wakes up with a headache and a sense of dread about the night ahead.

I am fine and moving forward, she repeats as she cleans and tidies, eventually saying the words aloud in the hope that she will believe them.

FIFTEEN
CHARLOTTE

Charlotte watches as Emily takes off after her friend Tamira, heading for the play equipment before the bell rings for the start of the school day. It is warm standing in the winter sun with the cloudless sky above, and she lifts her face, briefly seeking the heat.

'They're such good friends,' says Tamira's mother, Anika.

Tamira is just like her mother, with dark hair and dark eyes and a slim build. It is easy to look around the playground and match children with their mothers and fathers. Charlotte and Emily do not look alike at all, the little girl taking after her mother completely in looks. Charlotte wonders what it would be like to be able to look at your child and see your own eyes or mouth or chin reflected back at you. She doesn't think she could love a child any more than she loves Emily, even one who came from her own body, and she finds herself resentful at the 'evil stepmother' stereotype that exists. She is Emily's mother, and all that means is that Emily has two mothers – one of whom is not exactly good at the job. She could see Sarah was tired this morning, worn out almost, as though she was sinking back into old habits. She will mention this to Gideon at the right moment, because she doesn't want to appear to be criticising his ex-wife. Timing is everything, as her mother says.

'Do you think they're old enough for a sleepover?' asks Anika.

'Hmm,' says Charlotte. 'Not quite yet. Gideon and I have told her that she needs to wait until she's at least seven, so we're a couple of years away. The kindy year is such a big deal; we don't want to overwhelm her with too much. It's hard enough already...' she begins, and then waves her hand. Anika knows what she's referring to, and Charlotte is careful with playground gossip. Sarah still has a lot of friends at this school, friends made when Emily started pre-school at three years old and things were different for her. 'But maybe in the holidays we can discuss something?' she says brightly.

'Absolutely,' replies Anika, 'they'll love that. Ah, look at the time. My first patient is already in the waiting room, I guarantee it. Speak soon,' she calls as she runs off.

Anika is a dermatologist and one of the first people Charlotte bonded with at Emily's school. 'You must be Emily's stepmother,' she said, approaching her one morning as she stood awkwardly in the playground. She hates that she stood out so obviously, that she looked so uncomfortable among the casually chatting parents.

'I am, I'm Charlotte,' she said, grateful to be speaking to someone.

'She's a lovely little girl. She and Tamira are best friends.'

'Oh yes, of course. She talks about her all the time,' Charlotte responded, and they chatted about their girls and their jobs and Charlotte stopped feeling awkward, instead seeing herself as just another mother at morning drop-off.

She watches Emily climb the ladder to go down the slide, then returns to her car, thinking about the pick-up this morning. Despite the fact that Sarah looked tired, she is still beautiful, even dressed in an outfit Charlotte would never wear. How long will it be until she simply crumbles again? Days, weeks, months? She is obviously not a strong person. Charlotte has always hoped to be a full-time mother, and now that she's here, it feels terribly unfair that she will have to give it up, that Sarah will soon be dropping off and picking up from school and resuming her friendship with Anika.

It has come as a surprise to Charlotte that there are so many women she feels she can be friends with at this little school. Once she and Anika started talking, she was introduced to other mothers, and everyone has gone out of their way to be kind. A lot of the women work, and they all help each other out, and she's even picked up a couple of commissions just from chatting in the playground. She doesn't want to step back. But she can feel herself being pushed. Her space in Emily's life is under threat and she doesn't like that at all.

Last night she was absolutely furious with Gideon. He knew she was preparing a special dinner because it was just the two of them, and yet as the minutes and hours ticked by, she realised that he was wasting time at his ex-wife's apartment. Dropping Emily off and making sure she was settled should have taken no more than half an hour. In a fit of anger, she tossed the whole meal in the garbage, then left Gideon a note and headed for her mother's house. At the last minute, though, she decided against that, not wanting Carol to counsel her once again to not rock the boat. Instead, she took herself off to a boutique hotel where she knew she could get a late-night massage and divine room service.

She deliberately hasn't answered Gideon's calls or texts, which have come in regularly. She has let him stew because he needs to know that he can't treat her like this. He sat and ate rubbish food with his ex as though Charlotte was not waiting at home with a delicious meal, and that is something she refuses to tolerate. She will not just step out of the way now that Sarah is back. The woman hasn't earned the right to be Emily's mother again, no matter what Gideon says.

She turns the heating up a little in the cold car, planning her route to a house about forty minutes away. It's nearly finished being built and the owner wants her to get a feel for the place. Charlotte loves her career, loves creating a home from an empty shell of steel and timber and concrete, but her enthusiasm for the work has waned a little over the last few months. Motherhood has changed her.

'Maybe we should think about having a baby together now,' she suggested to Gideon last week, trying to keep her voice light as she hoped, once again, for excited agreement from him. She had just finished reading to Emily and was making herself some tea while she went over a set of plans sent to her by an architect. After she had finished reading, Emily had slung her arms around her and said, 'I love you, Charlotte,' and Charlotte had hugged her back, telling her she loved her as well and wishing that Emily had called her Mum instead.

She would be calling her Mum if Sarah hadn't returned, Charlotte was sure of that.

She tried to keep her tone casual as she spoke, hoping that perhaps Gideon might be more open to the suggestion now that he realised how good a mother she was. Surely he could see that she would manage a baby and their life? She was not Sarah, would not fall apart like Sarah had.

He was standing in the kitchen with her, rummaging in the freezer for the ice cream he liked, but he stopped when she mentioned a baby, turning around and closing the freezer door. 'Are you serious?' he asked, and for a moment she didn't know how to answer him, because the question could be heard two ways and only his incredulous tone gave away the fact that he thought the suggestion ridiculous.

She shrugged her shoulders.

'Well,' he said, 'I mean... It's just that... your age, and there's a lot... I mean, I haven't... I really don't want to go back to that. I made that clear when we started dating.'

'It was just an idea,' she said curtly, picking up her tea and leaving the room, her face flaming. She hated feeling vulnerable around him, hated asking him for something he didn't want to give.

She finds herself sweating as she remembers this, and she has to turn off the heater and open the window, allowing the icy air to blow in. She switches on the radio and turns up the music, concentrating on that until she arrives at the house she needs to see.

Stepping out of the car, she pushes her shoulders back, determined to impress with her thoughts about the house. Here, at least, no one is better at the job than she is.

A couple of hours later, she is home with the plans for the house and hungry for lunch. She sends Edward a message, reminding him about some scatter cushions he needs to pick up, which leads to a five-minute text exchange as she reminds him of which store he needs to go to and how to get there. *I'm doing my best*, he finally types, but she doesn't respond. If he was doing his best, she wouldn't have to keep directing him.

Just before she sits down to eat, she takes Emily's sleepover backpack and empties it, returning Bunny to his rightful place and putting everything else in the laundry basket. At the bottom of the bag is a small box of Smarties, the kind that come in multipacks. Charlotte stares at it for a moment, something niggling her about the slightly crumpled box.

Picking it up, she gives it a shake, and when she hears only a few of the sweets rattle, she opens it, wondering if it's an old packet that needs to be thrown out. The box does not contain Smarties; instead it holds three small white pills. Charlotte tips them out and then takes them into the bathroom to look at them clearly under the bright light. They are definitely pills. Emily has somehow got hold of some of Sarah's drugs.

'Jackpot,' she whispers to herself.

She opens the bathroom cabinet, comparing the pills to ones she has for headaches, but while they look similar, they are definitely not the same, and she knows this because she recognises the logo imprinted in the side. She has seen these before. They are sleeping pills, dangerous and possibly lethal for a child. Imagine if she hadn't found them.

In Charlotte and Gideon's bathroom, all the medication is up on a very high shelf in the cabinet, impossible for a child to reach without dragging a chair in, but Sarah has left some of her medication on a lower shelf – she must have. Perhaps she even has a chair in the bathroom. It's the kind of thing someone who is not used to taking care of a child would do. She may have only been away for a few months, but she is clearly not ready to care for Emily again. It's completely unacceptable. Charlotte's cheeks redden, anger making her hot. Sarah should not have Emily to sleep over.

While she eats her salad lunch and finishes her work, she debates whether to talk to Emily after school or to wait until Gideon gets home. She thinks about calling Sarah, but doesn't want to give the woman a chance to wriggle her way out of this. Instead, she picks Emily up from school and listens to her talk about everything she has done.

'We learned about words that start with c and h, like chips and chocolate, and Tamira had some crackers for lunch but crackers don't start with c and h but with c and um... r, and I went on the slide five times and so did Tamira.'

Charlotte makes dinner and helps Emily with her reading and spelling, and when Gideon walks in with a large bunch of flowers, she is finally ready.

'I'm really sorry about last night' are his first words, his sheepish smile nearly hidden by the enormous bouquet of gardenias, her favourite flower.

She sighs, some of her anger easing. He is very hard to stay annoyed at. 'You knew I was preparing dinner and you just stayed there,' she says, her tone even, only mild rebuke in her voice.

'I just got caught up with getting Em sorted out. I didn't want to leave until I was sure everything would be fine.' He's lying and she knows it.

She takes the flowers from him and finds a vase, busying herself with filling it with water and arranging the stems with a practised eye.

'So how was she when you fetched her this morning? Did everything go okay?' The eagerness in his voice makes her want to spit, and she can almost feel her mother standing next to her, whispering in her ear, 'Don't lose your cool, Charlotte. You have something to show him, keep calm now.'

She takes a breath and shakes her head, then turns to look at Gideon, who is sitting on a stool by the white stone kitchen counter, a beer in his hand. 'To be honest, I'm worried about things,' she says, making sure that her tone doesn't contain even a trace of the anger simmering inside her.

'What do you mean?' asks Gideon, the pitch of his voice a little higher.

'Well,' she says, making sure she has his full attention, 'first of all – and I do hate to say it – Sarah looked quite tired this morning, as though she hadn't really slept. I've never met her before, but it was very obvious. I know that lack of sleep was a huge contributor to what happened before and I don't want Emily to ever go through that again.'

'Of course not,' agrees Gideon. He takes a long swallow of his beer. 'I'll have a chat with her, see if she's okay.'

Charlotte clenches her fists, fury making her hold her body stiffly until she can calm down. She doesn't want Gideon checking up on his ex-wife, all kindness and concern. He needs to know she is not good for Emily. The last thing she wants is for him to spend more time talking to his ex-wife. His desperate need to see her as completely recovered and able to simply go back to her life is beyond irritating. If Charlotte had it her way, she and Gideon would have moved away before Sarah came home, and she could have visited Emily every now and again – not that she would ever say something like that to her husband.

'And there's something else, something a lot more concerning,' she continues.

Gideon sighs, long and loud. 'What's that, Charlotte?' He thinks she's being difficult. Even though she is only a stepmother, she has a duty to protect Emily, whom she loves with everything she has. She opens a high cupboard in the kitchen and takes out the Smarties box, handing it to Gideon. 'I found this at the bottom of Emily's bag.'

Gideon smirks. 'Yes, chocolate, very bad. I know your mother doesn't believe children should have junk food.'

Rage makes Charlotte lower her voice so that Emily will not hear her spit out her words. Children should not hear their parents fight. 'Open the box, Gideon, before you judge me. Maybe give me just a little credit. While you've got yourself all tangled up supporting Sarah and helping Sarah and believing Sarah, I've been here supporting you and taking care of Emily. Open the box.'

Gideon doesn't reply, but he opens the small box and pours the three white pills into his hand, studying them for a minute before lifting one to his mouth and touching it to the tip of his tongue. 'Shit,' he says at the bitterness he must have tasted. 'Where do you think she got them? They look like sleeping pills. You had some at one stage, didn't you?'

'I did, but that was sometime last year,' says Charlotte, waving her hand, remembering the difficult few months she had when she and Gideon first started dating and she began obsessing over how much he talked about his ex-wife. Not sleeping was intolerable to her and she went to her doctor for help. But the worse Sarah became, the less Charlotte worried about the woman's place in Gideon's life, and she threw out the pills he'd prescribed for her before she was taking care of Emily full-time. 'She didn't get them from here. I checked all our medication.'

'Daddy, Daddy,' Emily says, coming into the kitchen, 'me and Tamira are going to sing a song in the talent show. Mrs Watson said we could and it's next Friday and maybe Mummy can come and watch me and you and Charlotte and Granny Carol, because I am the best singer and Tamira is also the best and we're going to sing "Brave". It's a song about being brave and strong and Mrs Watson said Tamira and I were brave strong girls for singing in front of everyone. Jason is going to juggle but I think he will just drop the balls and I don't know if you can come but if you can I'll get you a ticket, except it's in class and–'

'Ladybug, that is a lot of things for me to listen to. Come here and give me a hug,' says Gideon. He has returned the pills to the Smarties box. He picks Emily up and hugs her and then sits her on his lap. 'Now listen, there's something I want to ask you. Today Charlotte found this box in your bag.'

He shows the box to Emily, who wriggles on his lap as her cheeks colour. 'It's mine,' she says.

'Ladybug,' says Gideon, pouring the pills into his hand, 'these are not Smarties. They are pills for adults and only for adults. They're very dangerous. Where did you get them?'

'They're my sweeties, mine,' protests Emily, pouting as she folds her arms.

'They are not sweets, Emily,' says Gideon, his tone stern.

Emily immediately begins to cry. 'I got them from the bathroom at Mummy's house.'

'How did you get them, Emily? Weren't they up high?' says Charlotte, making sure to ask the right question.

'Mummy has a chair in her bathroom and...' The little girl stops speaking, not wanting to confess.

'Did you take some of Mummy's pills, Emily? You need to tell me the truth now,' says Gideon.

Emily slides her eyes sideways.

'You won't be in trouble if you tell the truth,' says Charlotte, earning herself an exasperated look from Gideon. She shrugs her shoulders. It's more important that they know.

'I thought they would taste nice,' says Emily, and she bursts into noisy tears again.

Charlotte comes around the kitchen counter and picks her up off Gideon's lap. 'It's okay,' she croons, 'it's okay, it was a mistake.'

'I'll call Sarah,' says Gideon, and Charlotte cannot help a small smile. He looks devastated. Sarah is obviously not ready to take care of a child. It's best they find this out now rather than after something awful happens. She can't wait to tell her mother what happened. This is such a rookie parent mistake. Charlotte has only known Emily for a year, and the first thing she did when she moved in was to make sure all her medication was inaccessible to the little girl.

By the time Gideon is done with his phone call to Sarah, it's time for Emily to have her bath and her bedtime story. She is very contrite, and while Gideon is reading to her, Charlotte hears her promise again and again never to go near Sarah's medicine cabinet. She feels sorry for the child. It wasn't her fault. Kids will be kids.

Once she has served up their dinner of salmon with sauteed vegetables, Charlotte opens a bottle of red wine and hands it to Gideon to pour. She prefers a dry white with fish, but Gideon likes a fruity Shiraz. She watches the light red fill the glasses and forces away thoughts of all the other ways she accommodates what her husband wants.

They eat in silence for a moment, Charlotte swallowing her need to know what her husband said to Sarah with every bite of perfectly cooked mushroom. She knows that Gideon will eventually feel the need to say something.

'She said she's really sorry and she was absolutely devastated. She hasn't had to think this way for a few months and she's never had any medication in the house before. She told me to apologise to you – she said there is no way she will ever let it happen again.' He takes a bite of his fish but seems to have no appetite, preferring to finish and refill his wine.

'I don't know that Emily should sleep over again just yet,' says Charlotte, her voice indicating that this idea has just occurred to her.

Gideon puts down his glass and looks at her. 'She's her mother, Charlotte. I'm sure she's not the first parent to make a mistake, and I'm not going to yank Emily away from her every time something happens.' His tone is firm, his decision final, and not for the first time, Charlotte wishes that Sarah had never returned. It feels like her opinion about Emily is being eroded daily, as if her place in the child's life is moving further and further away, as if she no longer matters.

'I'm not hungry,' she says, standing up. 'I'm sure you can clean up.'

She takes her glass of wine to her study, where she locks the door and sits in furious silence at her Scandinavian light timber desk, her laptop open to some work she wanted to complete tonight.

After a few minutes, knowing she will get nothing done but not caring, she drains her glass and calls her mother. At least there she knows she will have some sympathy and support.

SIXTEEN
GIDEON
ONE WEEK AGO

He is worried about Emily sleeping over at Sarah's tonight, worried and not willing to tell anyone. The incident with the pills still really bothers him. He lied to Charlotte when he said Sarah apologised, when he told her she was devastated. She was devastated, but she was also defiant.

Because she didn't believe him.

'What?' she asked, when he told her what had happened. 'What do you mean? That's ridiculous. There's no way she got those pills at my apartment.' Her tone was strident and defensive.

'Sarah,' he said, 'that's the only place she could have got them. Our tablets are locked away and she told us she got them from your bathroom.' He spoke gently, softly, not wanting her to keep up the charade because she was afraid of his reaction.

'I don't...' she started to say, and then, 'Hang on. I'm going to check right now, because I know my medication is too high up for her to get. I made sure of that. Even if she had taken a chair, she still wouldn't have been able to reach them. I'm opening the cabinet right now and I will take a picture of...' She fell silent.

'Sarah,' he sighed, 'you need to tell me if you're not feeling well.' He knew she was looking at her bathroom cabinet and seeing that the pills were within Emily's reach.

'I'm fine, Gideon... I don't understand. I was so careful to put them up high. I don't get it.'

'Can you just move them higher, or better yet, lock them away,' said Gideon patiently, his hand squeezing the phone tightly to try and quell his anxiety.

'I'm sorry,' Sarah said, her voice catching in a way that he knew meant tears. He had always hated it when she cried, when tears slipped down her cheeks and her whole body sagged with despair. All he wanted to do was to stop her from feeling that way, and he still does, though it's a feeling he tries to quash.

'Please, Sarah... it's okay. It was a mistake, don't cry. You're doing so well; you just need to let me know if you stop sleeping. You don't want anything to happen to Emily, I know that. It was a mistake, but it's the kind of thing that can't happen.' He kept speaking, raising his voice slightly over her sobbing.

'I didn't mean to. I don't know what happened,' she cried.

'Are you sleeping? Can you just answer me that?' he asked.

'Yes... I'm sleeping well. I'm fine,' she said, but there was a tone in her voice that made him question her statement.

'You can tell me the truth,' he said.

'I told you, I'm fine. I made a mistake and I will not let it happen again.'

Gideon rubbed his hands through his hair. The turnaround was so quick, he couldn't believe it. She was lying about something, hoping to distract him with tears and then anger. He was pretty sure that she'd had some sleepless nights, and the thought crept in that the whispering man had made a reappearance. He immediately felt sick. He wanted to say something, to ask her, but he couldn't directly accuse her of lying. If she was fragile and teetering, he didn't want to push her over the edge. He also couldn't leave Emily in her care.

'Maybe we should leave the sleepover for this week, let you get some rest,' he said softly.

'Please, no,' she begged, her voice a whisper. 'I'm fine. You have to believe me. Don't take her away from me again, Gideon.'

'I didn't...' he began, but he was suddenly tired of the conversation, tired of the whole thing. He knew that Charlotte was waiting for him and he didn't have the energy to force Sarah to confront what was happening to her. He would allow her one more sleepover and if anything happened, anything at all, he would get the courts involved.

'There is something I'm a bit...' she began, then stopped.

'Something you're a bit worried about,' he prompted, sitting forward in his office chair, his body tensed with alarm. Charlotte had decorated his study with heavy timber furniture and tall bookcases. He would have preferred something light and airy, but he would never dream of questioning her. He always felt like he should be smoking a pipe when he sat in the leather chair. While he waited for Sarah to answer, he ran his hands over the soft leather inlay on the desk, feeling the brass studs as his fingers passed over them.

'Yeah... but it's... I mean, there's no reason for me to be... Look, I'm going to tell you just so that you can't say I kept anything from you, okay?'

'Okay,' he answered, wary of what he was about to hear.

'There's a guy,' she said, and he was shocked at the weight that immediately settled in his chest, so heavy that he lifted his free hand to press down on the ribs over his heart. He didn't say anything, knowing that if he did, she would realise how much those words had affected him.

'He's someone I met at the clinic and he's nice enough, but he's still there and he's been sending me emails. I mean an email every night. I'm trying to distance myself from him, but he's causing me some stress.'

'I don't understand – who is he? Why is he contacting you? What do you know about him?' he barked.

'You see?' she replied, raising her voice. 'This is why I didn't tell you. You think I'm incapable of running my own life and making my own decisions. You've always done this, Gideon; you've always tried to solve every problem I had, like I was a child. It must have been nice for you to have me finally break down and really need your help.'

'That's not fair,' he protested, feeling a rush of despair at her words.

'You're right.' She sighed heavily. 'God, I am so sorry, really sorry. I just... I'm going to sort this guy out. I'll send him a goodbye email, and if he contacts me again, I'll call the clinic and speak to someone. I just wanted you to know, that's all. I am truly sorry about the pills. I will not let it happen again.' Her tone was firm, controlled, and he knew she meant what she said.

'Fine,' he replied, needing to let it go. He would ask about the guy in a couple of days, and if Sarah hadn't done anything about him, he would contact the clinic himself and maybe even the police – though she didn't need to know that. 'Emily will see you tomorrow afternoon,' he said instead.

'Thank you,' she replied, and hung up.

The night of Emily's next sleepover was a restless one for him. He slept lightly, waking constantly to check his phone in case Sarah had tried to contact him. All night long he went back and forth over what he should or should not have done, what he did and didn't need to worry about. Should he have let Emily sleepover after what happened with the pills or should he have stopped sleepovers all together? Was the guy from the clinic a real problem or not a big deal? In the morning he was weary with the lack of sleep but jumpy with apprehension at the same time.

Charlotte was meant to pick Emily up but he needed to see Sarah so he could judge for himself how things had gone.

'I'll go get Em,' he told Charlotte when she got up to have her shower.

'I'm fine to do it,' said Charlotte.

'I know, but I want...'

'To make sure she's coped,' Charlotte finished for him. Still in bed, Gideon closed his eyes and nodded, not wanting to get into a conversation.

'Fine,' snapped Charlotte and she walked into the bathroom, closing the door behind her with a soft, deliberate click.

He showered in the guest bathroom and was relieved to be able to get out of the house before Charlotte finished getting ready for her day. All the way over to Sarah's apartment his stomach twisted as he tried to imagine everything that could have gone wrong.

He knew Sarah better than most people or at least he hoped he did. Whatever the truth was, he needed know. She opened the front door dressed immaculately, her hair done and a full face of make-up on.

'Oh,' she said when she saw him, 'I thought Charlotte was coming to get her.' She tucked her hair behind her ears.

'I decided I would,' he explained. 'I missed my Ladybug,' he added, knowing she could never argue with that. His whole body was weak with relief, everything had seemingly gone well and his middle of the night fears had not been realised.

Emily was delighted to see him, jumping into his arms, telling him about her night with her mother.

'Carry me to my room, Daddy,' she commanded. 'We need to get Bunny.'

He laughed and took the few steps to her bedroom, letting her wriggle down so she could grab her toy from the bed. Sarah's room was right next door, and he glanced inside at the unmade bed and the pile of clothes on the floor. He experienced a rush of anxiety when his gaze landed on the small walk-in wardrobe at the side of the room. The mess didn't bother him, but the flower-print duvet, lying crumpled half in and half out of the wardrobe, did.

He didn't know Sarah was behind him until she said, 'We were playing a game.' He startled and then laughed to cover his unease. 'Looks like you had fun,' he said. He wanted to ask about the guy from the clinic, but sensed she would react badly so didn't say anything.

In the car on the way to school, he listened to Emily's chatter, on the alert for anything that might give him a chance to ask about the whispering man. But there was nothing and he didn't want to bring the spectre up, to drag him into Emily's mind again. His daughter was so happy, excited for the next time she got to 'be with mum all of the night.'

He kept his concern to himself, knowing that it would be a few days until Emily slept over again, but now today is that day.

Today, he cannot stop worrying. The fear over the pills and the man contacting Sarah is right there and once again he is questioning himself. Everything went well last time but would it go well again and would there ever be a time he didn't have to worry about his daughter spending the night with her mother?

He looks at his watch and sees that it's 2.30. Charlotte will pick Emily up from school and drop her off at Sarah's apartment, and then he and Charlotte have dinner plans at a restaurant in the city. He knows he should be looking forward to some time with his wife, but he is anxious and jumpy and can't concentrate on anything.

He pulls out his phone and sends her a text.

Hope all goes well tonight. You can call me any time. Any time at all. I mean it. Xx

He picks up the document he was reading, but looks at his phone again when a message comes through.

You sent this to me, but I presume you meant to send it to your ex-wife.

He buries his head in his hands. He needs to pull himself together. He can only imagine what dinner will be like now. This is all getting too hard, just too hard.

SEVENTEEN
SARAH

As Sarah leaves the grocery store, she mentally goes through her list again, making sure she has every possible thing Emily could ask for. Charlotte will be dropping her off after school. Sarah is a child at Christmas, beyond excited about another sleepover with her little girl, even as worry threatens to strip her joy. She wants to make sure she gets everything right. If she can make this sleepover perfect and the next one and the next then maybe one day soon... it will simply feel like a normal part of her life.

She is trying not to be resentful about how closely Gideon is watching her.

He saw the evidence of her insomnia last time Emily slept over. When he had left after picking their daughter up, she cursed her own stupidity at not moving the duvet back onto the bed. The whispering man had returned, though she didn't want to admit it even to herself.

He'd appeared as she dropped off into sleep, as he usually did. *Saarah, Saarah.* His voice, his nails – the screeching scrape of them rippled through her body. Once again she forced herself to switch on her light and fling open the curtains to the small balcony off her bedroom. She searched for him in the eerie silence of the late night, finding nothing.

Emily, thankfully, slept through it all. She stayed asleep as Sarah lifted her from her bed and took her into the walk-in wardrobe, laying her gently on the floor. Sarah had sat up the whole night, her torch in her hand, listening for him, then, when she was sure he was gone, lifted her daughter gently and returned her to her own bed. In the morning, Emily found her lying on her duvet on the floor and asked, 'What are you doing, Mum?' and Sarah lied about a game, telling her the flower duvet was a forest floor where fairies lived.

She is hoping today, tonight, will be different. She wishes she could just relax and enjoy this time with her little girl, but she feels tightly wound, anxiety plucking at her insides.

Last night she took a pill and heard him again, heard the whispering man with his long, curled fingernails. She pulled the duvet over her head, hoping she'd been imagining it, but she needed to check, finally getting out of bed, her torch ready in her hand to shine around the balcony. There was no one there, of course, and she put it down to the effects of the pill and her worry over tonight. She slept deeply after that, and this morning she feels much better, more in control, if a little woozy. All the pills she has are now locked away at the top of her cabinet and have been since the incident at her first sleepover with Emily. She is hoping that her nerves will settle and she can put all the skills she learned at the clinic into practice.

After breakfast she took one more step towards feeling better again by sending an email to Damien. As Dr Augustine pointed out, 'If you don't tell people where your boundaries are, how will they know they've crossed them?'

Dear Damien,

I thought I would write and let you know that getting an email every night is not working for me. I know you will understand that I'm being honest with you in order to protect and help myself. I really value our friendship but I need to take some time to be with my daughter and to find my place in her world again. I'm asking you to give me a little space so that I can do that. I know and you know that Dr Augustine would not be happy to hear that you're contacting me every night. It's not good for either of us. I wish you all the best and I hope we can catch up when you leave the clinic.

Sarah

He has not replied, which is fine. She hopes he doesn't, and that she has managed to put an end to things. It was a mistake to get so close to him. She felt like she knew everything about him when they talked, but she wonders now if he kept things back. She regrets telling him so much about her life, but she was unwell at the time, working towards getting better, and what's done is done. She also wishes she had never shown him pictures of the new apartment, but when Gideon sent them, she was dizzy with excitement at the possibility of getting her life back.

'It looks like a nice place,' he told her, his face showing little emotion.

'I'm sure it will be, and you can visit when you get out of here,' she said, not thinking about the casually uttered words.

Damien knows where she lives and it would be hideous to have him just turn up. But right now he is still at the clinic, still hoping to get well, and she needs to let it go. Hopefully he will simply back off and get on with his treatment and eventually his life.

She would have preferred to collect Emily from school herself, needing to try and get back to some sort of normality. She hates that Charlotte and Gideon are dropping her off and picking her up. It feels like they are the adults and the treat of spending time with her daughter is being doled out in small pieces because she isn't responsible enough to handle it herself.

Can't I just pick her up? Sarah texted when Charlotte let her know what would be happening.

You're not on the list and the school is quite diligent about these things.

I don't understand. I was on the list four months ago. Why would I not be on the list now?

She waited for a response, trying to control her breathing and the mounting anger she was feeling. Why would Gideon have removed her from the list of people allowed to pick Emily up from school, knowing that she would return, knowing that she would one day be sharing custody with him again? She hated that she was having this conversation with Charlotte. It was something that she and Gideon should be talking about. Charlotte was not Emily's mother and it was time for her to step back a little now.

After waiting in vain for a reply, she called Gideon, who didn't pick up.

She decided it was easier to leave it, to let Emily be dropped off and then talk to Gideon another time.

At least she was getting to drop Emily at school tomorrow morning, so that was something. She shakes her head at herself as she has this thought. This is not how things should be. She was a perfectly fine mother to Emily before she lost a baby and both her parents. Anyone would have struggled under the circumstances and she's not going to have her daughter held hostage. She makes up her mind to talk seriously to Gideon about this when they next speak. He needs to know that Charlotte especially is crossing a very significant line.

But right now, all she wants to concentrate on is her daughter.

Only one more hour, she thinks, and then she'll be with me. Charlotte said she would bring Emily at around half past three. She glances at her phone and sees it's nearly three.

At her car, she loads the bags of shopping into the boot and climbs in, glad of the clear weather. The air is crisp and cold, but there is a park near her apartment and she has a new multi-coloured scarf for Emily to wear when they take a walk before dinner.

Her phone rings, and she answers before she starts the car, not looking at the screen, just sliding her finger across the glass.

'Hello, Sarah, it's Charlotte,' she hears. Her stomach flips, because she is afraid that Charlotte is going to tell her that she will not be bringing Emily over this afternoon.

'Oh, hey, is everything okay?' She feels herself sitting up straighter, as though the woman can see her through the phone. She wonders if she will ever stop being intimidated by Charlotte's cool grace.

'Everything is fine, but I'm in a meeting and running late. Do you think you could get Emily from school?'

'Of course,' says Sarah, 'but I thought I wasn't on the list?'

'It's fine. I called ahead. They know you're coming.' Charlotte's voice is clipped, professional, and Sarah understands that she is probably sitting in front of clients right now. Charlotte's business is very exclusive, and Sarah cannot imagine what it would feel like to be sought after in your career, to be married to a lovely man and in complete control of your life.

But you have Emily, and she's the best thing in the whole world.

'Oh, good, okay, I'll go there now.' Relief washes through her. She is not being denied the chance to spend more time with her daughter.

'Yes, you don't want to be late. Speak soon,' Charlotte says, and hangs up.

School ends at 3 p.m., and Sarah can see that she will already be a little late, ten minutes at least. She wishes Charlotte had thought to call her earlier but dismisses the thought, needing to concentrate on getting there. She remembers doing the school pick-up as easily as doing the laundry. It was just another chore, something she didn't even need to think about, beyond wondering what kind of day her daughter had had. Her time away has taken so much from her and she is surprised to find herself slightly sweaty in the heated car, her nerves getting the better of her. She can't mess up this simple task.

She arrives ten minutes later and parks, then heads towards the office, because that's where children waiting to be picked up are taken. She keeps a smile fixed on her face so no one doubts she belongs here. Looking around, she can see a group of children outside the office, and tries to spot Emily amongst them. She recognises one or two faces and moves towards them.

'Can I help you?' asks a man holding a clipboard. He's not a teacher she's met before.

'Yes, I'm Emily Greenstein's mother and I'm here to get her because her stepmother can't make it. I'm a little late because plans changed and...' She stops talking. He is no longer listening to her but running his pen down a list on the clipboard.

'Sorry, her name isn't on the list,' he says, and touches the orange sash he's wearing emblazoned with the words *Pick-Up Monitor* in black letters.

'Oh... Maybe she forgot to call? But she said she had.' Sarah looks around. Only a few children are still waiting for their parents or carers.

'Just give me a moment. I'll contact the office.' He takes out his phone and dials, even though they are standing close enough to the office for him to just walk over there.

Sarah peers around a wall so she can see the playground

area, in case Emily is there. But it's empty. The school is quiet. She looks down at her phone. It's 3.20. Where would she be? Tiny pinpricks of panic travel through her body, and she tries to take a deep breath but feels like she can't. Where is Emily?

'Hi, yeah, I'm sorry,' says the teacher, walking towards her holding up the clipboard, 'but we don't have any record of a plan change. What did you say your name was?'

'Sarah Greenstein, Emily's mother,' she says, unable to help a surge of fury inside her at having to identify herself. 'I know I was taken off the list of people authorised to collect her, but—'

'I'm sorry, but Emily has already been picked up.' He is kind but firm. He wants her to leave.

'Are you sure she's not somewhere in the school grounds?' she insists. Who would have picked her up? Has some stranger taken her child? How is that possible? How could this man have let some stranger take her child? She can feel herself sinking into full-blown panic. She clenches her fists and tries to breathe slowly.

'She's not here. I need to ask you to leave,' the man says, still polite but a little bit pushier now.

'Can I go and ask at the office?' she says, her voice high and desperate.

'I have just spoken to them. She is definitely not here and we would know if she was. Children have to stay in a certain area until they are picked up. Perhaps you made a mistake?' As he talks, he is guiding her towards the front gate and she finds herself going with him because what else can she do?

'Okay, fine,' she says. She lifts her phone to call Charlotte, but it rings as she does.

'Sarah,' says Gideon, and he sounds angry.

'Yes, I was just—'

'Charlotte is waiting for you at your apartment. She has a meeting to get to. Why aren't you there?'

'She said... She told me to pick up Emily. She called me and told me.'

'Why would she do that? Her whole day was structured around collecting Emily from school. Can you just get home quickly now? She really needs to leave. I hate doing this to her.' Gideon's voice is strained.

Sarah feels fury rush through her, replacing panic and strangling her words. She wants to shout and scream, to tell Gideon how worried she was, but he has already made up his mind. Arguing is pointless, so she spits, 'Fine,' and hangs up.

It's only a few minutes' drive to her apartment, and there she finds Charlotte standing by her car, her eyes on her phone as Emily balances on the edge of the sidewalk on her tiptoes, her arms wide.

She doesn't pull into the garage, but stops in the driveway and gets out.

'There you go, Ladybug,' says Charlotte, and her use of Gideon's nickname for their daughter grates on Sarah. 'I told you she'd be home soon.'

'Charlotte, you asked me to pick her up. You called me and told me to get her from school.' Sarah tries to control her tone but she can hear that she fails. She sounds hysterical and strange. She experiences a moment of wanting to actually hit Charlotte.

'But you're not on the list. Why would I have done that?' Charlotte's forehead creases a little, as though she is trying to understand Sarah's odd behaviour.

'I don't know, but you did call and I went to the school...' Her anger fades. Her certainty that she received a call is suddenly wavering. Did Charlotte call her? What if she didn't? She wouldn't lie about something like that. She wouldn't do that to Emily. 'I...' Sarah stutters, 'I...' but she has no idea what to say. She sags back against her car, takes refuge in silence as Charlotte stares at her.

'Mummy, Mummy, are we going to make popcorn tonight? You said we would,' Emily says.

'I, um... yes, yes we are,' says Sarah. She stands up straight again. She has to get it together, absolutely has to.

'Look, I really have to go. I am sorry you got a bit confused. It's easily done. But I'm late now. Bye bye, Ladybug, see you tomorrow,' says Charlotte, and Emily wraps her arms around her, holding tight.

Sarah feels sick. She knows she cannot get into an argument out here in the street. A car pulls up behind her and hoots because she is blocking the entrance to the garage.

'Hop in, love, and we'll go and park,' she says, helping Emily into the car with shaking hands.

Charlotte waves and gets into her own car.

Once they are inside the apartment, Sarah gives Gideon a call, but he doesn't pick up and her phone dies as she hangs up. Irritated, she finds her charger and plugs it in. She goes back and forth over what happened, but eventually decides that she did get a call. She will check that when the phone is charged, and she is certain that Charlotte's number and the time of the call will show up. It has to. Charlotte called her. She will not accept that anything else happened. Charlotte deliberately misled her, she knows it. Why would she have done something like that? It's cruel and disturbing that she would put her through this. What is the woman's agenda? Perhaps she is trying to paint Sarah as a poor parent. Perhaps she would rather that Sarah had not returned. If that's the case, she has underestimated her – how far she will go to protect her child and to make sure she stays in her life. 'I'm her mother,' Sarah mutters. She will not be pushed out by this woman, she will not.

EIGHTEEN
CHARLOTTE

Charlotte pulls away from Sarah's apartment block and calls her mother.

'Darling, how are you? Have you and Gideon got lots planned for your night off?'

'Oh yes, we have. We're trying out that new Greek restaurant in the city – the one you recommended. It has wonderful reviews and you know how Gideon likes his lamb.'

'You'll enjoy it. It's lovely to have some time off together. It will be almost like a little holiday, I guarantee it.' Her mother is trying to be upbeat about Emily staying with Sarah. She wants her daughter to see it as a good thing and Charlotte is trying to, trying but failing. She wishes, not for the first or even the tenth time, that Sarah had never managed to recover, certainly not like she has, and then she feels immediately guilty. Sarah is Emily's mother. But so am I now, she reminds herself. So am I. She could not feel any closer to Emily if she had given birth to her. And Sarah is not really recovered. She is putting on a good show, but Charlotte knows better.

'I suppose,' she says. 'By the way, the strangest thing happened. I picked Emily up from school and took her over to

Sarah's apartment, but she wasn't there, and when she finally arrived, she said that I had called her and asked *her* to fetch Emily. So now I'm running behind for my next meeting.'

'Have you contacted your client to explain?' asks her mother, always concerned with Charlotte's reputation.

'Obviously I did, Mum, but I'm worried about what she said. I never called her.' She makes sure she sounds firm. Her mother was always able to catch her in a lie when she was a child, and eventually it was easier to just tell her the truth. But she's not a child any more.

Her client – an officious businessman with a large empty apartment overlooking Sydney Harbour – was not understanding. 'I do work, Charlotte, you know,' he said. 'I had to rearrange meetings in order to get here. I'm beginning to think you don't value my time.'

Charlotte apologised over and over, and reassured him that she would be there soon. He wasn't the first client to complain in the last couple of weeks. She is finding herself distracted as her mind churns over the problem of Sarah. She has completely missed one appointment and had to send a sofa back to a store because she ordered the wrong colour. It was easy enough to blame that mistake on Edward at least. When talking to clients, she paints him as almost comically stupid and details her frustration at having to employ him because he's family. He's a useful scapegoat and he's willing to do anything she needs him to do.

Her mother is quiet for a moment, then she says, 'Charlotte, darling, you have every right to feel upset about having to share Emily. I know you love her – we both do – but if you try to get in between her and her mother, Gideon won't appreciate it.'

'Mum,' says Charlotte, exasperated, 'I didn't call her. Why would I do that?' Even as a child, she hated it when her mother didn't believe her about something, though she was usually right not to.

'I'm sure you didn't,' agrees her mother. 'It was probably just a mix-up, but if it happens again, you need to have a better system in place, maybe email or text. No one can dispute that.'

'We do–' begins Charlotte and then another call comes in and she recognises her client's number. She hopes he's not calling to cancel, since she is already halfway there. He'll get over his upset because she will soothe and compliment him, but after this little mishap, she is sure Gideon will start thinking more critically when it comes to his ex-wife.

'I have to go, Mum. I'll call you tomorrow.'

'Not too early now,' laughs Carol. 'You two need a lie-in.'

Charlotte ends the call with her mother. 'Barry,' she says, 'I'm nearly there now.' She listens as the man lectures her about her tardiness and his general importance.

How easy life must be for Sarah, she thinks. All she has to do is spend time with gorgeous Emily. She tries to imagine what it would be like to be some fragile, beautiful woman who no one expects anything from, but it's impossible. She despises weakness in people, wants to shake some of the women she works for who dither and can't make a decision and have to call their husbands. But maybe that's what Gideon really wants. She allows herself a moment of resentment towards her husband for putting her in this position, then pushes those thoughts aside, instead thinking about what she is going to advise her client. She is supposed to be arriving with a full brief, but in reality she hasn't done much work on the plan, which is not how she likes to run things.

Pulling up near the client's building, she begins circling the block to find a parking space. As the minutes pass, she can feel herself beginning to sweat with frustration and anxiety. Her life seems to be spiralling out of control. Only three weeks ago she had it all, and now she feels like she's losing things bit by bit, piece by piece. First Emily, then she is sure Gideon will follow, and by that point her reputation will be so tarnished she won't have a career either. If only Sarah had stayed where she was. If only.

But perhaps she can go back there, back where it's safe and there are people to take care of her and she cannot make anyone's life difficult. If she returned to the clinic, everything would be fine, and this time Charlotte would make sure that social services were involved. She's only trying to protect Emily, like any good mother. Sometimes hard decisions have to be made.

Finally she finds a parking spot and shouts, 'Yes!' triumphantly as she manoeuvres into it, her confidence returning. Getting out of the car, she pushes her shoulders back, ready to talk Barry into some very expensive art from a gallery where she gets a nice commission. She is back in control and she means to stay that way.

NINETEEN
GIDEON
SIX DAYS AGO

Instead of calling Sarah to discuss what happened yesterday, Gideon decides to stop by on his way to work. He doesn't mention this to Charlotte.

Last night, what was supposed to be a nice dinner in a good restaurant with no concerns about being back for the babysitter turned into a two-hour lecture from Charlotte about how irresponsible Sarah was.

Finally, over crème brûlée and the last drops of a bottle of Merlot, he held up his hands and said, 'Okay, I give up, Charlotte. I will tell her it was unacceptable and that she needs to be completely committed to the schedule. I will make sure she understands – again – that you were inconvenienced. But I am not going to stop her from having Emily, because that would mean punishing Emily for a mistake Sarah made, and that's not fair.'

Charlotte sighed, her lower lip drooping, and she looked for a moment older than she was. Dark shadows under her eyes told him that this was all taking much more of a toll on her than he'd realised. He reached across and touched her hand. 'Char... she's always going to be in Emily's life – she's her mother – but it doesn't change what you and Emily have. You're also a mother to her. You've been amazing with her.'

Charlotte snatched her hand away. 'Please don't placate me, Gideon. I know Sarah is her mother, but I'm worried that she's not ready to be a mother all the time.'

'It won't be all the time. We will eventually be two weeks on and two weeks off.'

'Emily will hate that. She's a child who likes structure and routine. Can't you talk to Sarah and... I don't know, maybe get her to allow Emily to be with us full-time and she can visit.'

'No,' he said, biting down on his anger. 'Sarah is her mother. She needs to be in her life.' He couldn't actually believe that Charlotte was making such a suggestion.

'If she was any kind of a mother,' Charlotte snapped, 'she wouldn't have been away from her for three months.' She leaned back in her chair and folded her arms triumphantly.

Gideon became aware of a few curious glances from other diners and lowered his voice.

'That's cruel, Charlotte,' he said. 'You know she needed time to recover from everything that happened to her. She was unwell.'

'My father died when I was only thirteen and I managed fine without falling into a heap.' Charlotte didn't look at him as she spoke, but rather around the restaurant at other tables, where people were smiling and talking and no one else was having an argument.

Gideon knew he was close to losing his temper and so he signalled to the waiter for the bill and they drove home in silence.

'How many more mistakes does she get to make before you admit there is a real problem here?' Charlotte asked him as she got ready for bed.

'Just leave it, Charlotte, I'll sort it out,' he snapped, and they went to sleep with their backs turned to each other, only the wine helping Gideon drift off.

This morning he left the house for a run before she woke up, to clear away the hangover, and when he got back, she was already out meeting a client.

Now he presses the buzzer for Sarah's apartment. He has already called the school and been reassured that Emily is there, safe and well. As he rides up in the lift, he takes a few deep breaths, knowing he needs to remain calm.

She is standing at the door to the apartment, dressed in jeans and a T-shirt, her hair tied up, and he wonders at his physical reaction to her, even after all these years. His heart speeds up and he feels himself flushing slightly, the same way he did the first time he picked her up for a date and she opened the door wearing a pair of jeans and a silky white top. He wanted to grab her and pull her to him but restrained himself when he saw her father standing behind her.

'Hi,' she says now, her voice wary.

'Can we have a quick chat? I think we need to clear the air about what happened yesterday.'

'Yes, I think we do,' she agrees, and she steps back, inviting him in.

He takes a quick look around the apartment, where there is evidence of his daughter everywhere, from the scattered toys to a multicoloured scarf lying on the coffee table. It is so different from his own home, where evidence of Emily is neatly stored away every night, packed into boxes and hidden in cupboards.

'Look...' he begins as he follows her into her kitchen, the worktop crowded with little craft projects she and Emily have obviously done together. Sarah turns around and holds up her hand to prevent him from saying anything else.

'No, you listen,' she says. Her green eyes darken slightly and he can see that she's angry. 'Your wife called me yesterday and asked me to fetch Emily from school. It's humiliating enough that I'm no longer on the list to pick up my own child, but when I arrived, I found that she had already been collected. And then Charlotte lied and told you she didn't call.' She speaks quickly, almost as if she knows that she has to get everything said before he can stop her. When she takes a breath, he dives in.

'Okay, first of all, your name should be on the list, but the school sends out a form for us to fill in every few months, and when the last one came, you were at the clinic and Charlotte filled it out. I should have done it, but in fairness to Charlotte, she didn't know when you'd be back. She was just doing what she thought was best for Emily.'

'I'll bet,' hisses Sarah.

'You were hardly in a position to fetch her from school anyway,' he barks, allowing his anger to surface. Sarah's face flushes and he immediately feels like the worst person on earth. 'I'm sorry,' he apologises quickly. 'That was unnecessary.'

'Yes.' She nods, and he is horrified to see her eyes fill with tears.

'I'm sorry,' he says again. 'Please, sweetheart, I'm so sorry.' The word slips out, and he quickly dismisses it as just an old habit.

'What about the call?' she asks. 'Why did she do it – and why did she lie about it to both of us?'

'Can I take a look at your phone?' he asks gently.

'Why?' She crosses her arms.

He doesn't want to raise his voice again. 'Give me your phone and I'll call her from it and then she can't lie about it, okay?' he says softly, soothingly.

She nods and pulls her phone out of her pocket, unlocking it for him. He looks at her last calls, searching for Charlotte's number, but it's not there. 'When did you say she called you?'

'Yesterday at around three. Why?' And now there is uncertainty in her voice. 'I was going to check that she called me so I could show you, but then my phone died and I... well, I had Emily and we were busy,' she says.

He looks at all her calls from yesterday. He doesn't recognise any of the numbers except his own.

'Do you have her number saved in your phone?'

'I do.'

He turns the phone to her, shows her the recent calls. Charlotte's name is nowhere to be seen, not for days. Fear prickles at the back of his neck. Charlotte did not call Sarah. He doesn't say anything, just stands there, his thoughts refusing to settle on the most obvious conclusion. Sarah has lied. She has lied or she believes that Charlotte actually called her, and he has no idea which is worse.

'Wait – that's impossible,' she says, grabbing the phone and scrolling through. 'Maybe she called me from another phone or something. Look – there's a call here at two fifty-seven...'

'Maybe you made a mistake,' he suggests, even as worry slides through his veins.

'No, look, I'll dial the number,' she says, frantically swiping at the screen and putting the phone on speaker.

'Graham's Garden Service,' a man's voice answers.

Sarah hastily hangs up. 'I don't understand. She did call me, she did. She said she was in a meeting – maybe that's where the meeting was...'

Gideon can feel her desperation, see that tears are starting to pool in her eyes, but he can't have this conversation any more. Rattling around his body is the same old fear he felt in the last few weeks before Sarah went to the clinic, the same panic about who this woman is now and about whether he can trust her with his child. There is a thread of despair running alongside that panic too. He thought she was okay, finally okay. He really wanted her to be fine. But she's not. He wants to hang his head and shed some tears of his own.

'I think... Can we leave this now, because I need to get to

work.' He is frightened for his ex-wife, and he is also angry with her, because she was supposed to be fine and he didn't want to have to do this again. He can't let her see that. She already looks broken as she stands in the small kitchen, her shoulders rounding, her whole body sagging.

'I promise you...' she mutters, still looking at her phone.

Gideon searches for something to say, to comfort her, but he can't come up with anything. He knows that continuing the conversation will not help, not at all. He's been up against Sarah when she's like this and he won't win. He wouldn't be divorced if she was easy to deal with in this state. He needs to give her time to realise that something is wrong. Maybe she's fine and she has just lied to him. It's such a strange thing for her to have done, though, because the one thing she has never been is deceitful, but perhaps she is so afraid of losing access to Emily that she is becoming a different kind of person.

He takes a deep breath as the prospect stretches before him of years and years dealing with Sarah and Charlotte and whatever is going on between them, while he worries about Sarah's health and Sarah's needs. He would like to scream out, 'Enough!' but he can't, because he's Emily's father and she is his number one concern. Still, he's not sure he has the energy for any of this.

Sarah bows her head. 'Never mind,' she sighs.

'Maybe you thought...' he tries, but he cannot come up with an explanation for what happened. She lied or she believed it happened. Which is it? Which is worse?

'Please call the school and add me to the list for next week. I want to pick her up,' she says.

'Um... okay,' he agrees reluctantly. He's not going to argue this point with her right now. He looks at the tiredness etched on her face and wants to ask her if she slept last night, but he keeps the question to himself. 'I'll speak to you later, okay?' he says instead as he walks to the door of the apartment. He wants to reach for her, because the need to hold her and make her feel better is stronger than his fading anger, but she just nods her head and steps back, and the door closes behind him with a quiet click.

What exactly is going on with her? It's such a strange thing to make up, because there was no way she wouldn't be caught out. He remembers one night before he knew about the whispering man, before he was aware of how bad things were. Emily was staying with him and the phone rang in the middle of the night, waking Charlotte, who had only just begun sleeping over. 'The old lady wants to know if you need some cake,' Sarah's voice said. And then she hung up. He contemplated going over there, but when he called her back, she answered the phone groggily. 'What is it?' she asked. 'Is Emily all right?'

'Are you okay?'

'Gideon, did you just wake me to ask if I was okay?' she said, and he apologised and tried to get back to sleep.

In the morning, she seemed to have no memory of the call when he dropped Emily off, and he assumed that she'd simply had a bad dream.

The whispering man filtered into Emily's conversation shortly after that.

Now, in the lobby, he walks past a corkboard filled with flyers advertising cleaners and painters. Right in the middle is a sign for Graham's Garden Service. As he stares at it, he wonders at the need for a gardening service in an apartment building. But then he recalls looking at an apartment on the ground floor that had a small, vibrant garden.

His phone buzzes, and he knows it's the office. He is late for a partners' meeting. Pulling it out of his pocket, he says, 'I'll be there soon,' even before his assistant can speak.

'I'll let them know,' she replies.

He studies the sign. It's on white paper with a large green tree in the middle. There are little tags with a mobile number that can be pulled off. Only one is missing. Gideon doesn't even have to look at the number to know that it's the same as the one on Sarah's phone.

Why would the gardener have called Sarah unless she called him first, and why would Sarah, who only has a few pot plants on her balcony, need a gardener?

He feels totally at a loss, unable to think straight. He shakes his head. *What now? What am I supposed to do now?*

TWENTY
SARAH

As soon as the door closes, Sarah begins cleaning, whirling around the apartment with energetic fury. She knows Charlotte called her, she's absolutely sure of it. *Why didn't you check your phone last night if you're so sure?* The question appears in her mind, as does an image of Dr. Augustine, eyebrows raised, waiting for her answer. An answer she doesn't have, doesn't want to have. *I was afraid to check, afraid to see that it didn't happen. I don't want to have to start questioning myself, not again. I'm better, so much better.* 'But what if I'm not?' she says aloud, her voice catching as she stops for a moment, standing still with her worry. She shakes her head, not accepting the thought, and returns to her frenetic activity.

She starts a load of washing and straightens Emily's room, opening the window to let in some fresh air, then she vacuums and dusts and wipes until the apartment is clean and she has run out of surfaces to shine.

At a loss as to what to do with herself, she grabs her phone and puts on a pair of sneakers, running down two flights of stairs and out into the street, where she walks quickly along the sidewalk, her arms swinging, her heart racing, lifting her face to the cold wind, feeling it slap against her cheeks. Charlotte called, she didn't call, she did call. With each step, she resists the urge to phone Gideon and accuse him of trying to make her out to be crazy, or to call Charlotte and yell at the woman for trying to drive her mad. Finally, after twenty minutes, she stops in front of a coffee shop, breathing heavily. Some part of her knows that it is better to feel this anger bubbling inside her, better than the uncertainty about her mind playing tricks on her.

She makes her way back to the apartment, rehearsing a text she is going to send to Charlotte, despite knowing it will only inflame the situation. She would love to never have to see or speak to the woman again, but they need to get along for Emily's sake. The little girl has had enough to deal with lately. Her happiness is the only thing that matters.

In her apartment, she takes a quick shower and then settles herself on the sofa with a cup of coffee, mulling over what to say. She starts and deletes the text a few times before she's happy with it.

Hi Charlotte, I'm sorry about what happened yesterday. I really did think you called me but perhaps I misunderstood or something. I know this is not an easy situation for anyone but I am sure we can make it work. I know you love Emily like I do and we all want the best for her. It will be easier for her if we can find a way to get along. I would love to be able to meet sometime so we can really talk, maybe even get to know each other better. I just want everyone to be happy. Sarah

Once she's sent the text, she feels herself getting anxious again. She didn't sleep last night, not just because she was afraid that the whispering man would return, but also because Emily cried out in her sleep and she thought it was easier to bring the child into bed with her. She sits on the sofa, her phone in her hand, willing a message to appear, but it doesn't surprise her when Charlotte fails to respond. Clearly the woman has no desire to get to know her, to be friendly with her or even to cooperate with her as they care for Emily together. Sarah realises she doesn't have the emotional strength to waste on her any more. From now on she needs to distance herself and keep things between her and Charlotte professional.

An early dinner and a long, hot bath with a glass of red wine make her drowsy, but just in case, she also takes a sleeping pill. Emily is with Gideon tonight and she can let go a little. She shouldn't be mixing alcohol and drugs, but she just wants to sink into nothingness and let her body rest.

She reads a little after climbing into bed, struggling to concentrate as her eyes keep closing, until she finally accepts that she is ready and switches off her bedside lamp, slipping quickly into a deep sleep.

It feels like hours later when her phone pings, dragging her from a dream about Emily's first birthday party in which she was trying to get her parents to stand still so they could have their picture taken, but they kept moving out of the frame until she got angry with them and yelled, 'Just stay there, please, don't move.'

Her body is heavy with the effects of the pill and the wine, but she picks up her phone and swipes at the screen, groaning aloud when she sees it's an email from Damien. She looks at the time – it's after 1 a.m., ridiculously late for him to be sending an email. She hoped, really hoped that he would just stop. For a moment she contemplates ignoring it, but it has to be dealt with. He will keep contacting her unless he gets a reply, she knows that.

Hi Sarah,

I was really surprised to get that message from you. I thought we were friends. When you hugged me goodbye when you left, I allowed myself to hope that perhaps one day we could be more than friends. Do you know how much courage it took for me to come up to you, to speak to you? Do you realise how hard that was for me? I thought you understood, I really did. But you're like all the other women who smile and say nice things to my face and then laugh at me behind my back. I never told you about them, did I? Perhaps I should have. Perhaps I should have mentioned my humiliation at their hands. But I thought you were different. I hope you are different. I'm going to give you a chance to be different. I need you to really think about the future and about the two of us together. It's going to happen sooner than you think. My time in here is almost over. So let's just forget your last email and plan what happens next. I can't wait to meet Emily. I hope she likes the new apartment.

Love, Damien

She reads the email twice as her body comes fully awake, the shock of the words prickling at her skin. What kind of a person sends an email like this? How could she have missed the signs? Their conversations run through her mind, bits and pieces she remembers and should have paid attention to.

A moment in the common room when they walked in together and there was a burst of laughter from some people on the sofa. Damien's face glowed bright red and his fists clenched. 'Bastards, bastards,' he muttered.

'What's wrong?' she asked, alarmed at the change in him.

'They're laughing at me,' he spat.

'They're not even looking at you, Damien,' she comforted him, and then she led him away to a small table at the back of the room where they could talk and play a board game.

Was that a red flag? Everyone had experience of thinking others were judging and laughing at them at some point in their lives, so how could that have given her any indication that Damien was the kind of person who would send an email like this?

Should she have given more thought to the things he said?

I've had my heart broken more times than is good for me.

It's always been impossible for me to speak to women, but you're different.

I think we get on because we've both been betrayed.

She didn't listen properly, she realises now. Her own recovery was taking up her thoughts, her feelings. Missing Emily, regretting letting Gideon go, and her need for sleep were at the forefront of her mind. She made a huge mistake becoming friends with this man and an even bigger mistake by replying to his first email. He has obviously attached himself to her and it needs to stop right now. This last email is a clear threat, and she is going to have to tell Gideon and maybe even get the police involved. And when she does tell Gideon, and confesses that this man knows where she lives, he will stop Emily coming here. Charlotte will certainly stop Emily coming here. Sarah can feel her child slipping away from her. She has done everything she can to get well so she can be the best mother she can be, and yet she knows that her daughter will be taken from her again.

Wide awake now, she sits up straight in bed as rage takes over her body. She's not going to let this man take anything away from her.

Her fingers hitting the screen hard and fast, she types a reply and sends it. Then she turns her phone to 'do not disturb' mode for everything except Gideon's number.

'Screw you,' she whispers as she lies down again.

Hi Damien,

We will never be more than friends. And now even that is not possible. Please stop contacting me or I will be forced to call Dr Augustine and the police.

Sarah

Just before dawn, she wakes thirsty and groggy, having struggled to fall asleep again. Knowing she shouldn't, but unable to stop herself, she takes her phone off 'do not disturb' mode, and feels a sickening fear in the pit of her stomach at Damien's reply to her last email.

Bitch. You made me love you. You don't get to reject me now. You just don't.

What on earth does he mean? Curling into a ball, she lets the anxiety and fear rampage through her body. She has no idea how to handle this, how to handle her life, and she can feel herself sinking back into the pit of despair she lived in after she lost Adam.

As the sun rises higher in the sky and the birds outside her window start their day, she picks up her phone again, wondering if it is too early to call Dr Augustine. She sees the message from Damien immediately and opens it quickly with shaking fingers.

Does he bother you at night, Sarah? Does he still call your name? It's your fault, Sarah, all your fault.

Her whole body feels cold, but at the same time she is covered in a light layer of sweat. Fear is part of her breathing. She has never told Damien about the whispering man. She has only told Gideon and Dr Augustine. Emily has experienced him and it's possible Gideon has told Charlotte, but she never told Damien about him, never wanted to admit to anyone that she assumed he existed to torment her.

And yet Damien knows. He knows.

TWENTY-ONE
CHARLOTTE

'Can you believe it?' Charlotte asks her mother after she has read Sarah's text out to her. It's Sunday afternoon and she is on her way to a Pilates class, hoping that some exercise will help her clear her head.

'I suppose—' her mother begins, but Charlotte interrupts her.

'Please don't lecture me again about all of us getting along and not rocking the boat. The woman is quite clearly mad and I don't see why she has to be in Emily's life at all.' She changes lanes quickly, cutting in front of another car, ignoring the angry tooting of a horn.

'What did Gideon say?' asks her mother.

Charlotte bites down on her lip as she turns into the studio parking lot. 'We're not really speaking right now,' she confesses.

'Oh Charlotte, how does that help the situation?'

'It's not my choice,' yells Charlotte, flushing as her eyes fill with tears. 'He won't speak to me. Every day since that woman came home he's been withdrawing from me. I can actually feel him getting further and further away, and now he's angry with me because I don't think she belongs in Emily's life, in all our lives.' She parks and then sniffs, finding a tissue, humiliated at her tears when she should be keeping her emotions under control. She doesn't want to be weak like Sarah. That's not the woman Gideon was attracted to. And yet she can feel herself becoming someone else as she tries to hang on to her little family. Her work is suffering, her skin is suffering, with a rash of stress pimples across her chin, and her heart is suffering, a heaviness on her chest all the time.

'All right, darling, now calm down and let's discuss this rationally. You need to really think about what you want. Because this woman will be in your life, it seems, no matter what she does. It's wrong, you and I both know it's wrong, but she is the child's mother. Unless she has another breakdown, I don't think she's going away. So, is it worth it?'

Charlotte takes a deep breath, exhaling slowly. 'Yes, Mum,' she says through gritted teeth. 'Gideon and Emily are all I want. And I'm ready to fight for them, I really am.'

'Okay then,' says her mother, 'let me think and we'll come up with something, I promise. What you're doing now doesn't seem to be working, so perhaps we need another approach.'

Charlotte nods. 'Thanks, Mum,' she says, comforted by her mother's words, ignoring the twinge inside her at all the things she has tried but not mentioned to her.

'You're my daughter, darling; what you want, I want. Are you going to reply to the text?'

'No,' says Charlotte, 'I have absolutely no desire to meet with her or to allow her to explain her behaviour.'

'I agree, and perhaps don't mention the text to Gideon – no need to stir things up. In fact, don't discuss Sarah at all. Just work on getting the two of you back on track. We'll figure something out.'

Charlotte knows this is good advice, knows that she pushed Gideon a little too far on Friday night, something she has not fully explained to her mother. Carol would only cluck and criticise, and Charlotte doesn't need that right now.

'She's making things up, Gideon, you can see that, can't you?' she said as they discussed the mysterious phone call after Emily had gone to bed. Gideon told her there was no evidence of her having called Sarah, as she had known there wouldn't be. She has made very sure to only text or email the woman. Written words cannot be disputed. Phone calls, however, are a matter of memory and interpretation.

'I think it's very irresponsible of us to allow Emily to see her at all,' she added. 'We need to get social services involved and cut her out of Emily's life entirely.'

'Charlotte...' he began, and she could see his hand gripping his whisky glass tightly, his fingers turning white with the effort of containing his rage. She wondered for a moment if it was possible that he would shatter the glass, and for the first time since she had met him, she was a little afraid of him. He is a big man, but she has never seen any evidence of a temper until this weekend. 'You need to shut up about it. I'm warning you. I know things are not going well right now, but I am absolutely not going to cut Sarah out of Emily's life.'

Charlotte stood up from the sofa, wanting to be as far away from him as possible. 'You know what your problem is, don't you?' she asked, and then continued without waiting for his reply, fury coursing through her body. 'Your problem is that you are so concerned about Sarah, you have stopped worrying about Emily, about your only child. And I'm not going to stand by and watch her get hurt. I, at least, am only concerned about her, and *I* will call social services, see if I don't.' She lifted her chin, triumphant at the flash of fear that crossed his face, sure that he would capitulate.

But he slammed his whisky down on the marble side table so hard that he cracked the glass and chipped a tiny piece of marble out of the table, which flew across the room and buried itself in the carpet. Then he leapt up off the sofa and grabbed her wrist, pulling her close and spitting, 'I dare you, Charlotte. I dare you.'

She wrenched her trembling wrist away from him and went to her study, locking the door behind her and sleeping in there on the small sofa when she was finally able to doze off. She was afraid to be in the same room with him, afraid that lurking underneath his nice guy image was something dark and terrible.

Her back and neck ached on Saturday morning. He hasn't spoken to her since then. Every time she walks into a room, he walks out of it, and she cannot think how to begin a conversation that doesn't end with her issuing a grovelling apology. She shouldn't have to apologise. He's the one in the wrong. Him and his crazy ex-wife.

In the class, Charlotte tries to concentrate on moving her body and freeing her mind, but the problem of her husband and his ex-wife won't let go. She cannot help but feel that if Sarah didn't exist, her life would be perfect, just perfect. She allows herself a quick fantasy of Sarah taking an overdose of sleeping pills, even imagining the funeral, which would be sad for everyone but would allow her to show Gideon what a tower of strength she could be for him. She can see herself standing at the graveside as the rain pours down, her long black coat tightly belted at the waist, Emily's little hand in hers as she holds an umbrella over both of them. 'At least the child has her stepmother,' she can imagine people whispering. She would be a mother, finally Emily's only mother.

'Swap machines,' says the instructor, and Charlotte releases the fantasy, feeling no guilt at all over it.

Everything she has done has been to protect Emily, but Gideon won't see it that way. And as she pushes herself harder, feeling sweat cover her face, she hates Gideon as much as she hates Sarah. The only person she loves purely and unconditionally is Emily. She is the only one who really matters.

TWENTY-TWO
GIDEON
TWO DAYS AGO

Gideon is happy to leave home on Monday morning, to drop Emily off at school and disappear into other people's lives. Sunday was hideous. He and Charlotte avoided each other all day while keeping their enmity towards each other from Emily, who was delighted to go out with each of them separately. He took her to the park in the morning and Charlotte treated her to a late lunch in the afternoon. Last night, he lay down next to his daughter on her bed as she discussed all the things she and Sarah were going to do at her next sleepover and felt his heart break for his little girl, who had no idea that the adults around her were in chaos and confusion. He fell asleep next to her and only woke up at 5 a.m., when he got up and took himself for a run, guilt pounding the pavement beside him over how he had behaved as he rehearsed an apology to Charlotte.

Did Sarah imagine the call from Charlotte or did Charlotte lie about calling Sarah? It would be easy enough for her to use another phone – but why would she do that, and why some random gardener's phone? He doesn't trust either of them, not fully. And he has no idea what to do now.

He concentrates on work instead, making sure he reads his contracts thoroughly, making sure he controls what he can.

He is in the middle of a client meeting, talking an older woman through her options now that her husband has decided, after fifty years of marriage, that he's looking to start a new life, when his phone lights up on his desk. He quickly slides it into his pocket. The client he is talking to reminds him of Carol, Charlotte's mother, as she perches stiffly on a chair opposite his desk, her handbag on her lap and her hand constantly patting her hair, making sure it is still in place. She has not cried, which is unexpected. Perhaps she is still in shock. He is used to many, many tears from both men and women in this office, and has tissue boxes everywhere on standby.

While he speaks, outlining what he thinks is the best way forward, his phone vibrates constantly in his pocket, over and over, distracting him and causing him to lose focus more than once. Eventually the meeting is over and he ushers the woman out, promising to give her a call and let her know when things are under way. Alone in his office, he takes out the phone to see seven missed calls from Sarah. His fingers tremble as he taps her number. *Oh God... what now? What now?*

He is worried about her picking up Emily today and has called the school twice already to make sure that her name is on the list and that Emily knows her mother will fetch her. This has all become so complicated so fast. Sarah needs help, he's sure of it, but he also knows that suggesting it will only result in an argument. In the middle of all this is a little girl who adores her mother and her stepmother and deserves a childhood free of the terrible tension that exists between these two women. And it is his responsibility to make sure that this gets sorted out. Emily is sleeping over at Sarah's tonight, but if one single thing goes wrong, if there is any hint of Sarah not coping, he has vowed to himself that things will change, that he will take control. Sarah may need more time at the clinic, more help than she has had, but whatever happens, Emily will not pay for the problems of the adults in her life.

'What is it?' he asks, panic making him more abrupt than he means to be.

'It's... I'm so sorry, Gideon, I know that you're at work and I wouldn't have called unless I absolutely had to, but I'm so scared...' He can hear she is on the verge of tears and he takes a deep breath, steadying himself so that he can listen to her and hopefully help her.

'Okay, calm down. Just tell me what's wrong. I'm sure we can figure it out. If you need to take a few days of... rest, that's fine, it's good.'

'No, that's not it at all. It's Damien,' she says, and he has to think for a moment before she reminds him. 'You know, the guy I became friends with at the clinic?'

'Oh yeah, yes, I remember, the one who was emailing you.' He relaxes a little, because this is not about Emily, or Charlotte, or something in Sarah's imagination. 'Damien who?' he asks.

She hesitates. 'He told me... Turner, Damien Turner.'

'You said you would ask him to leave you alone,' he says.

'And I did,' says Sarah. 'I did, but then he sent me another message saying he didn't think I meant what I said, so I told him again that I didn't want to hear from him and he... he called me a bitch. And then he asked... he asked about the whispering man – but I never told him about him, I never did... I swear.'

The words come out quickly as Sarah gulps and sniffs, and he knows she is crying, knows she is terrified, but he can only think about her forgetting that she has shared information with someone, like forgetting where she put her pills, like forgetting that she was supposed to meet Charlotte at her apartment and then inventing a random phone call. He slumps onto the small sofa in his office, his legs weighed down by a terrible sadness as all the hope he had dissipates into thin air. Charlotte is right. Sarah should not be alone with Emily. The realisation breaks his heart, and he feels the same way he did on the day Sarah told him to leave – completely and utterly hopeless.

Who is this man she is talking about anyway? Does *he* actually exist?

'I think we need—' he begins, but she interrupts him.

'I'm worried that he may come here when I have Emily. He can leave the clinic if he wants to and he knows where I live. He said he can't wait to meet her. I told him about the new apartment because you rented it for me when I was still there and I even showed him pictures on my phone. I'm worried he's going to come over and I just don't know what to do. Should I call the police? I've left a message for Dr Augustine so maybe he can speak to him, convince him to stay there and get some more help, but he hasn't returned my call yet.'

Gideon stands up and paces up and down his office. Maybe this is real. She sounds so sure of what happened. What if this man does exist and he actually does want to hurt her?

'He hasn't threatened you, has he? I mean, he said something horrible, but...'

'No, but... he scares me. How does he know about the whispering man?' Her voice is small and frightened, and he feels the same way he does when something is bothering Emily, like he has to solve the problem. His first instinct is to yell at her for getting involved with such a person, but he knows that will get him nowhere.

He sighs. 'I tell you what,' he says, as he stands at his office window and looks across the city and the harbour, watching a large cruise ship make its way under the bridge. He briefly contemplates telling Sarah to come and stay with him and Charlotte until she has spoken to Dr Augustine but dismisses the idea quickly. Charlotte would never stand for it. There is only one thing he can do. 'Pick Em up,' he says, 'and I'll come there after work and maybe stay the night. I can sleep on the sofa. I can be there in case... just in case he decides to come round. I think you should ask the psychiatrist at the clinic what his state of mind is. I don't think it's something you need to worry about, but I'll stay the night and then we'll see.'

'Thank you. I wish you didn't have to... but thank you,' she says, obvious relief in her voice.

He will stay at the apartment and let Sarah have one last night with her daughter. In the morning she will be calmer, he hopes, and he can explain that she needs more help, more time at the clinic. He will talk about it logically and he hopes she will understand.

His assistant opens his office door and pops her head in. 'Mr Armstrong is here,' she whispers, and Gideon nods and holds up his hand, asking for five more minutes. Charlotte won't be happy, but she'll have to understand. He tries to think straight. He's not really worried about the man turning up, but he is worried about Sarah's state of mind, and if he can see how she and Emily are together and maybe allow both of them to feel safe, it may help things a little. There is something going on and he needs to find out what it is. Their daughter cannot be put in danger.

'I'll be there for dinner, okay?'

'Okay,' Sarah says softly. 'Okay. Thank you.'

As he starts walking towards his office door to invite Mr Armstrong in, his phone buzzes again. He feels a tension headache start at his temples when he sees it's Charlotte. He doesn't want to speak to her but he answers so he can let her know that he will not be home tonight, bracing himself for the fallout.

'Hey,' he answers, 'now's not really—'

'Barry fired me,' she says, her voice strangled with fury or despair, he can't really tell which.

'Oh sweetheart, that's... Look, he was difficult to begin with—'

'That doesn't matter,' she shouts. 'They're all difficult, that's why they pay me the money they do. Don't just dismiss this. It's an indication of what's going on, what I'm dealing with. You have no idea how hard it is handling all this crap from your ex-wife and still trying to run a business. It's not as if I can just take to my bed. I have to do all of this and cope with you not speaking to me like you're a child. It's no wonder I can't concentrate any more.' Her voice has risen until the shrill tone is coming through the phone straight into his head, tightening the headache and making him grit his teeth against the throbbing.

Even though she can't see him, he raises a hand to get her to calm down. 'What do you need from me, Charlotte?' he asks, tense and irritated. He's sorry about the client but he is at work and he cannot be lectured about Sarah again right now. He has enough to deal with. He didn't like the man he became on Friday night, the anger that made him see red and grab her wrist. It's not who he is and he cannot allow it to ever happen again.

'I need you to take some time to just be with me tonight. Everything is falling apart, Gideon, and I can't stand it. We need to talk so I can get my head around things. You need to hear and understand how worried I am about Sarah and Emily. Please tell me we can have a real talk tonight.' Her tone has softened till it's almost pleading, and guilt lodges itself in his throat. She's not asking for a lot.

'I can't. I have to spend the night at Sarah's,' and before she can start arguing, he explains about Damien Turner, the patient at the clinic. Even as he doubts everything he is saying, he uses the man as an excuse.

It is only after he has been talking for a few minutes that he realises that the silence at the other end of the phone is not because Charlotte is listening, but rather because she has actually hung up.

He cannot control his fury. He picks up a cushion from the

sofa in his office and covers his face, screaming into it, hoping that no one can hear him outside the office.

Then he turns off his phone and opens the door to a bewildered-looking Mr Armstrong. 'Bad day,' he says, shrugging his shoulders, and the man nods sagely, well acquainted with the concept.

He gives his full attention to Mr Armstrong until the meeting is over and he knows that the rest of his day is client-free. When he turns on the phone again, there is a message from Charlotte.

Thought you might like to know that I called the clinic. No patient named Damien Turner is there or has ever been there. Your ex-wife is mad and is trying to ruin our marriage.

She doesn't answer her phone when he calls her, not the first time or the fifth, and eventually he gives up, knowing he will have to deal with everything in the morning. Tonight he will help his ex-wife and tomorrow he will, once again, apologise to his new wife, but beyond that he will make sure his daughter is safe. Everything else can wait.

TWENTY-THREE
SARAH

Sarah stands on her balcony with a cup of mint tea in her hand, watching the painters from next door clean up their cans and brushes. They are done and leaving. She hates just having a wall to look at when she is on her balcony and she knows she will buy an apartment with a view of trees and grass one day – maybe even the ocean. She would like to be able to look out at the sea, to watch it change colour from blue to grey with the weather.

Gideon should be here soon, and because he is coming, she feels an easing of tension across her shoulders. Dr Augustine has not returned her call but she is sure he will get back to her soon, although she knows that discussing another patient is tricky.

Emily is inside the apartment, playing a game on her iPad, and a chicken casserole is in the oven, filling the apartment with the rich smell of tomato and herbs. Pick-up went perfectly. Emily was waiting for her by the office, and the teacher in charge barely glanced at Sarah before allowing Emily to go with her. Her little girl was filled with stories about school, talking without drawing breath, telling Sarah how many times she got to go on the slide at lunch.

She feels a momentary sense of well-being. If Gideon is prepared to stay tonight, he is not going to try and stop her from seeing Emily, she is sure of it, and at the very least she will get some rest knowing he is here.

As she watches, a painter in white overalls walks over to the ladder leaning against the wall of the next-door building and picks it up, lifting it at an angle and then losing his grip, dropping it against the concrete with a loud clang. Sarah jumps, some tea spilling, and as he turns to look at her, she steps back inside. She wishes she wasn't so jittery.

She lifts a hand to her mouth and bites down on a nail. Maybe she should take a pill tonight. With Gideon here, she'll be able to sleep deeply and not worry about anything. Sleep is what she needs, deep, restful sleep.

She has been thinking about Damien's mention of the whispering man and has admitted to herself that it's possible she did tell him about her tormenting spectre. At the beginning, her time at the clinic felt elastic, stretching out and springing back, and she never knew if it was time for lunch or dinner, despite being able to see the day darken outside the windows. She also knows that she talked to him too much at first, remembering conversations where she just babbled about whatever was in her head as her body adjusted to finally sleeping and her mind fought its way out of depression. She needs to tell Dr Augustine that Damien is bothering her. While he's at the clinic, she's safe, but he can leave whenever he wants to and Dr Augustine needs to know that he's not ready to be out in the world yet. Why hasn't the man returned her call? She should have told the woman she spoke to that it was urgent, but is it? Questioning her own judgement is something she struggles with every day. The assertive, positive women she once was disappeared with those she loved and she wonders if she will ever get her back completely.

When Gideon arrives, Sarah can see the toll all this is taking on him. His shoulders are slumped and he looks like he forgot to shave this morning. Dark shadows under his eyes let her know that he is not sleeping well.

She grabs him in a quick hug. 'Let's just let it all go tonight,' she whispers, and she feels him nod against her shoulder. She doesn't ask him about Charlotte, who she knows must surely be angry about him being here, but she doesn't care. She has tried to like the woman, to get along with her, and she's done trying now.

The next few hours are like a return to a time before Adam, before she lost her parents and descended into a nightmare. It feels like an ordinary night during the week, Emily revelling in having the undivided attention of both parents. The little girl chats away over dinner, telling them about what she learned at school that day in between bites of chicken.

'Maybe stop talking and eat for a few minutes,' says Gideon. 'Mummy has ice cream for dessert.'

'Ice cream is filled with calories,' says Emily.

'And what's a calorie, Ladybug?' asks Sarah, moderating her tone. She is so sick of hearing Charlotte's voice come out of her daughter's mouth.

Emily shrugs. 'Charlotte told me but I forgot.'

Sarah throws a glance at Gideon, but he is looking down at his phone and she decides to leave it. She will have to spend a lot of time countering what Charlotte tells her daughter, she can see that.

'Well, I'm going to have some ice cream,' she says, and Emily smiles.

'Me too, me too.'

'Something wrong at work?' she asks Gideon.

He sighs and puts the phone on the table, rubbing his head with his hands. 'Charlotte had a bad day,' he says.

Sarah opens her mouth to say something, but swallows her reply, standing up and gathering the dishes on the table. 'Do you want to go home?' she asks when Gideon follows her, carrying the salad bowl.

'No,' he replies. 'I don't.' He doesn't invite any more conversation, so she leaves it.

'Ladybug, you can have your ice cream in front of the television,' Sarah says, and Emily jumps up from the table and settles down in front of a favourite show about a magic school bus.

'Have you spoken to Dr Augustine?' asks Gideon.

'No, he hasn't returned my call, but he will. I'm sure he will. I told the receptionist it wasn't urgent because I didn't want to pull him away from a patient, but perhaps I should have said it was. I'll call again in the morning.'

'Can you tell me more about Damien?' Gideon says, and Sarah looks at him, sees something in his gaze.

'He does exist, Gideon. I know you think it's possible that I made him up, but I didn't. As soon as I speak to Dr Augustine, I will tell you. You can even give him a call yourself, if you haven't already.' Gideon colours and Sarah knows it's because he is indeed planning to call her doctor. She can't blame him for that, but it still upsets her. Taking a deep breath, she spoons out ice cream into bowls and adds chocolate sauce and sprinkles, craving something sweet to take away everything but taste and sensation.

'I can show you the emails he sent me,' she says a little while later, as she scrapes her bowl for the last of her ice cream.' Gideon sighs, taking his own last spoonful. 'I suppose it's easy to make up an email address,' she adds, understanding that this is what he's thinking.

'I know you're telling the truth about him,' he says, and even though she is happy to hear the words, she is not sure he means them.

Determined, she gets up and retrieves her phone from the bedroom, opening the emails. She hands the phone to him without saying anything and watches as he reads through them.

'I can see why you're worried,' he says. 'Perhaps I can send him a message and kind of warn him off.'

'No, no,' she says, alarmed. 'He's... I mean, he's at the clinic for a reason and I wouldn't want to do anything that would interfere with his treatment. I think we need to let the professionals handle this.'

'Okay,' he says lightly, handing back the phone. She can see that he wants to ask her why she doesn't want him to speak to Damien. She does have her reasons. Damien is fragile, and even though she is scared of him, she knows that he needs to be handled delicately. She wouldn't want to be responsible for him getting worse or making any drastic choices – something he told her he thought about often before he came to the clinic.

'It's been such a good evening, let's not talk about any of this anymore,' Gideon says, and she is relieved. She cannot blame him for doubting her, especially when she is doubting herself.

Later, after Emily is tucked up for the night, Gideon comes and lies next to Sarah on her bed, and they talk, not about Damien or Charlotte, but rather about things they remember, places they have been together and things they have done. 'Remember the first night of our honeymoon?' Gideon says as they listen to the wind whipping around the building.

'I was terrified,' laughs Sarah. 'I thought we'd never survive the cyclone, especially when they told all the guests to take shelter in the hotel kitchen.'

'Yeah, but it turned into a great night – the chef made us all brownies.'

'I remember those,' says Sarah.

'Emily loves brownies,' says Gideon.

'She should. I ate plenty of them when I was pregnant with her. I couldn't get enough chocolate.'

'You made me go out to 7-Eleven at midnight one night,' laughs Gideon.

'I had to have my fix,' she giggles. 'It's probably why she's the sweetest child, all that sugar.'

When Gideon falls asleep, Sarah doesn't wake him, but settles down and sleeps herself. They both need the rest.

In the morning, she is excited to realise that Emily spent the night in her own bed and that she has actually slept. They have all slept.

'Maybe I can have her again tonight,' she suggests to Gideon after they have shared a breakfast of pancakes and Emily is brushing her teeth. 'I feel like I'm ready,' she adds.

He hesitates for a moment until she says, 'Dr Augustine will call me back today, or I'll call him again. I'll tell him about Damien and it will be fine. Damien's not going to come looking for me. Emily spent the whole night in her own bed and I just want to cement in her mind that this is a safe place and that everything is okay. I think it would be really good for her.' She smiles at him as she tops up his cup of coffee, the rich, earthy smell filling the air.

'Sure,' he smiles, also rested and looking a lot better. 'I'll let Charlotte know. I'll drop Emily off at school, okay?'

When Sarah is alone again, she cleans up and tries not to feel guilty about sleeping next to her ex-husband. Charlotte would be furious if she found out, and she doesn't want to risk getting between the two of them.

Feeling optimistic, she sits down at her computer and starts looking at job ads for history teachers as she waits to speak to Dr Augustine. If he tells her anything she can take to the police, she will try and get some help from them.

She changes her scrolling to a real-estate website. She needs to think of the future. Moving into her own place – somewhere she owns rather than rents – will be a good idea, and today she feels ready to start looking for somewhere she and her daughter can share for ever. She imagines a small house instead of an apartment, close enough to Emily's school and to Gideon, with a fenced garden where she and Emily can keep a puppy. She doesn't know how much she will have to spend, but if she gets a job, she is sure a small place will be possible.

As she scrolls through properties that fit the budget she thinks she will have, an email arrives from the agent telling her that the sale of her old apartment has gone through. A rush of relief makes her smile. That terrible part of her life can finally be put to bed.

That's wonderful. Can you tell me who bought it? she replies, pleased with the price the agent got for her.

> *Strangely enough, a woman who owned it before you. She has another apartment in the building and she owned this one but put it on the market last year. She wants it back, knowing that it's a good investment.*

Sarah doesn't know what to make of that. How strange to sell an apartment only to buy it back.

What's her name? she asks. But the agent doesn't reply to that email.

TWENTY-FOUR
CHARLOTTE
TODAY

Charlotte stands at the phone store, tapping her foot impatiently as she waits for a young woman to explain to an elderly man that his phone is not broken, it merely needs to charge.

'What can I do for you?' The young woman finally turns to her. Charlotte tries to see her myriad of tattoos and piercings as a good thing in terms of youth and technical skill. She needs getting a new phone to be simple and quick.

'I broke my phone,' she says, holding up her phone with its violently smashed screen.

'Wow,' the young woman says. 'How'd you do that?'

Charlotte shrugs. 'Dropped it. Can you sell me a new one, the latest model, and transfer everything over so I can get back to work?'

'Sure, though it may take some time. What were you thinking in terms of memory and price?'

'I have clients to call and every minute I stand here I am losing business. I don't care what it costs, I'm on a plan with unlimited data, just please sort it out. My whole business is on that phone. Give me exactly the same brand I have now, just the newest model.' She purses her lips, not wanting to get into any sort of conversation.

The young woman nods her understanding and sorts out a new phone in thirty minutes.

'You're good at your job,' Charlotte tells her as she takes back her credit card.

Back in her car, she familiarises herself with the new phone, which is just an updated version of the old one, and signs into everything. She didn't drop the phone. She threw it across the room and into a wall and then, using the heel of her shoe, she stood on the screen, her fury uncontained after receiving a text from Gideon letting her know that Emily would be spending another night with her crazy mother.

The rage that had bubbled inside her all night at Gideon spending the night over there, at him daring to try and fob her off with some weak explanation about Sarah being afraid of some man she met at the clinic, had erupted with the final straw of Emily spending more time with Sarah, time that was supposed to belong to Charlotte. She had barely slept as her anger churned inside her and only managed to eventually drift off by continually reassuring herself that Emily would be back with her the next day.

The text this morning was more than she could take.

She also smashed a couple of glasses in the kitchen and then had to clean them up herself, which made her even more irritated.

No matter what she tells Gideon about Sarah, he will not take Emily away from his ex-wife and cut the woman out of their lives.

She is losing this battle but she cannot lose the war. If she imagined that Barry firing her was the last straw, she was wrong. Gideon letting Emily stay another night with that woman is the last straw, and she's not going to deal with this crap any longer.

She fantasises briefly about taking Emily from school and

just getting on a plane with her to anywhere in the world. She could sell her investment properties, some of which Gideon has no idea about, and live off the capital for ever. But then she would never be able to see her mother again, and she wouldn't want that, though she would be more than happy never to set eyes on Edward again, lazy sod. If he'd done what she'd told him to do she wouldn't be in this position. Barry wanted to see the artwork the moment she mentioned it and Edward refused to pick it up, among other failings. He disappoints her every day, and she wishes her mother would let her just fire him.

She needs to think of something else – to do something else that doesn't involve kidnapping a child. One way or another this is going to get sorted out, and the first thing she needs is some sound advice, so she swipes her hand across the smooth, clean screen of her new phone.

'Mum,' she says when her mother answers, 'you need to tell me what to do.'

TWENTY-FIVE
GIDEON

Gideon puts down the papers he is reading and stands up to get himself some water. At least he's got some work done today, but he is aware that what he is mostly doing is trying not to think about Sarah and what he's going to do about her.

Last night felt like old times again, like being with the old Sarah, and it was wonderful. He was more comfortable in her company than he has been in a long time. But he knows that what he's really doing is avoiding thinking about everything that is worrying him. Last night he wouldn't have believed she could make up a phone call and invent a stalker, but if what Charlotte has discovered is true, then it seems she has done. Why wouldn't she let him contact the man and threaten him to make sure he stayed away? If Damien doesn't exist, what does that say about her? And what does that say about Gideon for allowing her more time with Emily? But this morning she seemed so capable, so in control, that it was almost impossible to believe that there was anything wrong at all. Maybe Damien does exist. Maybe Charlotte made a mistake. He feels like he's the one going mad.

Whatever is going on, he needs to get to the bottom of it. He picks up his phone and scrolls through his contacts, finding the Pacific Green Clinic. He calls and leaves a message for Dr Augustine, though thinking about it once he has hung up, he knows the man won't tell him anything about Sarah. He is also unlikely to tell him if someone called Damien Turner is there and has a history of harassment, which is what he really wants to ask. He has no idea how Charlotte got any information out of the clinic at all.

At this thought, he shakes his head at himself. Obviously the clinic wouldn't have given Charlotte information about Damien. They wouldn't even have told her if he was there or not. All those details are protected under the health act. How could he have been so stupid?

Charlotte has lied, and he doesn't need to think too hard to know why. Her extreme jealousy has caused a few problems in the past – like the times she's pulled him away from other women at parties, accusing him in a furious whisper of flirting – but it has never been this bad. What if she is the one losing control?

He cannot get any information out of the clinic, but he does know someone who could help. He uses his office phone to call Shana, the medical litigation partner in his firm.

'Gideon, to what do I owe the pleasure of a phone call from you?' she says, unable to conceal her surprise. Gideon usually avoids her. Before he started dating Charlotte, Shana was keen to spend time with him, but he knew that dating anyone in the office would be a disaster.

'I'm sorry to bother you,' he says, going for humble to get her on side. 'I'm just... I have a thing with a client I can't really... Well, you know the drill. I need to find out if a man named Damien Turner is still at the Pacific Green Clinic.'

'They don't like to give out that sort of information, you know that.'

'I know,' he says, 'but if anyone can get information from a clinic, it's you. You have a way of getting the support staff to talk,' he says smoothly, and he can hear her smile when she tells him she will try.

He knows that it will upset Charlotte if he spends another night with Sarah. But he's not entirely sure he wants Emily to be alone with her mother, and he's also not sure he wants to take Emily away from her. He's also fairly angry at his wife for the lie about Damien. She's desperate, but it's unacceptable.

'It makes my heart happy to be with Mummy,' Emily told him on the drive to school this morning, and he wanted to cry for her, for everything she was dealing with at such a young age. The three adults in her life need to find a way to make this work – unless it's too late for that. His parents will, thank God, be back from their long trip in two weeks, and he is looking forward to discussing this with them and having them around more often.

His office phone rings and he picks it up.

'Gideon,' says Shana.

'That was quick,' he laughs.

'Yes, well it was easy enough. I think you may have the wrong information there. No man named Damien Turner was ever at that clinic. Are you sure you have the right place?'

'I... um,' he stutters, 'I must have made a mistake,' he says quickly as he recovers himself. 'Thanks, Shana, I'm really sorry to have bothered you.'

'You can take me out for a drink to make up for it,' she says, and he laughs drily.

'Sure, as soon as I get out from under this paperwork, but thanks again for your help.'

He picks up his phone to call his ex-wife, because now he doesn't know what to think. Maybe the man gave her a false name... maybe? He sighs. He keeps trying to find a way to believe that Sarah is okay, but it's not working. There are too many things that don't make sense. He needs to call her out on this and demand she tell him the truth, demand that she returns to the clinic for more help.

Before he can dial her number, though, his phone rings and he looks down and sees that it's Carol, Charlotte's mother. He doesn't want a lecture from the woman, but he knows from experience that she will keep calling until he responds. Dropping his head onto his desk, he wants to howl with frustration, but he can't lose it now. Emily needs at least one person who is thinking of her and only of her. He needs to keep the peace until he can sort this out.

The phone stops ringing, and he sighs with relief and sits up, but as he had known it would, it immediately starts up again. Carol is persistent. She's a lot like her daughter that way. Sighing, he answers the call, greeting her curtly. 'Hello, Carol.'

TWENTY-SIX
SARAH

Sarah is not sure what makes her call the school – intuition, perhaps, or maybe it is fear that she will be denied entry again because her name is not on the list. Yesterday she collected Emily from outside the office and everything went well. But today the little girl has a drama class for half an hour after school, something she loves because they play all sorts of fun games, and Sarah will have to walk into the school and wait for her. She goes back and forth over the idea before she rings them, worried that she will sound strange when she asks if her name is on the list to pick up her own daughter. Gideon said he made the change and there is no reason for him to lie.

It was wonderful to have him stay over, and now that she's had some sleep, she feels like she can manage things better. When thoughts of Adam or her parents pop into her mind, she takes a few deep breaths and releases any lingering guilt she is holding onto. Damien is more of a concern, but hopefully she will have heard from Dr Augustine by this afternoon and she can leave the matter in the capable hands of the psychiatrist.

She is sure that the few appearances the whispering man has made recently were just anxiety and nerves. She doesn't quite know what to think about Charlotte calling her and her number not appearing on her phone. Could she have used someone else's phone? She is in and out of other people's homes all the time as part of her job – perhaps she used one of the gardeners' phones.

Charlotte is not the kind of person Sarah would have imagined Gideon ending up with. She knows he dated a few other women after their divorce, most of whom were easy-going and down to earth. Charlotte feels like a bad fit for him, but perhaps that's exactly what Gideon was looking for – someone who was the complete opposite of his broken-down ex-wife.

'I'll make sure they know that it's you picking up again today,' he told her this morning. 'I may come over just to see everything is all right as well, if that's okay?'

'Fine,' she smiled, willing to agree to anything for another night with Emily.

'Anyway, you're now back on the list, where you will stay for ever,' he said.

She laughed. 'I hope so.'

He was quiet for a moment. 'I hate that you're doubting yourself, Sarah. I hate that you're doing that to yourself.' His voice was soft, his concern real, and she wished more than anything that she could reach out and touch him, have him hold her tight. But Gideon belonged to Charlotte, and even though they could both feel there was something between them, something deep and special, there was no way she would ever come between him and his new wife. She'd made her choice, and whatever her issues with Charlotte, Gideon seemed mostly happy with her. Sarah was not going to spoil that.

'I'm not doubting myself,' she said, forcing another laugh. 'I'm just joking.'

But she does doubt herself, all the time. It's hard to come back to a life when you messed things up so spectacularly. She doesn't ever want to go through that again, or have Emily go through it either. It can't hurt to make sure. So just before lunch, despite Gideon's assurances, she calls the school, her excuse all prepared.

'Beacon Wood Primary School, Diane speaking,' she hears.

'Oh, hi, Diane, it's Sarah, Emily Greenstein's mum. I was just wondering exactly what time drama ends today. I know they were thinking of making the class a little longer, but I'm not sure if they did or not.'

'Let me check for you,' says the receptionist.

Sarah hears her tapping on her keyboard. She doesn't care if the class runs late or not – she's happy to sit and wait for Emily – but she needed an excuse to check that she is on the list.

'They finish at three forty-five. An email about that went out last week.'

Diane sounds just a tiny bit judgemental, but Sarah doesn't pay any attention to that. Charlotte or Gideon should have told her that the class was ending later, but in comparison to not being on the list, this is a small oversight.

'Right, sorry,' she says cheerfully. 'I'm sure I saw it but forgot. While I'm here, I just want to make sure of the names on Emily's pick-up list.'

'Just a moment,' says Diane, and Sarah hears the muffled sound of a hand going over a receiver. A tiny shiver of anxiety runs along her skin.

'Um, Sarah, you do know that Emily has already been picked up, don't you? Her stepmother said she needed to take her to a dentist appointment. She was collected an hour ago. She's not coming back today. I know Mr Greenstein said that you would be picking her up but her stepmother said that he'd made a mistake and she didn't want Emily to miss the appointment.'

Sarah grips her phone tightly, her heart thumping faster. Perhaps Gideon forgot about the appointment? But it's June, and Emily sees the dentist once a year in September, unless she has a problem, which she would have mentioned to Gideon or Sarah.

The school are aware that she and Gideon are divorced and that Emily goes back and forth between them. Her not knowing where her child is will be a red flag for them. They don't like to get into the middle of custody disputes, but sometimes they have to. She doesn't want to give them any reason for concern, not when she is questioning herself already, so she lies. 'Oh my goodness, I am so embarrassed. Of course I knew. It's my day to fetch Emily and I just forgot that Charlotte called me this morning to tell me about the dentist. Honestly, sometimes I don't know where my head is.' She lets out a trilling little laugh, hoping that she doesn't sound crazy.

'Yes, well, we all make mistakes,' says Diane, but she doesn't sound convinced.

'Thanks so much,' replies Sarah, and she quickly hangs up.

She calls Charlotte's phone, but there is no answer. Then she calls Gideon, but his phone goes straight to voicemail, and the feeling of anxiety gets stronger as she paces her apartment calling them both again and again.

Where is her child? Where is her little girl, and why has no one told her anything?

TWENTY-SEVEN
CHARLOTTE

'Where are we going?' asks Emily. 'Why did you fetch me from school? School isn't finished yet – I haven't even had my lunch. Mummy said she was fetching me.'

'Well, because I have a special surprise for you. You're having an afternoon of fun,' says Charlotte brightly, hoping that Emily won't sense her unease. She glances in her rear-view mirror to see the little girl with her arms folded, a look of concern on her face.

'But why did Diane tell me good luck with the dentist? I don't want to go to the dentist. My teeth aren't sore. Mummy always tells me when it's the day for the dentist so I can brush my teeth extra hard.'

Charlotte glances in the mirror again and catches Emily's gaze. She looks so like her mother, it's disconcerting.

'Don't worry, there's no dentist. I just told Diane that so she would let you come with me.' Charlotte laughs so that Emily knows this is something funny, but Emily isn't buying it.

She frowns. 'Mummy says you mustn't tell lies. Was that a lie?' she asks, curious more than upset. Her hand goes to her hair, which she plays with when she is thinking. Charlotte would never have tied it up in those messy bunches. Charlotte prefers a neat plait.

'It was... No, just something I needed to say,' she says brightly. 'Now, the surprise is that you get to spend the rest of the day with Granny Carol. She wants to bake with you and play all sorts of games and it will be lovely. She may even give you some more of that perfume you like.'

'I like the one that Granny Carol says smells like flowers,' says Emily, sitting forward in her booster seat, excited now. 'Where are you going to be?' she asks, and Charlotte lifts her eyes from the road and glances in the mirror again, meeting Emily's intense green-eyed stare. 'Will you be talking to people who want pretty houses?'

'No,' says Charlotte, stopping at a traffic light. 'I'll be there too, and the most fun thing is that Daddy is also going to come. It will be a family day of fun at Granny Carol's house.' She is really selling this, wanting Emily to be enthusiastic so that she behaves well, although that's never really a problem with Emily. Her voice is pitched so high she's annoying herself.

'Yay,' shouts Emily, always delighted to see her father during the week, when he's usually at work. 'A family day of fun, a family day of fun,' she sings, and Charlotte sees her look out of the window. She puts one hand on the glass, using the other to trace around her fingers as she sings. Charlotte will have to clean that window later.

She is not quite sure what her mother thinks this is going to achieve, but she's giving it a shot anyway.

As she sat in the parking lot on her new phone to Carol, Charlotte was unable to stop the tears as she blurted out the story of losing a client, and of Gideon staying the night at his ex-wife's and letting Sarah have Emily for yet another night. He hadn't even had the decency to call her, only sending a text letting her know. But what he also let her know by this callous gesture was that he was not going to apologise for last night, for not being there for her – and what is a husband for if not to be there when you need him?

Her mother listened quietly as the whole story poured out, only saying 'Oh dear' every now and again.

'Well, this really has gone too far,' she said when Charlotte had finally run out of words and blown her nose. 'I know you're worried about Emily being with her mother, and I know that you feel Gideon's affections are waning. I don't think it's something you can ignore any longer. You need to know where you stand. You need to communicate that to Gideon, and you also need to express the full level of your concern about Sarah. She is quite clearly not capable of taking care of Emily. The things that have been going on are ridiculous, and Gideon needs to face what is really happening.' Her mother's voice was firm, and Charlotte understood that she was right.

The previous day she had hung up on Gideon, not willing to listen to him explain himself for even one more moment. She'd had the most horrendous day. Barry, the client who'd fired her, was rude and abusive, calling her entitled and talentless, forcing tears from her eyes even as she managed to make herself sound businesslike on the phone.

All she had needed after that was some comfort and reassurance from her husband, and yet he had chosen to spend the night with his ex-wife, doing who knows what. It was completely unacceptable. Her small lie about calling the clinic had been self-defence, and it had been rash. Gideon is a lawyer, and he wouldn't have had to think very hard to know that there was no way she would be told if someone was a patient there. She had just hoped that it would bring him home to her, so they could at least have a conversation, especially when she didn't answer her phone. If Sarah didn't answer her phone, he went running over there.

But he had stayed with Sarah, leaving her alone with her pain and her failure.

'Time to bring this to a head, I think,' her mother told her.

'I don't know how I'm going to do that, Mum,' Charlotte said, even though it was exactly what she wanted to do.

'Come here, spend the day, bring Emily. We'll call Gideon and go from there. You deserve to know where you stand.'

If Gideon is planning on ending their marriage, she needs to know. As she has this thought, she has to swallow quickly, because the lump that forms in her throat threatens to choke her. She cannot lose Emily. She will not lose her.

The text this morning from Gideon had made her beyond furious, hence the broken phone.

'He wants Sarah to pick her up, Mum.'

'Yes, well, I am tired of hearing what Gideon wants. What about you? Just pick her up early, right now in fact. Make some excuse to the school,' her mother advised her. 'Emily was supposed to come home to you tonight. They can't just go changing things whenever they want.' Charlotte knew it wasn't that simple. Emily belonged to Gideon and Sarah, and since the courts were not involved, Gideon was free to chop and change arrangements. He was free to disregard everything Charlotte said, everything she wanted, and only the fact that they were married meant Emily got to stay in Charlotte's life. If their marriage ended, she would not see her again, and that could not happen.

'Bring her here, we'll bake and play. I'll tell Gideon she is here and that I will only let him pick her up, and when he comes over, the two of you can talk. An uninterrupted conversation goes a long way to sorting things out. No phones, no work, no child; you'll sort it out, you'll see.'

'And what if he won't come?' asked Charlotte.

'Oh, he will, darling. I'm sure he will. Emily will be with us. He will have no choice.' Her mother giggled at her own cleverness.

Charlotte wasn't convinced, but she agreed. 'I'll have to tell Sarah. We can drop Emily over at hers later.'

'No need to mention it,' said her mother. 'Let her figure it out for herself. She's messed up enough over the past few weeks. No need to take her into consideration. It's time to fight for your man, Charlotte, if you still want him. You do, don't you?'

As she drives, Charlotte ponders this question. Does she still love Gideon, or is it only Emily and being Emily's mother that she loves?

Things have become a little jumbled in her mind.

'Can Mummy come as well?' asks Emily, dragging her away from her thoughts. She experiences a wave of visceral hatred for Sarah that is so strong she can't answer for a moment. She stops at a traffic light and concentrates on the clicking of her turn signal until she has her breathing under control.

'Mummy's busy,' she says, glad that she has not told Sarah what is happening, imagining her walking into school only to be told that Emily is not there, pleased at how she will question herself, as Charlotte knows she has been doing.

When they reach her mother's house, Emily skips up the garden path, jumping only on the pale slate stones and not the dark ones. Carol is standing at the open front door and Charlotte feels relief wash over her. Her mother is so capable and calm. Surely she will help them get this sorted out? Perhaps if Gideon hears it all laid out for him, he will realise that Sarah needs to be removed from their lives.

'Hello, darlings,' says her mother, leaning down to drop a kiss on Emily's cheek. 'Change of plan,' she says to Charlotte. 'I have a surprise for you.'

TWENTY-EIGHT
GIDEON

'I was wondering if you could come over for a chat?' says Carol.

Gideon rubs his hands through his hair. 'No, I'm sorry, Carol. I have a lot of work to do. Now is not a good time.' He knows he sounds rude, but he is not going to waste time talking to his mother-in-law. Charlotte tells her everything anyway, and he is sure that some of the things Charlotte says come straight out of her mother's mouth. He needs to speak to Sarah. Maybe she made a mistake with the man's name, at least that's what he hopes. The idea that no such person exists, that she has been making up these emails, is so far out of left field he can't even contemplate it. Sarah doesn't lie. But if she is struggling again, she may believe that a man is messaging her, may have even created a fake email address to support her delusion – and that would mean that she is even worse than she was before.

'I really think you need to make the time to talk, Gideon. Why don't you come here to my house so we can all sit down together and talk about what's been going on?'

'Carol, I don't want to be rude, but this is between me and my wife. I know things have been difficult with Sarah's return, but Charlotte knows that Sarah is always going to be in our lives. She is Emily's mother.'

'Yes, so you keep pointing out to her, as though she has not been raising this child alongside both of you for the last year and very much as a primary caregiver for the three months Sarah was away. She has grown to love and adore Emily. You have no right to simply shove her aside now that Sarah is home. Charlotte is your wife.'

Despite the time of day, Gideon walks over to a low chest of drawers where he keeps a bottle of whisky to offer to those clients who may need a quick drink before telling him how their lives have fallen apart. He pours himself a shot and gulps it down quickly, hoping that it will give him the patience to deal with his mother-in-law.

'I understand that, Carol. But Sarah needs my help.'

'Did she need you in her bed as well?' Carol spits in reply, and Gideon swallows his shock at the assumption Charlotte has made, despite knowing the kind of man he is.

'I slept on the sofa,' he lies. 'There was a man who was—'

'Yes, yes,' says Carol, and he can picture her waving her hand at him. 'I've heard the explanation, but I know that my daughter needed you last night and you weren't there. Things cannot go on as they have been. New ground rules need to be established. It's not fair to Charlotte to treat her this way.'

'And Charlotte and I will sort it out. Thank you for your concern. I need to go now, but I will speak to her when both of us are ready to do so.'

'Oh Gideon,' she laughs lightly, 'you are so stubborn. I want you to come over so we can all talk. Emily will be here as well. Charlotte has picked her up from school.'

'But Sarah is supposed to pick her up,' he bursts out, rage and frustration making him yell as he imagines Sarah walking into the school only to find Emily gone, her worst fear realised.

'Oh dear, well I didn't know that,' she says, and it's obvious that she is not even attempting to cover up the lie. 'If you want her to see her mother today, feel free to come and get her, otherwise I think she will be delighted to spend some time with me.'

'Carol, listen—' he begins, but she has hung up.

Carol lives outside the city on a large property. It will take him close to an hour to get there in the daytime traffic, but he has no choice.

He lifts the empty glass and chucks it against the wall of his office, the heavy crystal bouncing against the cream paint and dropping onto the carpet. 'Shit,' he curses and goes to pick it up, grateful that it hasn't shattered. As he grabs it, his finger catches on a chip, nicking the skin, causing a drop of blood to form. He feels his hand shake as fury and frustration gallop through his body. He wants to scream and smash everything in this office. Things have got completely out of control.

He grabs his jacket and goes to tell his assistant to clear the rest of his day, barking the order at her without waiting to explain. As he makes his way down to the parking garage, he calls Sarah.

'I've been trying to reach you,' she says when she answers, her voice high-pitched with panic. 'Emily isn't at school. She isn't at school!'

'I know, I know.' He quickly explains to her what's happened and that Emily is safe. 'I'll pick her up now and bring her to you, okay?' he says when he's done. 'We need to talk about Damien.'

'I'll speak to Dr Augustine about him. Just leave that to me,' she says, and her tone makes her sound so sure that he questions his doubts again. Maybe Sarah got his surname wrong. Maybe the receptionist just wouldn't give Shana the information.

'Where does Carol live?' asks Sarah, and he tells her, but adds, 'Don't worry, I'll bring her to you. It's fine.'

'Oh, I'm worried,' says Sarah. 'I'm very worried.'

TWENTY-NINE
SARAH

Sarah writes down Carol's address, wondering what she should do now. She doesn't have the patience to simply sit and wait in the apartment. Her hands are shaking a little with the skittish feeling of panic running through her. *Find something to take your mind off it. Gideon is on his way to get her.*

In the kitchen, she starts taking everything out of the fridge so that she can wipe down the shelves. As she works, her mind mulls over what Charlotte has done. She lied in order to take Emily out of school. It's a display of power by someone Sarah can no longer trust, not now that she knows more about her. Why would she take Emily from school in the middle of the day? Her movements get faster and faster, her anger refusing to dim. Where is Emily now? Is she safe? Is she actually safe with this woman? Panic makes her drop an overripe banana on the floor, and furious, she kicks it, sending it smashing into the side of a cupboard, its brown-spotted skin bursting open. What is Charlotte playing at? She slams the door of the fridge closed. She can't just stay here and wait like a good girl. She has tried to do everything the right way, but Charlotte is not interested in that.

She tries Charlotte's number, but it goes straight to voicemail again, as she knew it would.

She drops her phone onto the kitchen bench, her heart racing. She has no idea what to do now. When it rings, it startles her, making her jump. She picks it up and swipes to answer without looking at the screen.

'Hello,' she says curtly.

'Yes, hi, my name is Graham Withers, from Graham's Garden Service. I got a call from this number about a week ago but then the caller hung up. I realised I hadn't tried to call back when I was going through my phone. I'm just checking that it was a mistake and that you weren't after a quote for some garden work because I have some time available.'

Sarah takes a moment to admire the man's tenacity. She is about to tell him that she dialled a wrong number, but then decides to explain why she called. 'This is going to sound strange, but I got a call from your number and I thought it was... a friend of mine asking me to pick up her child from school, and... Look, sorry, don't worry, it doesn't matter,' she finishes, aware of how strange she sounds.

'Oh, right... Wait a minute, are you talking about the call you got from Carol?' Graham asks.

'Carol?' says Sarah, and she feels her body tense as she stands in the kitchen, the sickly-sweet smell of banana everywhere. 'It was Carol who called?' she asks, her voice high.

'Yes, Carol Owens. I've been working for her for a while. She's the one who advised me to leave a leaflet in all the apartment buildings I could get to, and she was right, I've had heaps of business from it.'

Sarah picks up the cloth she was using to clean, and squeezes it hard, letting tiny drops of water fall onto the kitchen counter. 'I don't understand. Why did she call me from your phone?'

'Well, we were out in her garden and she remembered that

she needed to fetch her granddaughter, but she didn't have time to get there so she needed to call the school or have someone do it for her. Her phone was dead, so I offered her mine since we were quite far from the house – it's a big property, as you know.'

How does Carol know her number? *Why* does Carol know her number?

'And did... did you hear what she said?' she asks.

'No, she walked away a bit. Look, is there a problem of some sort?' The man sounds perplexed.

'No, I'm sorry, it's nothing, thanks for your help,' says Sarah, and she ends the call.

She immediately calls Gideon, but he doesn't answer, and then she tries Charlotte again, whose voicemail turns her stomach as fear courses through her. Why would Carol have pretended to be Charlotte, and what is the woman doing with her daughter?

She needs to get there, to go and find her child, because she is starting to think this is not just a power play from Charlotte, not just done to irritate her. Charlotte has deliberately taken her child from school so Sarah can't get to her, and her mother is involved as well. Who are these people and why has Gideon been so quick to trust them with Emily?

She picks up her jacket from her bed and is on her way out the door when her phone rings again and she sees it is Dr Augustine. With a quick irritated shake of her head she debates whether to answer, then slides her thumb across the screen.

'Dr Augustine, hello,' she says.

'Sarah,' he replies, 'is everything okay? I was given a message that you needed to speak to me. They said it wasn't urgent, and we've had some difficult days, so I thought I would wait until things were calmer so we could really talk. How are things going?'

'It's...' she begins. She wants to tell him that she's fine, that everything is fine, but she knows better than to lie to her doctor.

She shuts the front door behind her and speaks as she makes her way to her car. 'Things are a little difficult. I haven't been sleeping and I—'

'Sarah, if you feel you need to return, if you are still in need of guidance and help, then it's better to come back and make sure that you're fully well. You don't want to be in a situation where you're not sleeping again and the hallucinations return.'

'I know,' she says as she gets into the car, 'and I will if I need to, but right now I wanted to ask you about Damien, because he sent me some emails that kind of crossed a line, and I wanted to ask you if he was... capable of anything more, you know.'

Dr Augustine hesitates for a moment. 'Sarah, who is Damien?'

She feels her body tense, her hand clenching into a fist. 'What... what do you mean?' she asks. 'The man I was friendly with, the thin patient with the beard and the blue eyes. I met him, I met him a few days after I arrived. He was there, he was...' She speaks faster and faster, the words spilling out as her fear grows. What if Damien doesn't exist? Dear God, what is wrong with her mind?

'Calm down now, Sarah, take a deep breath, a big deep breath, in slowly and out slowly,' says the doctor, and she follows his instructions as she drops her head onto the steering wheel, not caring if anyone sees her.

What is wrong with her mind? What is wrong with her?

THIRTY
CHARLOTTE

As Charlotte drives, her mind wanders.

She has so much work to do, but she is not heading for work; so many clients to call back, but she is not returning calls. It is no wonder that Barry fired her, but she cannot go on like this anymore. Gideon needs to make up his mind, needs to make a decision. The trouble is, she knows he is going to choose Sarah. She can feel it in the way he looks at her when she says something negative about Sarah, in the way he talks about his ex-wife, in the way his whole face seems to soften when her name is mentioned. She is going to lose him, she knows this. And she has tried so hard to hang on to him, to hang on to Emily, who is the light of her life.

She has learned in the last few months that she has a capacity for love way beyond anything she ever imagined. Her love for Emily consumes her, and she wishes that the little girl was hers and hers alone. She realises she has been having a fantasy, a terrible dark fantasy in which both Gideon and Sarah die and she is the only one left to care for Emily. She can see herself and the little girl living in a beautiful city apartment together, shopping and bonding, getting closer as she grows older. She would never mention this fantasy to anyone, because it sounds crazy. It's odd to think that Sarah leaving a clinic where she went because she was mentally unstable has somehow managed to drive Charlotte mad, but that's what it feels like. She wishes Sarah gone with every fibre of her being. The woman should have stayed where she was and left Charlotte and Gideon to raise Emily alone.

She didn't want to take the spa day her mother has arranged for her. 'It's all organised, darling. I gave them a call at Healing Hearts and they're expecting you,' Carol said after Charlotte had settled Emily in front of the television with a snack.

'But that wasn't the idea, Mum,' argued Charlotte. 'I was supposed to have some time to speak to Gideon, to sort this out.'

'I know, darling, I know,' her mother said as she flicked on the kettle to make cups of soothing camomile tea. 'But I've been thinking that perhaps what Gideon needs is to hear things from someone else's perspective. The two of you are emotionally entwined and there can be no real conversation until one or both of you is prepared to listen and consider each other's points of view. I'll ask him to come here for a chat and tell him what I've noticed about Sarah's behaviour. I can explain that I share your concerns and then you can come back looking divine and rested and we can all have a long chat about things. By the time it comes around to taking Sarah to Emily, I will have Gideon thinking about things with a little more clarity. I don't want you to give him an ultimatum or something like that and then look back and regret it. Take some time to think, get your ducks in a row, and when you come home, he'll be more open to a discussion.'

Charlotte slumped onto a kitchen chair and dropped her head into her hands, suddenly exhausted by all the effort it was taking to keep her marriage, her business, her life together, just because she loved Emily so much.

'I've tried to get him to agree to have a child with me, Mum,' she whispered, 'but he refuses... he won't even discuss it.'

'Oh darling,' her mother said, patting her lightly on the arm, 'don't you think I knew that all along? You would have had a beautiful baby together, and if he listens to reason and can see Sarah for who she is, you may still get that chance. Men change their minds all the time. Emily would love a brother or sister. Leave this to me, my darling. You take some time to breathe and leave this to me.'

Charlotte agreed, because she knew her mother was not one to be dissuaded. At the very least she will get to relax a little, even though she's not all that fond of spa days. Some time doing nothing might give her the space to really put into words what she wants Gideon to know. And one of the most important things for him to know is that he can't have his cake and eat it too. He cannot have two wives. This is not some sort of polygamous relationship. Sarah is not the other wife in this relationship; she is the ex-wife, and she needs to know her place.

As she pulls into the spa parking lot, she takes a few deep, cleansing breaths and then goes inside, happily leaving her phone in a locker provided for her in the luxurious marble bathroom so she doesn't have to deal with anything at all for just a few hours.

THIRTY-ONE
GIDEON

Carol steps back from the front door and lets Gideon in. 'Thank you for coming,' she says softly. 'I know you don't like to take time out of your work day, but I thought it was important that we talk.' She is, as always, immaculately dressed, with her ash-blonde hair perfectly styled. He has never seen her in casual clothes. She runs her fingers along the double string of pearls she always wears around her neck and then smooths her long cream skirt.

'No problem,' he says, thinking of the endless paperwork that has to be read through before he can send the documents to clients for signing. He has been taking constant calls all the way down here. It is a problem, but he cannot have an argument with Charlotte's mother. 'You sounded really—'

'Daddy, Daddy,' he hears, and Emily comes rushing from the study that Carol has set up for her to play in, grabbing him around his legs.

'Hello, Ladybug,' he says.

'Charlotte dropped me here to play for the afternoon. She said we were going to have lots of fun and you would be here, and here you are.'

'Here I am,' agrees Gideon. He looks down at his daughter, who is filled with joy at the unexpected afternoon off school and time at Carol's house, where there is always a new toy to play with.

'Granny Carol bought me a fashion Barbie set and she has pretty hair and lots of shoes and four dresses to wear.'

'Lucky you. Why don't you go and play for a bit while Granny Carol and I talk, and then maybe we can go for a milk-shake afterwards.'

'Granny Carol says milkshakes make you fat,' says Emily, her face falling.

Carol strokes the top of the little girl's head, a small smile on her face, and then wags her finger at Gideon. 'It's never too early for a young girl to learn to look after her figure. We don't want tiny little Emily turning into two-ton Emily, do we,' she laughs. It's not a nice laugh.

Gideon casts a quick glance at Carol and sees his wife many years from now, although there is a certain pinched look to Carol that her daughter doesn't have. He sometimes wonders what life must have been like for Charlotte growing up. There is a reason his wife is so rigid, so driven to be perfect, so in control. There's a reason why Edward can't hold down a proper job or maintain a relationship with a woman.

He wants to say something, but he is too irritated by the interruption to his day to attempt to correct what Carol has told Emily. He has no desire for his daughter to grow up thinking food is the enemy and that her body needs to be strictly controlled. But he can see that this is not the time. Emily should be at school, and then spending another night with her mother, and he just wants to get her to Sarah and then go back to the office for a few hours of uninterrupted work and some time to figure out what to do about this whole situation. He will check on Sarah and Emily before going home and see that everything is okay.

'We'll have a healthy milkshake,' he says lamely. 'Now go and play till I call you.' The words sound a bit sterner than usual, and he sees his daughter's face fall and feels like an absolute bastard. The complicated lives of adults should not be something she has to worry about. 'Off you go, Ladybug,' he smiles, and she smiles back and skips off to the study.

'I'll just get her a quick snack,' says Carol, and follows Emily.

Gideon stands in the entrance hall, looking up at the winding staircase with its polished timber banisters. It's a beautiful house; beautiful, but it feels like a show home, not like a place where people live.

He hears Carol say, 'Eat up all those little carrot sticks now so your eyesight stays bright and strong,' and then she returns and gestures that he should follow her into the living room.

He doesn't move. 'Where is Charlotte?' he asks.

'We'll get to that,' she says.

He cannot control his anger at the cryptic response. 'Carol, Emily should be at school. I really don't like the fact that Charlotte has taken her out early. She knew Emily was spending another night at Sarah's. It's not acceptable. What exactly is going on here?'

'There are so many things about what's happening that are unacceptable, but I am glad you're here. We can chat.'

'I have work to do and it's Sarah's night with Emily. Please just get Charlotte so I can speak to her. We will sort this out and then I can go.' He can feel himself growing furious, and he doesn't want to yell at Carol, doesn't want his daughter to hear him losing control.

'Look, Gideon, I asked you to come here because we need to discuss this. Charlotte has been trying and trying to tell you what's going on, but you don't listen and she's not...' Carol waves her hand in the air, 'strong like you and me.'

'I have listened to her, believe me, but the things she's saying aren't true. Sarah is fine.' He knows the words to be a lie, but he doesn't need Carol to know how concerned he is about Sarah.

'Look, why don't you come and sit down and relax and we can figure a way forward that works for everyone. I hate seeing Charlotte so unhappy and I'm sure you do too.' She turns and walks away, and Gideon has no choice but to follow her.

The living room is large and cold, with stark white walls. The thin rugs over marble floors lend the space no warmth. He looks around, still after all this time unsure where to sit because all the ornate furniture looks so uncomfortable.

'Sit here,' says Carol, patting the seat of the stiffly upholstered deep blue velvet sofa, and he does, draping his jacket over his lap.

He knows he needs to end this now. Things have become ridiculous. His new wife cannot keep his child from her mother, from the woman he wishes he was still married to. He allows himself to admit this as he waits for Carol to speak. He is still in love with Sarah, despite all her issues. He's been fighting it since she came back, but he cannot deny it anymore and it's not fair to keep going with Charlotte, to keep stringing her along, because it is clear to him that it is making her increasingly upset and unhinged. He makes a decision to say this to Charlotte now, and then he will take Emily to her mother.

'Listen, Carol, I need to get Emily to Sarah. Can you please go and fetch Charlotte,' he says.

Carol ignores him. 'Gideon, Charlotte brought Emily here instead of leaving her at school because we are both very concerned about Emily's mother. She is not a well-balanced person and she is not fit to take care of a child. I cannot stand by and allow Emily, whom you know I love deeply, to be negatively affected by her, and neither can Charlotte. We won't allow it, Gideon, we won't. If necessary, we will call in social services.' She sits back and folds her hands in her lap, triumphant at having delivered her message, and Gideon wants to rip the double string of pearls from her neck.

'Carol,' he says, using all his strength to control his voice, conscious that his daughter is in the house and does not need to hear him shouting, 'Emily is always going to see her mother. Sarah is always going to be in our lives. She is a very good mother who went through a very bad time and is now recovered. She is a wonderful woman and Charlotte is not going to get me to stop speaking to her, to stop sharing Emily with her, to stop loving...' He bites down on his lip, cursing the slip.

'Loving her,' says Carol bitterly. 'That's what you mean, isn't it?'

Gideon stands up and puts his suit jacket back on. 'This is not a good time. Let me take Emily to her mother and then Charlotte and I will talk.' He looks around, certain that Charlotte will walk into the room at any moment, wondering why she hasn't done so already. 'Where is Charlotte?'

Carol shakes her head, and then she seems to deflate, her shoulders rounding, her eyes filling with tears. 'We only want what's best for the child. We both love her so much,' she sniffs.

Gideon sits down and pats her shoulder. He speaks softly, gently. He doesn't like his mother-in-law, doesn't like the way she raised Charlotte, but there is no doubting her devotion to Emily. 'I know, Carol, I know, and we'll figure this out, I promise. But right now, I have a lot of work to do. Let me take Emily back to school or to her mother, and then Charlotte and I will talk tonight. Tell her that we will definitely speak later.' Perhaps Charlotte is lying down. When she's stressed, she tends to get headaches, and he knows that this situation is very stressful for everyone.

Getting up, he walks towards the door. Carol stands up quickly. 'Will you have one last drink with me, Gideon?' she says, drying her eyes. 'I feel like this is the end of something, I feel like you're going to leave us... I mean Charlotte.'

'No thanks, I'm good. And I don't know what's going to happen, not really.' He does know what's going to happen, and a pang of guilt hits him.

She smiles. 'That is a pity. A last drink would be appropriate; a last drink may be just what you need.' She walks towards a gold and glass bar cart and opens the whisky bottle, pouring herself a slug. As Gideon watches, a thrum of uneasiness runs through him. She usually only drinks sherry.

'I'll just get Emily,' he says.

'No,' she says, turning around. 'No, you won't.'

He registers her smile first, her perfect white teeth, pink lipstick bleeding into the cracks and wrinkles at the sides of her mouth.

And then he sees the gun.

THIRTY-TWO
SARAH

When she feels calmer, Sarah lifts her head and stares out of the windscreen of her car at the wall of her parking spot, the number 7 in black paint.

'Better now?' asks Dr Augustine. Sarah pictures him in his office, perhaps sitting at his desk.

'I am... and I'm sorry. I don't know... You saw us together, you did, I know you did. I can't have made him up.' She cannot believe that she was talking to someone who doesn't exist. It's just not possible. 'I have emails from him,' she says, opening her emails, seeing his name there, proving he exists.

'I'm afraid we don't have a Damien Turner here, nor have we ever had one. We do have a young man with the surname Turner, but obviously I can't discuss him.'

'That's not possible. He was with me often...' Was he? Did she imagine him? No, she did not, and she has not imagined those emails.

'I understand,' says the doctor. 'I did see you with someone, Sarah, but his name is not Damien. The man you spent some time with, the person I think you are referring to, is Edward. I saw you with Edward from time to time – is that who you're talking about?'

Sarah closes her eyes and drops her head again, catching a corner of her lip with her teeth, biting hard enough to cause pain. 'He told me his name was Damien,' she whispers.

'Really?' says the doctor, clearly taken aback. 'But he said you knew each other from... He said you used to live in the same building.'

Sarah's stomach turns as a memory returns, a strange encounter with the previous occupant of her old apartment. Something she has only recently understood about her time there is that the apartment felt tainted from the first day she moved in. The day the former occupant knocked on the door.

'I'm so sorry to bother you,' the pretty young woman with tumbling black curls said when Sarah opened the door, quickly wiping her dusty hands on her jeans. 'I know this is probably a long shot, but did you happen to come across a phone charger? I'm on my way to get a new one, but I thought I would just check.'

Sarah smiled. 'Actually, I did find one in a drawer in the kitchen,' and she went to retrieve it for the woman, thankful that she had not yet thrown it out. 'How long did you live here?' she asked her.

'Two years, but then all of a sudden we were told we'd have to move. The owner wanted to sell immediately. I'm getting married, and my fiancé and I want to buy a house, so we're back with my mum and dad for a few months to save some extra money.'

'Congratulations,' Sarah said, and she hoped she sounded sincere. The chance of a happy marriage and a wonderful life ahead was lost to her for ever.

The woman thanked her and turned to go, then stopped and turned back. She seemed hesitant as she said, 'Look... this may sound a bit odd, but... just watch out for a guy named

Edward. He lives in another part of the building, but he's around quite a bit, at the mailboxes and in the garage. It's not that he's a bad guy – he's nice and all – but,' she frowned, 'eventually my fiancé had to kind of warn him off.'

That night, Sarah checked three times that her door was locked before she was satisfied that it actually was. The next night, Emily woke up and cried about a monster, and when Sarah switched on her bedroom light, she heard a tapping noise. Fright made her freeze, but she had to make sure that Emily felt safe, so with her heart in her throat, she opened the curtains. A spindly tree branch was knocking against the window in the wind. Before going back to bed, she checked the door again, and the windows as well.

As the days went on, her sleep became even more disturbed as she listened for sounds and looked out for the man the young woman had mentioned. Every time she saw a man in the complex, she dropped her head, just in case it was Edward.

The less sleep she got, the more worried she became about everything. Every night her guilt mingled with her fear and the noises in the apartment grew louder. She had the branch cut down, but she still heard tapping and squeaking. If she ever did drift off to sleep, she would wake up in a panic, her heart racing.

She never met the man when she lived in the apartment, but she was always on the lookout for him. It increased her anxiety levels, which made the insomnia and depression worse and whittled down her time asleep further and further until the terrible night when she started hallucinating.

Now she rubs her head with her hand, pushing against the pounding ache she is feeling. 'I don't know him... I didn't know him before, I mean. I only met him at the clinic.'

She *had* only met him at the clinic, but had he been watching her all along? Had he been watching her in her home? With her child? Where had he been hiding? Why hadn't she seen him?

Her old apartment was on the ground floor, easily accessed by anyone. And that was where she was tormented by the whispering man. She knows now that she never told Damien about him – she's sure she didn't – and yet he knew. She didn't trust her memory, didn't trust herself, but she was right – she had never shared the information.

Is Damien the man from the apartments? Are they the same person, and is that person the one who was tormenting her? How else would he know about the whispering man? It doesn't make sense. Why would he target her like that? Why was he at the clinic?

'Sarah...' says the doctor. 'Sarah, are you okay?'

She feels her stomach twist, a light sweat beading her upper lip. 'I'm fine,' she says, the lie coming easily. 'I'm fine. I don't know why he gave me a false name, but it doesn't matter.'

'Perhaps you should come and see me. I'm free this afternoon. I can tell reception that you'll be here soon.'

'No,' she says abruptly, using one hand to pull her hair back. 'I have something to do. I just need to ask one thing. What did Edward do for a job before he came to the clinic?'

'I really don't see how this is relevant.'

She can hear Dr Augustine is uncomfortable having this conversation, so she sighs and starts the car. If he's not going to tell her, that's fine. But then he speaks again.

'He does very little. I believe he works for his sister on and off, but he's mostly unemployed.'

'What's his surname? What's his sister's name?' demands Sarah.

'I don't think it's appropriate for me to give out that information. If he continues to bother you, contact the police and they can give me a call. Now, I really must go, but I urge you to consider returning here for a week or so. Please tell me you'll think about it.'

She ignores this. 'Is Edward still there? I mean, is he still at the clinic?'

'No, Sarah, he checked out the day after you left. I thought... I thought you would know. You two seemed so close. Look, I'm not sure what's happening, but you need to come and see me.'

'I will, I promise,' she says, as horror churns in her stomach. For the last three weeks the whispering man has been bothering her. Why has Damien – Edward – done this to her? What does he hope to gain? If she had agreed to become something more than friends, would the whispering man have simply disappeared into the thin air he had emerged from?

She is not hallucinating again, she is not sinking again, she is fine. She never was hallucinating. She never was. She has been depressed and sleep-deprived and some sick man has taken advantage of that. She should have asked the woman who came to get her charger what Edward did to her, how he bothered her.

But she cannot think of any of that now.

She is certain that Charlotte and her mother are trying to steal her child from her – something she is not going to allow. Three weeks ago, she would have tried to talk herself out of this belief, three weeks ago she would have put her thoughts down to her own terrible issues, but today she knows exactly what's happening. She wonders if Gideon realises what he is walking into by going to Carol's house, wonders if she does either.

She cannot think about Edward right now. That is something she will deal with after today. Right now she needs to find out what these two women are trying to do. Something is wrong here and she is certain it's not her mind, her thinking, her beliefs. She is not insane; she knows that they are up to something, and whatever it is, she has to stop them.

She speaks aloud, telling herself to think about one thing at a time. First she will go to Carol's house, then she will get Emily, then she will go to the police about Edward... and then?

She reverses the car out and checks the rear-view mirror before putting the car into drive, and he's there, standing there.

Damien/Edward/the whispering man.

She freezes in horror, her foot on the brake. He smiles.

His smile, his terrible smile. He does not have the nails she imagined, does not have the long grey hair, but the beard is there. At the clinic it was neat, contained, but now it hangs around his face, jagged and messy. Her nightmare come to life.

He lifts his hand to wave, smiles again, calls, 'I'm here, Sarah, I'm here,' as her foot slowly lifts itself from the brake and moves towards the accelerator.

What if he's not real? What if he is real? Can you kill a spectre? Can you kill a nightmare?

As her foot comes down on the accelerator, she wrenches the gearstick into drive and screeches off, leaving him looking after her, calling, 'I love you, Sarah, I love you.'

A burning rubber smell fills the air as she speeds towards the exit, grateful that there is no security gate like there was at the last building she lived in. She turns into the street, narrowly missing a parked car, and her tyres squeal as she takes a corner too fast, and then another and another, looking behind her, expecting to see him, because he has superhuman strength and speed – or because he is not real and can be anywhere she is – but there is nothing, and finally she pulls into a side street and stops the car.

Her breathing slows as she tells herself to calm down. She is aware of a light sweat covering her whole body, and she switches the fan on, taking deep breaths until she is ready to drive again.

She has to get to Carol, to Emily, to Gideon.

She follows the sat nav's directions, getting lost once or twice. Carol's house is forty minutes away. As she drives, she tries to call Charlotte again and again, but the woman doesn't answer any of her calls.

She wishes, for what feels like the millionth time, that she had never needed to be away from her child, and then she pushes her shoulders back as uneasiness makes her tense.

The whispering man did not return to torment her; it was Edward, she is certain. The mistake she made in going to fetch Emily was prompted by a call from Charlotte's mother. Everything that has made her question herself has been something else. Perhaps she really did leave her pills on a lower shelf in the bathroom, but even as she thinks this, she has a memory of placing the box high up behind a small jar of face cream before her daughter spent the night with her for the first time. There's no way the little girl could have reached them unless someone had moved them – but only she and Emily were in the apartment.

'Bunny,' she says aloud as she stops at a traffic light.

The first time Charlotte came to fetch Emily, Bunny was lost and Charlotte was left alone while Sarah and Emily went to find him. But surely the woman would not have moved the pills? Because if she would do something like that, if she would actually put Emily in danger in order to discredit Sarah, then something is very wrong with her.

THIRTY-THREE
CHARLOTTE

The thing about getting a facial is that although Charlotte always looks forward to them, at the same time, even with the best intentions, she cannot relax enough to enjoy them. The therapist has just left the room while the mask on her face does its work, and she would love to scratch her cheeks with her fingernails.

Lying still like this as the melodic pipe music wafts through the speakers gives her too much time to think. She is finding it impossible to stay still. Gideon is going to leave her and there's nothing she can do about it. Her mother having a chat with him will not help. She wonders if Gideon will even agree to that. Everything is worth a shot, she supposes.

She squirms a little, not wanting to think about what she's done over the last few weeks to make sure that her little family stayed intact. Her mother would be horrified, she's sure, but she's done what she had to do. Moving the pills was quick and easy, and although there was a chance that Emily wouldn't have thought to take them, despite the bright colours on the box, luckily she did. Knocking on the door of the apartment and then leaving, making sure Sarah kept getting woken up, was silly and childish, but she was trying to prove how easily the woman could be manipulated, and she knew it would unsettle her. If Gideon had come home on time for dinner that night, she would never have had to resort to such silliness.

Sarah can't be trusted and all she needed to do was nudge the woman just a little and she could prove that. She refuses to feel guilty about what she thinks of as her little tricks. What kind of a crazy person hears someone outside their window anyway – and why would Gideon want such a person in charge of his daughter? Sarah invented a phone call from Charlotte, so she is obviously not sane.

Her mind drifts to her clients and all the calls she must be missing. She understands the benefits of having a few hours away from her phone, but it's not how she likes to do things. Some clients need advice on the smallest things – like the woman who calls her to ask what to do every time she needs a new throw pillow.

As she lies there, her heart rate speeds up. She is supposed to be feeling drowsy, to be relaxing, but she is getting more and more irritated. She realises she hates being here, hates the fact that she is out of reach of anyone. And what about Emily? What if her little girl needs her? This is ridiculous.

The door opens softly and the therapist pads back into the room. 'How are we doing here?' she asks, her voice just above a whisper.

'Actually, I need to go,' says Charlotte. 'Please take this off so I can leave.'

'But you have another half-hour booked and then a foot massage,' says the woman.

'I don't care. I need to see my phone. I'm a working mother and I need my phone.'

'No problem,' says the therapist, and she sets about cleansing Charlotte's face.

It feels like it takes forever as the woman's hands stroke and massage and rub, but finally Charlotte is back in the locker room, and she breathes a sigh of relief as she opens the locker and pulls out her phone.

She has twelve missed calls from Gideon. Ten missed calls from Sarah. And a text message from her mother.

Hope you're having a lovely time, darling. Don't rush back. Gideon and I are having a good chat. One way or another, everything will be different when we're done.

THIRTY-FOUR
GIDEON

'I didn't want to believe Charlotte, you know,' Carol says.

'What do you mean?' Gideon asks, his heart racing. How is it possible that this woman – his mother-in-law – has a gun pointed at him? He knew she had one, because she has told him that she and her late husband were members of a gun club, but he never imagined the weapon saw the light of day any more. Is this really happening? She must be insane. He moves his lips, trying to think of something to say to get her to put it down – and then a jolt of fear stops him saying anything.

Emily is in the house.

'When she told me you were still in love with Sarah, I didn't want to believe her. It's a terrible thing to watch your child in pain, Gideon, a terrible thing, and the last thing I wanted for her was to end her life alone as I have done. Motherhood is a kind of madness. They don't tell you that in the books or the blogs or whatever young women read these days, but it is. You grow a human being inside you, watching what you eat, what you drink, how you stand and sit and lie down. And then you give birth and they are your everything, but that doesn't last and soon you realise that they have to go out into the world, into a world you cannot control, and they will be hurt. They will be hurt again and again and no matter how hard you try, how much you try to control, you can't stop it happening. And that makes you just a little crazy – well, maybe more than a little.' She smiles.

'Carol, look,' he begins, 'this is not what you want to do. Let's talk about this, let's try and sort it out.'

'Isn't it lovely?' she says, glancing at the gun in her hand. 'This is a nine-millimetre Glock – something like what the police use. Paul bought it for me. It's lightweight and durable and sleek. It's a beautiful piece of equipment.'

'Carol, please,' he says, wondering if he could overpower her. She is a small woman, but the gun in her hand is not to be trifled with. They stand in silence. Carol will not miss if she decides to shoot. He knows that.

'You must understand, Gideon,' she says quietly, 'that I didn't plan to use this until just now. I mean, I have it here just in case, but what I really hoped was that you would arrive and be grateful that Charlotte and I had taken Emily to protect her, grateful and ready to fight your crazy ex-wife for custody. But that's not the situation at all. And so here we are.' She frowns, her brow furrowing as though she is confused by the situation, but he knows that's not the case.

'What do you want?' he asks. 'Tell me what you want from me.'

Carol waves the gun back and forth in front of him at chest height. 'I want you to love my child. I want you to make her feel like the beautiful, talented, wonderful woman she is, but you're not going to do that now. You haven't been doing it since Sarah came home, and that's not very nice, is it, Gideon? You, who are supposed to love her, are hurting her. And as hard as she tries, you will simply keep hurting her, because you love someone else. That's deceitful and awful, and something *you* should suffer for, not her. And to add insult to injury, you refused to have a child with her, refused to give her something just for her that she could love... that we could love. She gave up her last chance for you – her very last chance to have a child.'

'No... she understood... I... Please, you need to stop this before...' He takes a tiny step backwards. This cannot be happening.

Carol moves towards him. 'Emily is locked in Paul's study. There's a television in there and she has a snack and water and she's drawing you a picture, isn't that sweet? She won't ask to come out for a while, and who knows what will have happened by then.'

'Where is Charlotte?' he asks desperately. 'She wouldn't want you to do this. Where is she?'

'My poor darling. She's been so stressed and upset. I bought her a spa day, absolutely insisted on her taking it. It's very expensive and exclusive and they are strict about leaving your phone in your locker. I told her that her clients can wait, you can wait, everyone can wait if they need to get hold of her. The most important thing is that she has a few hours to just unwind.'

'Charlotte loves Emily,' he tries, 'and she loves me. There is no way she would want you to hurt either of us.'

'Well, you're a parent, Gideon, so you realise that children don't always know what's good for them.' She steps back to the bar cart and picks up her drink, the gun pointed directly at his chest as she throws back the slug of whisky.

'You can't... What are you going to do to Emily?'

'Well, that's the sad thing, Paul – I mean Gideon.' She shakes her head and then laughs. 'Funny how your mind plays tricks on you. Charlotte loves Emily, but if you're gone, Emily will be with Sarah, and if you're both gone...' she waves the gun again, 'then your parents will get involved and it all gets so complicated. What's important, I think, is a good clean break.'

Gideon snorts in disbelief. 'What are you going to do, Carol? Kill me and my five-year-old daughter?'

'Oh no, I would never do that. That's what you're going to do, and it's so sad.' She pulls her lips down in a clownish imitation of sadness. 'So sad,' she repeats. 'You knew I had a gun in the house and that's why you told Charlotte to fetch Emily from school and bring her here. You've been really upset about Sarah and worried, and the stress of everything has been getting to you and, well... men kill their families, don't they? Not always physically. Paul just blew us all up and tried to walk away, even as Charlotte and Edward and I lay bleeding on the floor. Edward has never really recovered, poor soul. It's hard for a boy to lose his father, but I think it would have been harder for him to see Paul with another woman. I'm lucky that didn't happen, and I want the same sad luck for Charlotte. She won't suffer seeing you with another woman, a woman like Sarah. I'm going to be devastated when I tell the police that I went for a walk, leaving you with your daughter, and returned to find... such a mess.' She bares her teeth at him in an ugly imitation of a smile. There is lipstick on the bottom row of teeth, faint pink and smudged.

'You're not thinking straight,' he tries, his hand sliding into his pocket where his phone is. This has gone on long enough. 'Charlotte will never forgive you.'

'Uh uh,' she says, waving the gun at him. 'Don't do that.' She lifts her whisky glass again, finishing the last of the drink quickly.

'No one will believe you,' he says.

'I don't care,' she replies, acid in her voice. 'I just don't care.' She drops the glass back onto the bar cart and it clangs against the glass shelf. She winces, but doesn't take her eyes off Gideon.

A tinkling sound dances through the house, and Carol grits her teeth. 'Who is that?' she asks.

Gideon shrugs. The doorbell rings again, not just once, but twice. And then again, three persistent times.

'Don't move,' says Carol. 'They'll go away.'

'Granny Carol!' They hear Emily banging on the door of the study. 'I'm locked in. Let me out, Granny Carol!'

'Carol,' says Gideon, 'please, just let her out, let her go. I'll stay and we can talk.'

The bell rings again, and then there is knocking on the door. 'Gideon,' Sarah's voice calls, 'are you in there?'

'Shit,' he mutters.

'You called her?' Carol asks, her voice high with disbelief. 'You called her to come here, even now, when it should have been just you and Charlotte? How could you, Gideon? How could you?' She sounds hurt, incredulous. She cannot see what she is doing; can only see what has been done to her.

'Mummy! I'm in here, can you hear me?' Emily shouts, and Gideon remembers that Paul's study faces the front yard.

'Emily,' shouts Sarah.

'Mummy,' calls Emily.

And Gideon moves. But Carol is quicker, her finger already on the trigger, a small smile on her face.

THIRTY-FIVE
SARAH

She pounds on the door as her daughter calls to her, shouting, 'Mummy! I'm locked in!'

Fear creeps over her as she thumps the wood again and again. What is going on? Why is Emily locked in? What is happening?

'Gideon!' she calls again, and Emily shouts as well. But no one answers the door and Sarah's panic grows, her hand burning as her body flushes hot with terror.

THIRTY-SIX
CHARLOTTE

Charlotte reads the text again, trying to work out why it bothers her so much. What is her mother trying to say? If Gideon decides to leave her, there is nothing Carol can do. There was nothing she could do about her father, though he died before the inevitable happened.

'Oh God,' she whispers. 'Oh God, oh God.'

She grabs her things and dashes for the car park, hearing the receptionist shout, 'You forgot your voucher' as she goes.

THIRTY-SEVEN
GIDEON

He doesn't feel anything except an enormous amount of pressure on his chest. He hears a loud boom in his ears and his body falls backwards. And then he is on the ground and he has no idea how he got there. He can't breathe; he gasps for air.

He is aware of Carol crouching next to him. 'Men kill their whole families, Gideon. How much you must have hated your ex-wife and child to do something like this. It's just terrible, tsk, tsk.'

Sarah rings the bell again, pounds on the door.

'Actually...' says Carol, and he notices as he tries to find a way to breathe that her perfume smells like gardenias, 'I have a new idea, a better one.' She laughs, a trilling, scratchy sound. 'It's so simple, so clever. Thank you for bringing her here to my house, my home, where she should never have been. Your ex-wife, your poor troubled ex-wife. I have no idea why she would do what she did. I was so scared of her coming to the house that I took the gun out for protection, and then look what happened. It's a wonder I wasn't killed myself.'

She stands up and he hears her walking towards the front door, then she stops and turns around. He moves his head to see her, his eyes burning, but all he can glimpse is the bottom of her cream skirt and her matching pumps. There is a black smudge on one of her heels, and he wonders if this will be the last thing he ever sees.

'You never liked my son, did you?' she says, her voice coming from above him. 'Well, no one does, not really. I love him, of course – he's my child – but he wouldn't be controlled, wouldn't allow me to make his life perfect for him the way Charlotte did. I tried, but in the end he was too stubborn. It was fortunate that an apartment came up in the building where he lived just as Sarah was looking for somewhere to buy. Fortunate, but not a coincidence. It was my apartment, just like the apartment he lives in is mine. Paul left me with a number of investment properties. Edward was most cooperative about Sarah after I explained her problems. I told him what he needed to do, especially if he wanted to continue living rent-free.

'And then, of course, he was happy to go off to the clinic for me. I don't know what happened there, but he failed to make Sarah go away for ever. It's not the first time he's failed. Poor boy. The thing is, you see,' she continues, walking back towards him, her face looming over him, the sagging cheeks and wrinkled skin forming shadows, her teeth slightly crooked this close, 'he wasn't supposed to fall in love with her, silly boy. But you can't have everything, can you, and this will all be much better. Now Sarah can go to prison, where she belongs.'

He hears her walking away again. 'You really were far too nice to her, Gideon,' she calls. 'You're not supposed to still love your ex-wife; you're supposed to hate her, those are the rules. You can only love a dead wife, a dead husband – like I loved Paul. It would have been very different if he had left me, but it was fortunate that he died. Best for everyone really. The way you felt about Sarah bothered Charlotte from your first date, and that sort of thing can't be allowed to go on. I'm only doing the best for my child.' She laughs again. 'Charlotte will be upset, of course, but a new start is needed. My poor darling has been through enough. A new start will do her good.'

As he struggles for air, he hears the click-clack of her heels across the marble floor.

She is going to let Emily out and let Sarah in. She is going to kill them both.

THIRTY-EIGHT
SARAH

The crack of sound, like a concentrated burst of intense thunder, shocks her, stops her banging on the door. She has no idea what it was. She steps back a moment and looks up at the house.

'Mummy,' she hears her daughter call again, 'Mummy, help me.' And she realises Emily's voice is coming from the window to her left.

What was that sound? What was it? It couldn't have been what it sounded like. What was it?

She rings the bell again and then darts towards the window, trampling over tiny white flowering bushes. Peering in, she sees Emily, her back to the window as she bangs on the door. The room looks like some kind of study, with a large desk and matching floor-to-ceiling bookshelves in dark wood.

She raps on the glass. 'Emily, Emily...' she calls, and her daughter turns around at the sound of her voice. But as she does, the door to the study opens and a woman she assumes must be Charlotte's mother walks in. She is dressed in a light-coloured skirt and top, a double string of pearls around her neck.

'Granny Carol,' shouts Emily indignantly, 'why did you lock me in?'

'Emily,' calls Sarah, rapping on the window again. 'Carol, please let me in. What was that sound? What's going on? Where is Gideon?' Something is wrong, something is very wrong. Her heart is racing, her cheeks flushed with panic.

The woman lifts her fingers to her lips. 'Hush up now,' she says, raising her voice so that Sarah can hear her through the closed window.

'Can you just let me in?' shouts Sarah, slapping desperately at the window. 'Emily is supposed to be with me.'

'You should never have left the hospital, Sarah,' says the woman. Emily looks at the window, her confusion obvious. Carol leans down and grabs her hand, and Sarah knows she is holding on tightly, because Emily tries to pull away. 'You should never have left,' she says again. 'How could you have come here and hurt your ex-husband and then your child? What kind of a woman does that, Sarah? What kind of a person? You need to be in the hospital. You're completely mad. I know it, Charlotte knows it.'

Emily is pulling at Carol's hand, trying to get her to release her. 'Let me go, let me go. It's too tight, let me go!'

Sarah feels hysteria rising inside her. What is this woman saying? What is she doing? She is hurting her baby. She takes a deep breath and looks around her. In the flower bed at her feet is a collection of fist-sized decorative rocks. She bends down and picks up a smooth grey one and holds it up. 'If you don't let me in,' she shouts, 'I'm going to smash this window.'

Carol doesn't say anything. It's not easy to read her expression, but as Sarah watches, a smile spreads across the woman's face, and then she raises her hand. It's only then that Sarah sees the gun.

Emily sees the gun too and struggles harder. All Sarah can do is scream. From deep inside her, she lets go of a shriek that pierces the air. At the same time, Emily wrenches her hand out of Carol's grip and darts out of the study.

'No,' shouts Carol, and Sarah lifts the stone to shoulder height and chucks it at the glass. It smashes through the window, the tinkling sound loud and rippling.

Carol turns and runs from the room and Sarah looks at the hole she has created. It's too small, so she picks up another rock and another, and another, frantically throwing them at the window pane. When she has created a large enough space, she leans in through the glass, feeling it pull at her clothes and slice at her skin. She finds a catch that allows her to slide the sash window up, creating enough space for her to get inside. She scrabbles awkwardly up the wall, her feet struggling to find purchase, then hoists herself through the gap, falling in a heap onto the floor of the study, landing on glass and stones, the breath knocked out of her. There is a pulsing pain in her arm and her shoulder and her neck, but she leaps up and runs out of the room, shouting, 'Emily, Emily, Emily...'

She has no idea where to go, which way to run, where to look. 'Emily!' she screams, going back and forth across the marble entrance hall, which is dominated by a delicate round table adorned with a giant flower arrangement. 'Emily!' she calls. The dark, exotic smell of orchids hits her skin as she dashes past the table again, and in a terrified fury, she swings her hand at the vase, feels her wrist connect with the glass as it smashes to the ground, leaking water and white flowers everywhere.

'Emily,' she cries, 'Emily!'

THIRTY-NINE
CHARLOTTE

She gets into her car, calling her mother and Gideon and Sarah in turn, but no one answers.

She needs to get to Carol, because something is very wrong. She pushes her foot down on the accelerator, praying that she will not encounter any police. Her heart races and her skin itches from the cream that the beauty therapist used. She lifts her hand and scratches at her cheek, feeling a sticky residue there. Her phone rings and her hands shake as she presses a button on her steering wheel.

'Mum,' she shrieks, but it's not her mother.

'Charlotte, it's Edward,' a man's voice says, and Charlotte feels a sick twisting in her stomach. He would pick today to bother her. She hasn't even given him any work that he could have stuffed up.

'What do you want?' she shrieks. 'Why are you calling me?'

'I can't get hold of Mum. I think she's angry at me, but I didn't mean to fall in love with her. I didn't mean to. I was supposed to make her even crazier, but then I met her and she's... I didn't mean to.'

'What are you talking about?' Charlotte screams. 'Leave me alone.'

'But I love her, Charlotte. I love Sarah. Mum sent me to the clinic to meet her, to hurt her, but I couldn't. Please tell her I'm sorry, but I couldn't. I just love her so much.'

Charlotte listens to her brother wittering on, horrified at what she is hearing, as she tears down the highway towards her mother's house, grateful for the lack of traffic lights. He was at the clinic with Sarah? How is that possible? Her mother sent him away to Europe, he was supposed to be on holiday.

'Oh Mum,' she moans, 'what have you done?'

'Charlotte, will you tell her I'm sorry?'

She wants to hang up on him, but she can't, because she knows without question that he is talking about Sarah, Gideon's ex-wife, Charlotte's rival.

Edward loves Sarah. Gideon loves Sarah. Everyone loves Sarah and no one loves Charlotte.

Edward lived in Sarah's building, but Charlotte assumed they'd never met. She was incensed when her mother told her to decorate the apartment for her brother.

'Make it a lovely bachelor pad,' Carol said.

'Why are you letting him live there? You would never do that for me. Tell him to get a better job so he doesn't have to work for me and can afford his own place.'

'He's not capable, darling. Edward is not made of strong stuff, and if you needed this kind of help from me you would get it. I help you all the time, sweetheart, sometimes even when you have no idea that I'm helping you. I just want my children to be happy.'

Was Edward watching Sarah in that building? Maybe even stalking her? It's a preposterous thought. 'Did you...' she starts, feeling like she wants to throw up. 'What did you do to Sarah?'

'It was just... Mum wanted me to spy on her. I had to watch her. It was my job to watch her and I didn't mind because she's so beautiful. I told Mum when she went out, when she stayed in, when she went to sleep and woke up. I was good at my job. She never saw me. I never met her until Mum sent me to the clinic. I wanted to hate her, Charlotte, I did, I know she makes you unhappy, but I couldn't.'

This cannot be possible. This cannot be how her mother was trying to help.

Trust me, darling. In the end your life will be improved by your brother having some time away.

Charlotte didn't pay too much attention to that statement, but was this the plan all along? Was Edward supposed to make sure Sarah remained at the clinic? Obviously he had failed at that, and now that she's back and causing such trouble, what is Carol planning to do? What is she capable of?

'Can you just tell Mum I'm sorry,' says Edward again, sounding desperate, and she can hear that he's crying.

'Leave me alone,' she screams, ending the call.

Her mother hated that she was jealous of Sarah, because she hated for Charlotte to be unhappy. It was fine when Sarah was in the clinic – that had been the happiest few months of her life – but now that she was back, the green-eyed monster crouched in Charlotte's heart, vicious and angry. What would her mother do to stop her feeling that way? What would she do to make her happy again? Because the one person who truly loved Charlotte was her mother.

Better to be a widow than to be betrayed.

The words come back to her, and she takes a hand off the steering wheel, holds it in front of her mouth. Her stomach heaves and she swallows quickly. 'Oh God, Mum, no...' she moans.

She speeds up, flying through the streets to her mother's house, to her husband, to her daughter.

FORTY
GIDEON

Where is he? What has happened? He is on the floor, lying down. Pain – God, the pain. He was in darkness, but now there is piercing light everywhere. He hears Emily scream, hears glass smashing and more screaming. He has to help his little girl – he has to help Sarah.

As he tries to roll on his side, black spots appear in front of his eyes and his body becomes nothing but agony. His chest is so heavy that he cannot move, but he keeps trying. 'I'm coming,' he says, but he can't hear the words in the air. He repeats them anyway. 'I'm coming, I'm coming.'

FORTY-ONE
SARAH

She cannot find anyone. She looks at a wide staircase carpeted in plush pale green and made out of smooth carved timber, and shouts again, 'Emily!' and this time her daughter answers.

'Mummy, Mummy – help me.'

Her voice, pitched high with hysteria, fear and shock, is coming from upstairs, and Sarah hurtles up the steps two at a time, her feet stumbling and her hand slipping as she tries to hold onto the banister. She looks down to see that her hands and arms are covered in blood, shards of smashed glass embedded in her skin glinting in the light. Above her a giant crystal chandelier catches the light from an overhead skylight, bright and twinkling. She looks down at her hand again, the blood a deep red, and feels nothing but terror for her child. She looks away, not wanting to see the damage that she has done to herself. *Not now. Not now. Not now.* She cannot let herself stop. Her heart pounds in her chest, fills her ears with its frantic sound.

At the top of the stairs is a long hallway carpeted in the same pale green, and at the end are large double doors, painted stark white. She dashes towards them, her heart loud, her breathing fast as a strange silence envelops her.

At the door, she almost stops herself, afraid of what she will see, but she keeps moving. The room beyond is large, the green carpet spreading into the space and merging with green silk curtains. The bed is enormous, covered in snow-white linen. Sarah looks wildly from one side of the room to the other until she sees her, her little girl, her terrified little girl. She is curled up tight in a protective ball, her head on her knees, her eyes closed so she won't see what is about to happen to her, dressed in red against the green carpet, a flower waiting to be trampled as Carol stands in front of her, the gun in her hand.

Carol doesn't acknowledge Sarah, doesn't seem to have heard her come into the room. She is facing away from the doorway, her long pale skirt ripped on one side, her hair sticking up at the back.

'You shouldn't have run,' she hisses, and lifts the gun so that it is pointing directly at Emily. Her hand moves slowly, as though the air is heavy, and her breathing is ragged with fury. 'You shouldn't have run,' she says again. 'You're not my grandchild, you're just some other man's child, some other woman's child. You're not mine. And I don't care if you're gone.'

'No!' screams Sarah, disbelief mingling with fury and horror inside her. The scream is long and loud, startling Carol, who turns towards her.

Emily looks up. 'Mummy,' she moans.

Sarah flies through the air as she launches herself at the woman, her body moving at lightning speed. She crashes into Carol, throws her off balance, causing her to fall onto the bed and lose her grip on the gun. As she struggles to get up, hissing, 'Bitch, bitch, bitch,' Sarah is on top of her, curling her hand into a fist.

'Run, Emily,' she shouts as she hits the woman once, twice,

feeling pain in her hand, glass shards forcing their way into her skin, her movements clumsy.

Carol is not young or strong, but she lifts her hands, fingernails reaching for Sarah's skin, tearing at what she can touch.

'Your fault,' she rasps, her voice transformed, the whispering man come to life, 'all your fault, Sarah.' It was never a man, never a man. It was this woman, this terrible, hideous woman all along. The months Sarah spent in fear of her own mind, the months she spent awake and on guard and the months she spent away from her little girl rush at her, one image after another assaulting her as a thick, dark fury rises inside her and she punches and punches and punches. She keeps going until she is sure that Carol is unconscious on the bed, her eyes closed, blood trickling from her mouth.

Then, her chest heaving, her face dripping in sweat, she looks around the room and finds the gun, picking it up, feeling the heaviness of the strange object. She dashes back along the hallway and down the stairs, her hands dripping blood, her wrists aching, her breath burning her lungs. As she gets to the bottom, the front door opens and Charlotte is there, her white pants paired with a green blouse, her face free of make-up, only two spots of colour on her pale skin.

The two women stare at each other, mouths open in shock, and then Sarah slowly lifts the gun and points it at Charlotte, unable to help the tears that trace their way down her face.

'Look what you did,' she says. 'Look what you did.'

FORTY-TWO
CHARLOTTE

Charlotte is frozen to the spot. Sarah is a madwoman, her brown hair slick against her face, her arms and hands covered in blood, her face red, her teeth bared. The gun belongs to her mother, Charlotte knows that, but she cannot even begin to ask the question. The entrance hall is a mess, the large glass vase her mother prizes shattered on the floor, water and flowers everywhere, white petals on white marble and a madwoman with red blood all over her.

Sarah is pointing the gun at her with intent, and she knows that she is going to die.

She lifts her hands a little, her palms towards Sarah, asking her to stop, as the enormity of what she has done lodges in her throat. She has driven this woman mad and now Sarah is here to kill her. Has she driven her mad or has her mother driven her mad? Or Edward? Have they all done this, separately and together? A fleeting thought crosses her mind. This will surely be the end of Sarah in their lives. If she can just get the gun and call the police, the woman will be sent away for years. She drops one hand to her pocket and grabs her phone, then raises it and starts filming.

'Look what you did,' screams Sarah, 'look what you did.'

Charlotte squares her shoulders. 'You're mad,' she whispers, 'you're mad and I'm calling the police.'

At that moment, they both hear Emily's voice coming from the living room. 'Daddy, Daddy, please wake up and help me. Please, Daddy, I'm scared.'

'Don't move,' says Sarah, deep menace in her voice, not caring that the phone is pointed at her, capturing her every move. Charlotte nods acquiescence, but she keeps filming, knowing that she will have to show this to the police.

Sarah darts off towards the living room, leaving Charlotte in the entrance hall. She looks around her and takes a step towards the study, then changes direction towards the stairs, but she has no idea where to go or what to do. Whose blood is Sarah covered in? Why is Emily telling her father to wake up? She feels paralysed, unable to think, unable to move, but finally she does the only thing she can think of. She closes the camera app on her phone and calls the emergency services. 'Help,' she squeaks into the phone, 'help.'

'Police, ambulance or fire department?' says a man quickly.

'Police, police. She has a gun. She's going to kill me. She has a gun.' Her voice rises as she speaks. She is going to die, here, now, today. She can feel it. Where is her mother? Where is her mother to protect her?

'Can you confirm your address? The police are on the way. Help is coming,' the man says calmly.

'Where is my mother?' Charlotte moans instead. 'Where is she?'

'Gideon, no!' screams Sarah, startling Charlotte, who drops her phone on the marble floor, hearing the screen shatter. She turns to leave, to run, but then she thinks of Emily. Her daughter. She has to save Emily from Sarah, who is obviously insane. She has to save her and make sure that the police know what

Sarah did. *I have to show them. I have to show them who she really is.*

She picks up the broken phone, sliding her finger against the screen to film again, the glass slicing the skin. She runs into the living room, the phone held out in front of her like a weapon.

Emily and Sarah are draped over Gideon, who is on the floor, his pale blue shirt covered in blood, his blue and red striped tie hanging by the side of his chest.

'Oh my God,' whispers Charlotte, and Sarah sits up, her face covered in tears, her nose running.

She lifts the hand holding the gun and says, 'Don't you dare,' her voice an anguished wail. 'Don't you dare come near us.'

'The police... the police are on their way,' stutters Charlotte, trying to sound strong but unable to stop her tears. What has happened here? She lowers the phone slowly.

'Good,' says Sarah. 'Now call an ambulance, call an ambulance before he dies! Gideon, wake up, please wake up, my darling, please,' she wails, and her body folds over his again.

Emily joins her. 'Please, Daddy,' she cries, 'please, Daddy,' and she puts her little arms around her father, his blood darkening her red dress. 'My daddy,' she whimpers, 'my daddy.'

Charlotte cannot process what she is seeing, but she does as she's told. She calls the emergency services again and requests an ambulance, wondering once more where her mother is, her mother who is the owner of the gun that is never removed from its locked box. Where is she?

Sarah looks at her again. 'Get out of here!' she shrieks. 'Get out, get out,' the gun moving through the air, her hand shaking.

Emily lifts her head and stares at Charlotte too, and for a moment, mother and daughter blur and merge into one. 'Go away,' commands Emily. 'Go away.'

Utter despair overwhelms Charlotte as she backs out of the

room. Turning around, she looks at the stairs, where she can see smears of blood on the banister. Where is her mother? She looks back at the living room, at the family on the floor, at the man and the child who were never hers to begin with, and then she races up the stairs, her heart in her throat, to find the only person who has ever really belonged to her, the only person who has ever loved her enough.

Carol is on her bed, her eyes closed, dark blood seeping into the snow-white lace duvet that she washes carefully by hand and steams to smooth perfection. Charlotte's first instinct is to ask her how to clean up the mess, and then she registers that her mother is not moving, and she steps over to the bed, laying her head against her chest, her heart breaking open.

'Oh Mum,' she whispers, 'oh Mum, oh Mum,' her voice rising as her desolation engulfs her until she is screaming the words. As she howls her distress, she hears the sound of sirens, hears raised voices and shouted commands of 'Drop the gun!' and Emily shrieking, 'Don't hurt my mummy.'

She cries for her mother, but mostly she cries for herself, for everything she has just lost and for everything she never really had.

FORTY-THREE
GIDEON

A jolting motion forces his eyes open, and he can feel something on his face. He winces, tries to move his hand to take it off, but his arms won't budge. He registers sirens, noise and movement. His head turns a little as he feels someone squeeze his hand, and he sees Sarah and Emily sitting together. Their faces are pale against the identical chestnut shade of their hair. They are moving.

'Sarah... Sar...' he tries.

Emily leans forward and touches his hand, light and soft, a butterfly landing. 'Daddy,' she says, and then Sarah puts her arm around their daughter, squeezes his hand again. 'Stay with us, don't leave us,' she says.

'Where...' he begins, but the words won't come. He wants to take this thing off his face.

'It's an oxygen mask,' says Sarah. 'Carol shot you.' He hears an intake of breath, sees tears on her cheeks. 'She shot you,' she repeats. Her clothes are covered in blood, one arm wrapped in a bandage.

Emily is next to her, blood on her clothing as well, her little face white with terror and shock.

'Please don't be dead, Daddy,' she says, her voice small and sad. She pushes against her mother, burrowing into her.

'Nearly there, mate,' comes a man's voice. 'Hang in there for me.'

His eyes open and shut, open and shut.

'She's safe,' says Sarah. 'We're safe. You can rest. It's okay to rest.' Her voice is strong now, sure and determined. He closes his eyes and lets go. He rests.

EPILOGUE

Dear Charlotte,

I do wish you would reply to my letters.

I understand you may need some time to process what has happened to your life, to the man you loved, to me, to the little girl you hoped to raise. I understand, and I am here for you when you need to talk, here for you until my last day on earth. I will keep writing and one day I know you will reply.

I won't bother you with what it's like for me here, except to say that my organisational abilities have come in handy. I am working in the kitchen, teaching and directing others, helping them improve their skills. I have begun to wonder if my life would have been very different if I had chosen to have a career, to be in the world working with people instead of in my home maintaining order. Perhaps I would have been fine with your father betraying our wedding vows and leaving the three of us, perhaps not.

Betrayal changes something in you, Charlotte, it forever alters how you look at the world, your perceptions. I didn't want that for you. I didn't want you to never trust again, to never love again, to find yourself alone because being alone is easier than putting yourself through the pain again.

I did what I thought was best for you. I know you can't see that right now, but it's the truth. You would have become a bitter and twisted woman if he'd left you. I saw it happen to friends. I saw so many of them lose everything including themselves when their husbands chose someone else, and I never wanted that to happen to you. I didn't let it happen to me.

It was so sad that your father had a heart attack, but the timing was impeccable for me. Well, sometimes you have to help things along, don't you. He was a clever man, your father, but he was also, in the way a lot of men are, too stupid to ascribe intelligence to the woman he was married to. He thought I would simply accept his decision. I remember him saying, 'I will always look after you and the children, but perhaps you should think about getting a job.' He said that the night he told me he was leaving us. I had a job. My job was to take care of my family and I was very good at it, but after all the years we had been together, he wanted me to go out into the world and find a way to provide for myself and my children.

And after telling me that, after cleaving my heart in two with his ridiculous affair – and here I have to smile at his stupidity – he simply kept taking his pills. Pills that I had counted out into his organiser for him while he made arrangements to leave us. Pills can only come in a certain number of shapes and colours. He didn't even look when he took them, just opened the organiser on the right day and threw them back before he ate the breakfast I'd prepared, sitting at the table I'd laid in the house I'd cleaned. I thought it would take longer than it did, but his heart was very weak. I'm only telling you this now because you need to know that I understand how terrifying it is to be betrayed, to know you will be alone, to have your heart broken. I didn't want that for you, my darling.

Perhaps if I hadn't involved your brother, things would have worked out the way we both wanted them to, but I do like to give him things to do. It was his idea to use Pamela's surname when he spoke to Sarah in the clinic, but of course he couldn't call himself James –James was already a patient, being treated once again for his addiction. I have to confess that I did hope that while Edward was there he might work out a few of his own troubles, but it was not to be. I didn't want you to ever have to worry about Gideon's ex-wife again. Your brother was supposed to make sure she was never able to leave the clinic, but he fell in love with her instead.

What is it with men and fragile women? Why do they want someone who needs constant rescuing? I will never understand it.

He was useless when she returned, took to mooning over her, pretending to be a painter to stay close to her, and I was the one who had to climb up and down ladders to make sure she understood she would never be free of the whispering man. It was all her fault anyway. She ruined your life and because of that she ruined mine as well.

I know you tried to take matters into your own hands with a few silly tricks, but Sarah needed more than a little push, determined little vixen that she was. She needed a giant shove, and nothing she did would make Gideon see her failings.

I did give him a chance to love you the way you deserve to be loved, but he was incapable of it. I had no other choice than to do what I did. The psychologist I see in here believes that I need to realise what I did was wrong, but on her ring finger, a small diamond glints in the yellow light of the office we sit in. She has no idea of the soul-killing depths of betrayal.

I'm your mother and I only wanted what was best for you, you know I did.

This place is... well, what can I say, except it's most

unpleasant. I find the close quarters, the endless smells and noise too much to bear sometimes, but bear it I will.

It was all for you, Charlotte, so I shall bear this for you.

Please write to me. I should love to hear how you're doing and if you've managed to find someone new.

With my deepest love,

Mum

Charlotte crushes the letter into a tight ball, tossing it into the garbage can in her father's study. This is where she spends most of her time these days, on the internet, googling Gideon, Sarah, even Emily, who played a fairy with silver wings in a school concert last month. There were lots of Facebook pictures of that, every mother in the class sharing details.

It is silent in the house, no trace of what happened here remaining. The new glass in the window in her father's study sparkles in the summer sunshine. It is a season she usually loves, but a season she is keeping out with the soft hum of the air conditioner, set so high she is wearing an old jumper that belonged to her father. She found it buried in a box in a spare room. She likes to think she can smell him on the worn fibres, but mostly what she can smell is the musty packed-away scent of old clothing. She should have washed the jumper, but doing the washing feels beyond her most of the time. She has taken to wearing her mother's clothes every now and again when she runs out of her own things, only forcing herself into the laundry room when she is desperate.

She taps on the keyboard of her laptop, clicking onto her website, where black lettering tells all who might look for her that her business is temporarily suspended. The clients have floated away quickly enough. Sydney is filled with interior designers.

It's been a few months now and she can feel that her business will be suspended for many, many more months, years even. What is the point of making the rest of the world beautiful when she can only see ugliness wherever she looks? She glances around the study, noting the empty chocolate wrappers and crumpled takeaway bags. The space is a mess, as is she, her hair shaggy, her skin covered in acne from all the rubbish food she has eaten, her pants uncomfortably tight, forcing her to leave the zip down. Fast food is comforting, quick to arrive and easy to eat as she stares at her screen.

There is no reason to work anymore because her mother has signed everything over to her. She had to so that Charlotte could pay for the lawyer, pay to keep the lights on in the house, pay to keep her brother fed and alive. Edward calls every few days, whining about lost love and how he was manipulated into doing terrible things. He is hiding somewhere in Queensland and he will stay there if she keeps sending him money. Sometimes Charlotte listens to his despair, sometimes she simply hangs up on him. She makes sure to keep sending him money.

The lawyer she hired, an elderly man who coughed and rasped through every conversation, managed to get her mother a plea deal. Fifteen years for attempted murder. 'She'll be out sooner than that,' he comforted Charlotte. Not too soon, she hopes.

She herself received only an apprehended violence order from Sarah and Gideon, instructing her to stay away from them, from their child. It was delivered by a very young policewoman, who lifted her eyebrows in reaction to Charlotte's unkempt appearance, judging her the way Charlotte once judged others. Charlotte ran her fingers over Gideon's signature, trying to feel his hand moving over the paper.

She did not know what her mother had planned, but she understands why she made the choices she did. Her anger is over the loss of precious Emily, over the loss of her daughter.

She is angry at her mother, but her worst fury is reserved for Sarah – the thief, the slut, the usurper.

They would have been a happy family if not for Sarah's return. The woman didn't deserve what she had. Charlotte could understand Carol's anger at that. It was her anger too, but her mother's interference ruined everything. With a little more time, Charlotte is sure she could have lured Gideon back to her.

But it's too late for all that now. She seems to be stuck here, in her childhood home, in her father's study, in his jumper, her heart fluttering with grief and loss.

It's been months now and she knows that eventually she will have to face the world. But not yet. Now she needs to be here, her laptop open, scrolling through Gideon's Facebook page, where he simply accepts friend requests without thinking about who they may be from. He doesn't post a lot, but what he does post she studies intently, trying to discern if he is truly happy in the photo taken on a beach somewhere with Sarah and Emily, a large white hotel in the background. His smile seems wide enough, and the caption *Holiday joy with my beautiful girls* may be genuine.

In the picture, his hand is on Sarah's stomach, her hand covering his, both of them protecting something – someone? It wasn't that he didn't want to go back to nappies and sleepless nights. It was that he didn't want to go back to them with Charlotte.

She looks at the photo again, at the photo of a family, a true family, her anger seething through her, warming her blood.

It seems real enough, but maybe it's just a facade. People lie all the time.

When her mother said that Charlotte's father had had an unfortunate heart attack, that was a lie.

When Gideon said he no longer loved Sarah, that was a lie.

When Charlotte promised that she agreed to never go near, stalk or harass Gideon and his family, that was a lie too.

Right now, she's stuck here, but soon, very soon, her energy will return and she will be able to leave this house, and then... and then, who knows.

A LETTER FROM NICOLE

Hello.

Thank you for reading *His Other Wife*. If you enjoyed it and want to keep up to date with all my latest releases, just sign up at the following link. Your email address will never be shared and you can unsubscribe at any time.

www.bookouture.com/nicole-trope

When I began this novel, I was unsure if Sarah would manage to recover and become the mother she wanted to be. Losing a child is devastating, and it's a pain that never goes away. I completely understood Sarah's emotional breakdown, especially when coupled with the death of her parents. At first my sympathy lay with Charlotte, who stepped into the role of mother so willingly. But as the novel progressed, I saw a much darker side to Charlotte. Her whole life was about appearance and control, something she learned from her mother, who could not bear to be left by her husband and took steps to ensure that wouldn't happen to her daughter. Carol is a chilling and disturbed character who gave herself permission to do the most awful things under the guise of protecting her children. I don't see her ever accepting her behaviour as wrong.

I feel sorry for Charlotte, who lost everything, but she made a choice to try and cut Sarah out of Emily's life and Gideon would never have stood for that. I can see Charlotte living in her mother's house for decades, alone and angry, nursing her grudges and pain. Emily is the one who suffered the most, as all children do when the adults in their lives are in chaos. I hope her future is brighter and easier.

If you have enjoyed this novel, it would be lovely if you could take the time to leave a review. I read them all and love when readers connect with the characters I write about.

I would also love to hear from you. You can find me on Facebook and Twitter and I'm always happy to chat to readers.

Thanks again for reading.

Nicole x

ACKNOWLEDGEMENTS

Thank you to Christina Demosthenous for being the very best kind of editor. Her first email to me asked me to revise a novel I had submitted to Bookouture. I was completely surprised when she responded quickly to a follow-up question I sent, letting me know that this was the editor and the company for me. Here's to many more novels together.

Thank you to Victoria Blunden for the first edit, where she gently sliced away repetitive text and let me know that the novel was working. Thanks to Jane Selley for the copy-edit and Liz Hatherell for the proofread, and thanks to Lisa Brewster for the beautiful cover.

I would also like to thank Jess Readett for spreading the social media word about this novel.

Thanks to the whole team at Bookouture for their continued support.

Thanks to my mother, Hilary – first reader, last reader, best reader.

Thanks also to David, Mikhayla, Isabella and Jacob, and Jax, who has slept through thousands of words and hundreds of edits. Walk time!

And once again, thank you to those who read, review, blog about my books and contact me on Facebook or Twitter to let me know my work moved you. Every review is appreciated.

Milton Keynes UK
Ingram Content Group UK Ltd.
UKHW010621280723
425939UK00004B/145